"HOW CAN YOU LET ME DOWN THIS WAY, MITCH? I NEED YOU!"

"Kristina, you know I can't help you. I have to turn your case over to another lawyer. Try to understand."

"Understand what? It nearly killed me to beg you to take this case in the first place, and I'm having to do it over again. Why do you want to hurt my pride and make me plead with you this way? My sister and I are going to lose everything now and all because you're too afraid to get involved."

"I told you before: Cowards live longer. People who get involved always end up getting hurt just like I did —and it nearly ruined me. I can't go through it again —even for you."

CANDLELIGHT ECSTASY SUPREMES

RISKING IT ALL

Caitlin Murray

A CANDLELIGHT ECSTASY SUPREME

Published by
Dell Publishing Co., Inc.
1 Dag Hammarskjold Plaza
New York, New York 10017

Dell ® TM 681510, Dell Publishing Co., Inc.

Candlelight Ecstasy Supreme is a trademark
of Dell Publishing Co., Inc.

Candlelight Ecstasy Romance®, 1,203,540, is a registered
trademark of Dell Publishing Co., Inc.

ISBN: 0-440-17446-5

Printed in the United States of America

March 1986

10 9 8 7 6 5 4 3 2 1

WFH

To Our Readers:

We are pleased and excited by your overwhelmingly positive response to our Candlelight Ecstasy Supremes. Unlike all the other series, the Supremes are filled with more passion, adventure, and intrigue, and are obviously the stories you like best.

In months to come we will continue to publish books by many of your favorite authors as well as the very finest work from new authors of romantic fiction. As always, we are striving to present unique, absorbing love stories—the very best love has to offer.

Breathtaking and unforgettable, Ecstasy Supremes follow in the great romantic tradition you've come to expect *only* from Candlelight Ecstasy.

Your suggestions and comments are always welcome. Please let us hear from you.

Sincerely,

The Editors
Candlelight Romances
1 Dag Hammarskjold Plaza
New York, New York 10017

CHAPTER ONE

Kristina Neilsen welcomed the cool breeze against her face as she entered the air-conditioned lobby of the Petroleum Building in Austin. It was hot and sticky, a typical mid-September afternoon in central Texas. Kristina reached in her cotton batik shoulder bag and pulled out a fresh tissue to blot the tiny beads of perspiration that dotted her brow. Thus far it had been a disappointing day for her, with a futile pilgrimage fifty miles east to the time-worn oil town of Gilbert, Texas. Would this be another dead end in her search? Kristina hurried across the lobby to the building directory, hoping to find at last the name of the person she'd been hunting all day. To her relief, there it was: *Mitchell McNaughton, Attorney at Law, Suite 508.*

For a moment her spirits rose. She tilted her head, arching her slim neck, and took a deep breath. Maybe help was close at hand. Kristina punched the elevator button, too preoccupied with her problem to notice the rotund stranger in a brown western-cut suit and cowboy boots who stood beside her, frankly admiring her blond, long-legged beauty.

Kristina stepped off the elevator at the fifth floor,

her sandals sinking into the lush gray-green carpet of the reception area of Suite 508, and she recognized the unmistakable aroma of wealth even before her eyes could absorb the visual impact of mahogany, leather, oil paintings, and brass.

An attractive, well-trained secretary inquired politely, "May I help you?"

Kristina repeated the words she'd said so many times already, "Yes, I'm looking for Mr. McNaughton." She felt the secretary's eyes roam over her bright-yellow slacks and teal-blue gauze top and for the first time she felt uncomfortable. Kristina had been so caught up in her problem—or rather, her sister Valerie's problem—that she'd given no thought to how one should dress for a visit to a lawyer's office. No doubt Mr. McNaughton would be wearing a navy-blue three-piece suit with a striped silk tie. Perhaps Kristina should've worn something tailored—maybe her beige linen suit with high heels and stockings. But she was already there, and it was too late to go home and change clothes. She smoothed a stray wrinkle in her yellow slacks, her eyes pleading with the secretary. "Please, is he in? I need to see him very badly."

"Let me tell him you're here. Your name, please?" The secretary pressed the intercom button with a long, polished fingernail.

"Kristina Neilsen. But my name won't mean anything to him. We've never met." Kristina listened as the secretary repeated her name to the man who was her elusive quarry and held her breath while the secretary murmured a few phrases into the intercom, then nodded and turned to Kristina with a pleasant smile.

"You can go right in, Miss Neilsen. He's working on a drilling application, but he said he could see you now if it won't take too long."

It was only a few steps to the inner office, and as she entered, Kristina could smell the polish that burnished the rich wood paneling as well as the carved desk and leather furnishings. The man behind the massive desk rose to greet her, a question in his blue eyes, as though something about her seemed vaguely familiar to him.

At five feet nine, Kristina was accustomed to meeting a male glance almost head-on, but with this man, she definitely had to lift her eyes. He was very tall, surely six two, with shoulders broad and thick-muscled like an athlete's. She didn't find him in the three-piece suit she'd expected. Instead he wore crisp khaki slacks with a navy polo shirt, its pocket embroidered with the logo of its famous designer.

He automatically reached out his hand to shake hers, his deep voice murmuring, "I'm Mitch McNaughton. Won't you have a seat?"

His hand was warm and firm against hers, the bone of the fingers well shaped with no hint of softness. It was the sort of hand Kristina liked in a man. "I thought lawyers wore three-piece suits," she was surprised to hear herself say as she sat down.

"Not oil and gas lawyers," he answered, the merest twinkle dancing in his blue eyes. "Most of us wear grubby jeans and even grubbier boots. And drive pickup trucks."

"You're an oil and gas lawyer?" she asked, feeling a sudden rush of confusion. Maybe Valerie had given her the wrong name.

11

"Yes, ma'am. Has somebody offered you an oil lease on your land that you'd like me to check out for you?"

"Why, no," Kristina answered hesitantly. "I guess there's been some mistake. I was looking for the Mitchell McNaughton who used to practice law in Gilbert."

"No mistake, then," the lawyer answered, feeling a sudden wrench in his gut at the memory of Gilbert, Texas. "That was a long time ago, though. I moved to Austin—oh, almost seven years ago." His eyes met hers in a puzzled glance. This visitor certainly looked like someone he'd met before, someone connected with Gilbert. Mitch leaned back in his chair and waited for some further explanation.

"If you're an oil and gas lawyer—" Kristina perched on the edge of the leather chair and tried to think. "Then maybe my sister got the name wrong. She's not thinking very clearly just now." Kristina brightened. "But if you used to practice law in Gilbert, maybe you'll know whom she meant. I'm trying to find the lawyer who handled the divorce for my sister, Valerie . . . Valerie Winston. She used to be married to John Ed Winston."

There was a crease in his brow as Mitch frowned. So that's why this attractive visitor looked so hauntingly familiar to him. She resembled his former client, Valerie Winston, whose divorce had nearly ruined Mitch's career. "I handled that case. In fact, it's the one that did me in as a general practitioner in Gilbert. The Winstons held a grudge against me for taking your sister's side. They had plenty of money and power, and when they blackballed me, they put me out of business." The anger that he'd repressed for years surged upward and Mitch felt the taste of bile in his throat.

"I'm sorry. I don't think Valerie knows . . . or she wouldn't have asked me to come see you."

"She was a nice kid, kind of helpless. I think the Winstons had probably given her a lot of hell over the years." Mitch let the conversation turn to his former client until he could get a firm grasp on his emotions. He didn't want to think about what the Winstons had done to him and his law practice. He'd been a young kid then, fresh out of law school, and they'd tried to ruin his life.

Funny thing, though. The Winstons had carried their spite so far it had backfired, and he'd gotten some new clients through sympathetic friends in the "oil patch." He'd then moved to Austin and built a lucrative oil and gas practice, far beyond anything he could ever have done in Gilbert. A lot of "wildcatters" had been glad to exchange part-ownership in oil wells for Mitch's legal services, knowing that if they didn't strike oil, they wouldn't have to pay him anything. His clients had been lucky, and by betting on their skill, Mitch wound up owning small royalty interests in a number of producing oil wells. His royalty checks were still rolling in, bringing him more income per month than he'd earned in an entire year in Gilbert. Mitch thought wryly that the Winston family would have a collective stroke if they had any idea they'd been indirectly responsible for the financial success and prestige he now enjoyed.

"Valerie should've left too, but she stayed in Gilbert

and let the Winstons browbeat her," Kristina said, interrupting Mitch's train of thought. "John Ed and his family believed that Valerie's children were Winstons and belonged to John Ed as if they were material possessions. He told Valerie he wouldn't pay her any child support if she didn't stay in Gilbert where he could see the kids anytime he wanted to. Poor Valerie, she never thought she could cope without his financial help. And of course John Ed did everything he could to destroy her confidence."

"So she's still there?" Mitch was surprised. What did a dull little town like Gilbert have to offer a pretty young woman like his former client? She should've moved on to a bigger town long ago and made herself a new life, maybe even found another husband. Poor thing, she must be the kind of woman who needs someone to prop her up. Mitch made a keen study of the woman on the other side of his desk. *Not a bit like her sister,* he thought. *This one is tough.*

"No . . . well, not exactly. She's been in Gilbert ever since the divorce seven years ago, but this summer she finally got up her nerve to move to Austin and get herself a job. Everything was all set for her to start work as a receptionist with one of the new computer companies that's moved into the city." Kristina glanced out the large window with its view of the Colorado River and the city skyline. Austin was such a lovely city.

"Sounds like she's finally making progress." Mitch's words were polite, guarded. He still didn't understand what all this had to do with him.

"She is, a little. Well, for Valerie, it's been a lot of

progress. She's pretty timid and insecure. But John Ed made sure her attempt to be independent didn't last."

John Ed was a true Winston, all right. It was just like one of that bunch to squelch anybody who didn't let them call the shots. Mitch squirmed in his chair. This office guest was bringing back memories he'd thought were dead and buried. Nothing she said was relevant to his present life as a successful oil and gas lawyer in Austin, but it all dated back to his old life in Gilbert, now defunct. His eyes scanned the drilling application on his desk. The papers were due at the Railroad Commission by five o'clock today. An important client needed a variance so he could start drilling for oil. It was time to steer this visitor, gorgeous though she might be, out the door. Mitch wanted no more painful reminders of Gilbert, Texas, and the notorious Winston family. "It was nice of you to stop by," he said, sure Kristina would take the veiled hint to leave. "Give my regards to your sister."

"She needs your help again, Mr. McNaughton." Kristina knew she was being coaxed to leave, but she couldn't, not until she'd accomplished her mission. "You've got to help her do something about John Ed."

Mitch's voice was firm. "I'm sorry, Miss Neilsen, but as I told you, my practice is limited to oil and gas matters these days. I don't handle family law cases any more."

"Please, Mr. McNaughton, you're the lawyer she trusts. Surely you can make an exception for an old client."

"I'm sorry, Miss Neilsen, but I haven't bothered to

keep up with all the changes in family law. I haven't even read the legislation in the past seven years."

Kristina's eyes fixed on his face, watching for the least crack in his cool composure. There was none. Kristina blinked back tears. Though it would be a blow to her fierce pride, she would beg if she had to. Valerie needed this man, and somehow Kristina had to persuade him to take Valerie's case. "But Valerie needs someone she can trust. It doesn't matter if you're not an expert."

Her jabs at his conscience were beginning to prick. Mitch felt an urgent desire to be rid of this woman who had intruded upon him and his hard-won sanctuary from the past—and the Winstons. "Let me recommend a friend who's a family law specialist and will be able to help your sister collect her child support from her ex-husband."

Kristina sat bolt-upright in her chair. "It's not *child support* she's after, Mr. McNaughton." She shook her head vigorously, as though the motion could dispel his misunderstanding. "It's her *children*. You see, John Ed took them on a trip to Disneyland in August and never brought them back. They're gone, and Valerie hasn't been able to find them anywhere."

Mitch leaned back in his chair and pressed the tips of his fingers together against his chin. This matter was getting more complicated by the minute. "Miss Neilsen, your sister doesn't need a lawyer," he said firmly. "She needs the police. Tell her to call them immediately."

"She did, several weeks ago," Kristina protested. "But they can't find John Ed and the kids."

16

"I don't want to be unkind," Mitch said, trying to avoid the haunted look in her green eyes, "but why did you come to me? I'm just one person, and not a private investigator at that. If the whole police force can't find your sister's children, how do you think I can?"

"I don't know."

"Then why did you come?" What a bizarre situation. It suddenly occurred to Mitch that his visitor had gone to a lot of trouble to find him today. She was obviously well educated, and those green eyes of hers flashed with the spark of intelligence. She must know that this was a matter for the police, not for a lawyer, and especially not for an oil and gas lawyer. Mitch had no intention of letting himself be drawn into this unpleasant situation. Thanks to the Winstons and the bitter lesson they'd taught him, he'd quit riding a white horse into battle a long time ago. Leave that to the young idealists. He had enough scars to last a lifetime and would be satisfied to devote his remaining career to the pursuit of oil and money. Mitch had paid his dues. No more. Today he had a drilling application to file with the Railroad Commission. More oil, more money—if first he could just get rid of this unwelcome guest.

Kristina's glance fell to her lap, and she willed her hands not to tremble. She could feel the heightened tension in the room. It was obvious that she should leave, yet if she did, there was no place left to turn. She took a deep breath and straightened her shoulders. She had to do this for Valerie.

"Why did you come?" Mitch repeated, then caught a sense of the growing purpose in the woman across the desk from him. Suddenly he wished he could retract his question. He wasn't sure he wanted to know the answer.

"Because Valerie thinks you can help her. It doesn't matter whether you can or not. What matters is that she *thinks* you can help her now—because you helped her stand up to John Ed once before."

"Look, a lawyer can't take cases just to give a client a feeling of security. If that's what she needs, you'd better get her a nurse. Or a psychologist."

Kristina's breath came faster with anger. He'd touched a raw nerve. "I have," she answered tersely. "She has several of each, plus two physicians. She's lying in the hospital right now, barely alive because she tried to commit suicide."

For a moment Mitch couldn't speak. It was such a totally unexpected response that it knocked the wind out of him. "I'm sorry," he said at last. "What—"

"The police have told her there's nothing more they can do. She didn't want to live any longer if she couldn't have her children."

"Look, Miss Neilsen, this is completely out of my realm. I'm really sorry about your sister, and I wish there were something I could do about it. I wish there were something *anybody* could do about it. But I'm afraid there's nothing until the police come up with some leads." He put on his best reassuring manner, nodding confidently. "And they will. Nobody can disappear forever. Tell her to hang on and be patient. Her kids will turn up eventually."

Kristina wanted to believe him. More than anything, she wanted Valerie to believe him. If only Vale-

rie could hold on to a little spark of hope, maybe—
"Would you mind going to the hospital and telling her
that?" Kristina asked in a persuasive voice. "I think
you might be able to convince her."

Mitch stiffened. He didn't want to go to the hospital, not at all. If he made the slightest move in Valerie
Winston's direction, or her sister's, he was going to be
drawn into this affair against his will. He'd had
enough of dealing with other people's messy personal
problems. Besides, he'd paid the price for standing up
against the Winston family seven years ago. Let Valerie find another sucker this time.

Kristina stood. She'd been able to read Mitch's refusal in his severe expression. She couldn't beg anymore, not even for Valerie. Blinking back tears, she
hurried from the room, out of the Petroleum Building
to the sweltering heat of her old foreign car. Mitch
McNaughton had been her last hope and he'd turned
her down. *What a jerk!* she thought in disgust. What
on earth had made her sister think she'd receive any
help from an emotionally shallow cretin like McNaughton, who was totally preoccupied with making
money and totally disinterested in human beings? Angry to have made a fool of herself, Kristina stomped
on the accelerator and headed north on I-35. She still
had a full day's work of her own to do before visiting
hours began at the hospital.

It was five o'clock by the time Kristina crossed the
bridge over the Colorado River and made her way to
her office on the campus of the University of Texas.
She parked in a vacant spot on the street and hurried

19

across the sidewalk, shaded by a natural canopy of huge oak and pecan trees, to the stately brick building where she taught political science classes. Her office was a tiny cubicle furnished, in the usual manner of a lowly assistant professor, with a cast-off desk and chairs, bookshelves and a filing cabinet. On the wall hung posters salvaged from Kristina's student days at Berkeley and Wisconsin, and beside her desk was a child's drawing of a kitten signed "Love to Aunt Kris from Shelley." Kristina glanced at the drawing and quickly averted her gaze. She had work to do, and for the moment, she must put Shelley and Michael and Jason—Valerie's children—out of her mind.

Kristina peeled off the top copy from a stack of freshly mimeographed papers left by one of the staff secretaries and scanned it. It was a handout for tomorrow's class, PolySci 201, State and Local Government. Kristina shrugged at the irony. The handout was entitled "Enforcement of Individual Rights."

Suddenly Kristina felt a great weariness. She'd intended to prepare for tomorrow's lecture in her office before going to the hospital to see Valerie. Now all she wanted was to go home, to the security of her own little nest. She could go shower away the day's grime and disappointment, change clothes and have a quick bite to eat, then prepare her lecture in the relative comfort of her own living room. There was no need to stay there in the eerie silence of an almost deserted building, not when her heart was full of pain and worry and anger.

Her mind made up, Kristina grabbed her textbook and thrust it into her batik bag with a copy of the

20

handout and a folder of lecture notes. The bag bulged and dangled awkwardly from its shoulder strap, bumping against the door frame as Kristina locked the door to her office. She supposed she really ought to get a leather briefcase like those everyone else carried, but so far she hadn't been able to bring herself to do it. She just wasn't the briefcase type.

Kristina fried strips of bacon for a bacon, lettuce, and tomato sandwich, the aroma kindling her appetite despite her inner turmoil. The shower had refreshed her sagging spirits, and she stood in her tiny kitchen with a towel wrapped around her wet hair, slicing a ripe tomato while the bacon cooked. With starchy Scandinavian self-discipline, she prepared a pretty tray with a ruby-red placemat and napkin to complement her berry-patterned dishes. She filled a stemmed red goblet with ice, then poured tea from a frosty pitcher. Her mother had always insisted on a beautiful table setting, and Kristina clung to the habit even when eating a simple meal alone.

She put the strips of bacon on a paper towel to drain and went out on the back steps to cut a fresh rose for her tray. As an afterthought, she cut several perfect blooms and placed them in a small vase to take to the hospital. Maybe Valerie would enjoy them. Kristina sighed. How she dreaded having to tell Valerie that her day's mission was a complete loss. Somehow Kristina would have to come up with another plan that would instill hope in Valerie, for at this point, hope was the only thing that would keep her sister alive.

Kristina took her tray into the living room and

turned on the local news broadcast to possibly catch a news item relevant to tomorrow's lecture on local government. By the time she'd taken her first bite of her sandwich, Kristina's brain had moved into its "professor" mode, classifying and analyzing information and planning its presentation. Like all truly gifted teachers, Kristina had a sense of drama. Her classes sparkled, her students responded, and her creative approach to her subject caused quite a stir.

Last year, in her first year at the University of Texas and her first year of full-time teaching since she'd earned her Ph.D. at Wisconsin, she'd won recognition as a "comer," a teacher to watch. She'd even been nominated for a faculty excellence award—unheard of for a first-year teacher. This year, if all went well, maybe she'd actually receive the award despite the fierce competition. This year she might win *if* she could discipline her mind and do her work in the midst of a family tragedy.

Kristina straightened her shoulders and squared her jaw. Of course she'd do her work. She wasn't Valerie. She wouldn't fall apart, no matter how tough things might get. She'd do her job *and* help her sister. There was bound to be a way. And with or without Mitch McNaughton's help, Kristina would find it.

Mitch McNaughton. Kristina scowled at the thought of the man. How adept he'd been at turning his back on her pleas for help. He must've had a lot of practice to be so good at it. Kristina's full lips twisted in a grimace. The only thing she didn't understand was where he'd gotten that twinkle in his eye, the one she'd noticed before she told him why she'd come, before he'd backed so far away from her he'd nearly fallen out his fifth-floor window. A twinkle like that usually marked a person with warmth and humor, not a human glacier like McNaughton. Definitely odd. Not to mention misleading. That twinkle had certainly fooled her—until they'd gotten past his glossy exterior to the vacuum underneath.

Kristina stacked her books on the coffee table and carried her dishes back to the kitchen. Tomorrow's lesson was outlined and clear in her mind; she could add the finishing details before she went to bed. Now it was time to blow-dry her hair and go to the hospital to see her sister.

She'd just shrugged out of her seersucker robe and into a brightly printed sundress with tiny straps and a snug bodice when the telephone rang. Barefooted, she leaned across the bed to the telephone and answered it while her foot groped for her sandals. It took a moment before she recognized the male voice on the other end of the line, and then she felt a wave of confusion. "Mr. McNaughton?" she inquired after a moment's hesitation.

"Look, I don't know for sure why I'm calling," Mitch replied, his own uncertainty obvious. "I can't help your sister with her legal problems."

A tense silence lengthened. Finally Kristina spoke. "You made that clear this afternoon."

"Yes. Well . . . but on the other hand, I truly feel sorry for her."

"Thanks, but your pity isn't going to be much help at this point." Kristina felt an overwhelming urge to strike out at Mitch, to hurt him for wounding her

23

pride. It took all her self-control to keep from being totally rude.

"I didn't call to offer pity," he snapped. "You mentioned that she needs reassurance that eventually the police will find her children and bring them back. I doubt that anything I might tell Valerie would make any difference, but you asked me to go to the hospital and console her."

"And you refused that request." Kristina was angry and didn't intend to make this any easier for her caller. She heard him clear his throat, as though he were strangling on words too difficult to speak.

"I've been thinking it over, and I've changed my mind. She's an old client. I owe her that much."

Kristina had won an unexpected victory, but its taste was bittersweet. There was no joy in it, only numbness. "Thank you," she answered woodenly. "It will mean a lot to her to see you."

"I'd prefer to go to the hospital when you'll be there, just in case she gets upset."

"I try to go every night at seven." She glanced at her watch. It was almost seven-thirty. "I'm running a little late tonight, but I'll be leaving right away if you'd like to meet me there. That is, if it's not inconvenient on such short notice."

"I'll be there as soon as I can," Mitch answered. "I live out of town."

"Where?" Kristina felt curious in spite of herself.

"Rob Roy." It was a new and exclusive development in the wooded hills overlooking the city.

24

"I might have known," she muttered under her breath. More clearly, she added, "She's at Brackenridge Hospital, Room 245. I'll be in her room with her when you arrive."

CHAPTER TWO

The September evening was only slightly cooler than the sultry afternoon had been, and Kristina was glad she'd chosen the sundress, which left her tanned shoulders and arms bare. She'd pulled her long blond hair up into a twist at the back of her head, and the agate earrings she wore matched the green of her eyes and the floral pattern of her dress. At the moment she looked more like one of her own college students than a professor. At twenty-nine, Kristina glowed with health and radiated energy as well as such beauty that every man in the lobby of the hospital turned his head and stared when she walked past on her way to the elevator. She took her good looks for granted, however, and was so devoid of vanity that she supposed men stared at her because of her height.

"How are you today?" she asked with a warm smile as she entered her sister's hospital room and tried not to notice the dark circles under Valerie's eyes and her sallow skin. The I.V. was still running to Valerie's arm, but some of the other technical apparatus had been removed since Kristina's visit last night. "See the pretty pink roses I brought you from the bush outside

26

my kitchen window?" she said in a cheerful voice, placing the vase on the nightstand.

Valerie's head turned listlessly on the pillow. "The doctor says I'm better today."

Kristina leaned over and brushed her sister's cheek with a light kiss. "You sound stronger, too." Kristina squeezed her sister's hand, wondering what to say next. She'd run out of words of comfort, she'd said them all so many times before: *Things will seem better later on. You still have so much left to live for. In time this pain will pass. Life is precious. I love you.*

Valerie turned away her head and stared out the window, silent tears dampening her tangled hair on the pillow. "What day is it?" she inquired after a long silence.

"It's Thursday. Would you like for me to turn on the television set? This is your favorite night for TV."

Valerie shook her head. She had no interest in any of the ordinary routines of life.

"Did they bring you anything good to eat today?"

"Broth and Jell-O."

"As soon as they take you off that bland diet, I'll bring you something really delicious. How about some chicken enchiladas from Fonda San Miguel?"

Again Valerie shook her head. The very thought of food nauseated her.

Kristina tried to hold on to her patience. Sometimes it was hard not to feel angry with Valerie for giving up, for making no effort at all. Valerie was two years older than Kristina, but somehow Valerie had always seemed more like a "little sister" who needed to be looked after. All her life Kristina had watched Valerie

27

shrink from problems and vowed she'd never live that way herself. No, she'd meet life on its own terms and grasp as much joy and victory as she could. She refused to be defeated by every setback as Valerie was. Kristina might get beaten, but she'd go down fighting. She drew a deep breath and plastered another reassuring smile on her face. She'd go down fighting for Valerie, too, by God, if Valerie wouldn't fight for herself!

"I went to see Mitch McNaughton today," Kristina said as casually as she could.

Valerie lifted herself, a question in her eyes. It was the first sign of life she'd shown in almost two weeks. "Oh, Kristina, that's wonderful," she said in a weak voice before she fell back against the pillows. "Is he going to help me? Did you tell him I'd pay his fee somehow? I'll go to work as soon as I can so I'll be able to start giving him some money."

Kristina's eyebrows lifted in surprise. This was the first indication that Valerie might do anything except lie in this hospital bed. How typical of Valerie, to take hope only if someone else would fight her battle for her. Yet Kristina couldn't tell her sister the truth, that Mitch McNaughton had refused to take her case and would fight no battle at all. Kristina tried to think of a reply that would be encouraging yet noncommittal and found herself at a loss for words.

Footsteps sounded in the corridor outside, slowed as they neared the door of Valerie's room. Kristina heard the clearing of someone's throat, a slight cough of nervousness. Then the footsteps came nearer and the small hospital room was filled with the presence of a new, powerful personality.

28

"Hello, Miss Neilsen," said Mitch McNaughton, with a cordial forcefulness that scattered Kristina's angry defenses. "And Valerie, my goodness, it's been a long time since that day when we pinned back John Ed Winston's ears at the county courthouse." Lawyers, like actors, must play many roles, and Mitch had carefully planned tonight's role of Medicine-Man-Who-Brings-Patient-New-Hope. He gripped Valerie's hand and seemed oblivious to her ghastly appearance. "I hear John Ed's up to another one of his dirty tricks."

"Oh, Mitch, you came," Valerie said, tears of joy springing to her eyes. "I told Kristina you'd beaten John Ed once before and you could do it again." She tried to sit up, but the effort was too much for her. She clung to his hand and fastened her desperate gaze on his handsome face, towering above her.

Mitch sat on the side of the bed and held her hand, trying not to reveal his alarm at her feeble condition. It was one thing to be told by a third party that someone had made a "suicide attempt." It was altogether different to view first-hand the human wreckage. No wonder her sister had pleaded with him on Valerie's behalf.

He directed his glance to Kristina, who was watching silently from the foot of the bed. Her unspoken question was unmistakable: *Now do you understand?*

Mitch shook his head in an effort to clear it, to bring forth reason and logic in the face of the tumultuous emotions that flooded the room. He'd gone there to reassure this former client because somehow her sister seemed to think his words would help. He had *not,* repeat *not,* gone there to take on her legal action. He'd put family law behind him forever, and nothing would induce him to take on a child custody suit, that most traumatic of all family law cases.

Using all his acting skills, Mitch projected a confidence and positive, upbeat manner to try to convince Valerie that in time the police would locate her children and return them to her. She hung on his every word until she was spent from the effort of listening. "You'll help me, won't you, Mitch?" she said, then repeated it until her lips could no longer form the words. Her head slumped against the pillows, her eyes closed. She was asleep.

Mitch tried to disengage his fingers, but Valerie held them in a viselike grip. Silently Kristina stepped to his side and helped him free himself, murmuring softly when Valerie stirred and whispered, "Mitch? Please, Mitch."

"She'll be all right now. You can go." Kristina lifted her eyes and saw his troubled expression. "Thanks for coming. I think you've helped her take heart again."

"I didn't realize—" he said, as though in some sort of belated apology for the afternoon's rebuff. He stared down at Valerie's blotchy, puffed face with the dark pools around the eyes. She'd been a gorgeous young woman, but she seemed to have aged at least twenty years since he'd seen her last.

He glanced at his own reflection in the mirror and wondered if the years had been so unkind to him. He'd never thought about it before. Except for an occasional thread of silver in his dark-brown hair and a few laugh lines around the eyes, he didn't notice much

30

of a change since those years in Gilbert. He'd weathered well, and even though he might be biased, he thought he'd held up okay for a man of thirty-six. Maybe it was his daily tennis/golf/swimming, but somehow Mitch suspected that his physical condition was due less to biology than to an abundance of money and a scarcity of personal problems. Poverty and trouble were the great aging forces of life.

Kristina had observed the direction of his glance and could almost read his thoughts. "She looks much prettier when she's well," she said, defending her sister. "That's why it's so frightening to see her like this."

"I remember how beautiful she was when I saw her last. I figured some lucky guy would marry her within six months." Mitch compared his memory of the younger Valerie with the sister who stood beside him now. No, even then Valerie hadn't had that extra something that marked her sister's beauty. Kristina Neilsen had a glowing vitality that made the whole of her significantly greater than the sum of her parts. Her silver-gold hair had a silky sheen that came from good health, not shampoo bottles; her green eyes, the sparkle of intelligence and wit; and in her facial expression and smile, she revealed a great, caring heart. If he were ever in trouble, he'd want someone like Kristina Neilsen on his side. Valerie was luckier than she realized to have such a sister. Mitch stood and looked down for a final time at the morose face sleeping fitfully on the pillow. "Well—"

"Thank you again for coming." Kristina's gratitude was genuine. No matter how much he'd irritated Kris-

31

tina, Mitch had inspired a little hope in Valerie. At this point, the slightest progress was a milestone. Kristina owed him her courtesy.

Mitch took a step toward the doorway. "It's dark outside. Can I see you to your car?"

"Thanks, anyway, but I'll stay a little longer and be sure she's sleeping soundly." Kristina brushed the stray tendrils of hair back from her sister's face, but Valerie didn't stir. "The nurse will be in soon with her medication, and I'll leave after that." She turned to Mitch and made an effort to smile. "Good night, and thanks again."

Mitch hesitated, but Kristina had turned back to her sister. It gave him an odd feeling to walk to the door, leaving Kristina to cope with her problem all alone. Yet she had great strength. She could deal with it. He took two more steps. And she wasn't a whiner. She'd accepted his visit on his own terms, without another word of request. He reached the door and paused. Kristina didn't look up.

But she heard his footsteps echo as he walked slowly down the corridor away from her.

Thirty minutes later Kristina emerged from the elevator and crossed the hospital lobby, her mind already skipping ahead to tomorrow and the lecture that must be put into final form before she went to bed tonight. She didn't see Mitch McNaughton rise from a chair in a darkened corner and move toward her until she'd almost bumped into him.

"Oh!" she exclaimed in surprise. "I didn't realize you were still here."

"I thought maybe you might join me for a cup of coffee." Mitch couldn't understand himself at all. Why had he sat there thirty minutes waiting to talk to someone who could only spell trouble for him? Why couldn't he just drop the whole messy situation? But somehow he couldn't. And so he'd waited for her, berating himself the entire time. Yet when Kristina tilted her head just enough to meet his gaze and ponder his intentions, he was very glad he'd waited.

"I have to prepare for my class tomorrow." Kristina knew she had work waiting at home for her, but for some reason, Mitch's invitation was tempting. Usually she wasn't a procrastinator, but this had been a hard day. Maybe she could use a coffee break.

"The Old Pecan Street Café isn't far, and they have wonderful Colombian coffee."

"Ummm . . . well, I *did* get my lesson outlined earlier. I could probably finish it in an hour."

"They have chocolate cheesecake."

"Yes, I remember. And sometimes chocolate mocha cake."

"You can't go wrong with their Southern pecan pie."

"Are you offering to buy me one of each?" She grinned, for the first time in days, and looked like a seventeen-year-old imp.

He cast an appreciative eye at her figure. "With that body, you can probably eat anything. But I have to watch my weight. Men in my family tend to get beefy if they aren't careful."

He was lean and trim and anything but beefy, Kristina carefully noted. She also noticed the intriguing twinkle in his blue eyes. "You can watch me eat, then. There aren't any calories in looking."

"Does that mean you'll join me?" His smile flashed, revealing white, even teeth.

For a moment her eyes held sorrow. "On one condition."

He bantered, trying to bring back the grin. "That I not ask for a bite of your pie?"

She shook her head, though she appreciated his effort to be lighthearted. "That we don't talk about Valerie. For six weeks I've thought about nothing else, and I'm exhausted from worrying about her. For a little while, for thirty minutes, help me take a break from it, okay?" This was the first night Valerie hadn't become hysterical; the first night she'd shown any interest in the future; the first time Kristina could let down her guard for a moment and relax. She was very glad Mitch had waited for her to come downstairs. She desperately needed a touch of normalcy right now.

Mitch extended his right hand. "Agreed." They shook hands. "Come on, let's drive over in my car and I'll bring you back afterward to get yours. The parking will be wild over on Sixth Street at this hour."

The Old Pecan Street Café was crowded but somehow they managed to get a table near the window where they could watch the throngs of people outside. Austin's Sixth Street, which in the nineteenth century had been known as Pecan Street, had been rejuvenated in recent years, with its historic buildings converted to shops, clubs, and restaurants that drew crowds of university students, politicians and government workers, and other professionals. People strolled from place to place, street vendors plied their wares, and occasional bursts of music escaped club interiors and wafted in the summer breeze.

Their waitress brought dessert and coffee, as delicious as Mitch had promised, then left them in the relative privacy of the crowd.

"So how long have you lived in Austin?" Mitch asked. He still knew almost nothing about Kristina herself.

"Oh, I grew up here. Our parents moved here from Fredericksburg when we were little kids."

"Did you go to U.T.?" Mitch himself had done his undergraduate work at Texas A&M, zealous archrival of U.T., though he'd later capitulated and gone to the U.T. School of Law.

"No, like all eighteen-year-old kids, I wanted to get away from home, so I went to Berkeley." She took a bite of her cake and waited for his reaction. She almost always got one.

"Berkeley, huh? So you were a student radical?"

"No, those days were pretty much over by the time I arrived on the scene. Actually, I'm at the awkward age: too young to be a hippie, too old to be a preppie."

"But just right to be a yuppie." There was that twinkle again. Yet if questioned closely, Mitch would have to admit she didn't fit the mold of the typical young, upwardly mobile professional.

"Nope, can't qualify there, either, because I don't say *awesome* and I don't drive a BMW. You should see my beat-up Volkswagen." Five years of graduate

35

school on top of four years undergrad had taken its financial toll, and Kristina would keep her old Beetle until her student loans miraculously disappeared someday. "What about you?" she asked. "You're about the right age to have been a hippie."

He hated to admit he'd been totally square and gone to that squarest of institutions, Texas A&M, where the biggest student protest had to do with nothing more momentous than food in the dorm cafeterias. So he tried to pass it off with a breezy wave. "Oh, I've always hated confrontation, so I chose a place where I knew there wouldn't be any: A&M."

"You didn't!" She quickly checked his haircut, but it was very un-Aggielike, a nice length brushing his ears and collar. Very nice hair, actually, thick and— She lowered her eyes to her coffee cup. "If you hate confrontation, why on earth did you become a lawyer?"

"That's a good question, and one to which I've not yet found the answer." He sipped his hot coffee. "It certainly explains why I got out of family law." It occurred to Mitch that this conversation was quite unlike the ordinary get-acquainted session with an attractive member of the opposite sex. He actually found himself wanting Kristina to understand what made him tick. Maybe their initial meeting this afternoon, penetrating as it did to the very marrow of their personal values, had stripped away the superficial, leaving them to meet now as genuine, authentic persons. It was a little scary. Nothing like this had ever happened to him before. "On the other hand, law isn't necessarily confrontation, not unless it's courtroom litiga-

36

tion. There's also a lot of mediation and negotiation, and I'm pretty good at that."

He wasn't afraid to be candid about his strengths, yet he wasn't egotistical. Kristina liked that. It was rare. "You don't miss the drama of the courtroom?" she asked, puzzled. She thrived on the drama and role-playing of the classroom, and had she gone into law instead of teaching, she'd have been a litigator.

"No." His answer was too abrupt, but how could he explain the all-or-nothing stakes of the courtroom? The best solutions to legal problems were usually negotiated and settled in advance of trial, with a give-and-take that was fair to both parties. When the case couldn't be settled and went to trial, one party emerged in total victory, the other in total defeat. And the odds were seldom any better than fifty-fifty, so the risk of losing was always high. Losing—God, how he hated it! "No, I've never missed the courtroom. The lawyers who thrive on that are the ones who like to fight just for the sake of fighting. They're welcome to it."

Their eyes met, searching for common ground. Each recognized something vaguely familiar in the other, yet they were also quite different. Why, then, didn't the differences, obviously substantial, drive them apart? Or was it really true, that weary old cliché, that opposites attract?

Because there was no denying the fact that they were attracted. Throughout their conversation there'd been a heightened tension and awareness, surreptitious glances at skin and hair, shape and color, eyes and hands. Their speech had become softer, creating a sense of intimacy as they strained to hear over the tumult of other voices. Mitch had delighted in the soft ripple of Kristina's laughter, she in the crinkle at the corner of his eyes as he smiled.

"More coffee?" asked the waitress, checking her tables during a lull.

Mitch lifted an eyebrow in Kristina's direction.

"No more for me, thanks. I need to get home and finish up my work."

"I guess we're ready for the check, then." Mitch felt a curious dejection. The evening was ending too soon. He caught sight of Kristina's smile and reconsidered. On the other hand, maybe the evening was ending too late. Suddenly he found it hard to breathe. It was time to get out of there.

Mitch threaded his Nissan 300-ZX through the maze of Sixth Street traffic and worked his way to Red River Street for the short hop back to Brackenridge Hospital. His hand had fallen casually across Kristina's bare shoulders for a brief moment as he'd helped her into the car. That same hand now rested lightly on the steering wheel while Mitch wondered what it would be like to stroke that silky skin of hers. His fingers curled into a knot from the wondering.

Kristina leaned back against the leather cushions and stretched. What a day it had been, exhausting in some ways, yet oddly exhilarating. He was a comfortable man to be with, sure enough of himself to show a sincere interest in his companion. She thought of the guys she'd dated in the recent past, most of whom had looked upon an introductory meeting as an opportunity to brag about their many achievements. Yet Mitch, who had obviously attained a considerable measure of success, didn't boast at all. His quiet confidence was more impressive than all the self-aggrandizement of lesser men.

She studied his profile in the shadows of passing streetlights. His nose was straight, his jawline solid, his cheekbones high. His dark lashes, she now noticed, were a thick fringe for the crystal-clear, almost aquamarine blue of his deep-set eyes. Tiny laugh lines danced at the corners of his eyes, and there was the faintest growth of beard along his chin and upper lip. She glanced at his right hand, gripping the steering wheel, and was surprised that it took such effort for him to steer the car. His knuckles looked white in the glow of the light from the dashboard. Impulsively she reached out her left hand to the steering wheel and placed it over his. She felt the pulse throb in his thumb.

"There's my car, under the streetlight," she said.

Saying nothing, Mitch pulled into the parking lot and drew up beside Kristina's battered, beloved Volkswagen. His right hand turned upward and caught her fingers, pressing them into his palm.

The silence and the darkness enfolded them, wrapping them in a cocoon of mutual awareness. They remained silent, experiencing the flow of warmth between their locked hands. The interior of the car felt charged with an electromagnetic force, and as the silence lengthened, Kristina realized that neither of them was daring to breathe. A portentous hush filled the car.

Kristina caught her breath. She knew what was about to happen. It was inevitable. She wanted Mitch McNaughton to kiss her. And he wanted to kiss her. In the soft glow of the streetlamp she felt far more than she could see, and what she felt was a growing magnetism between them. She tilted her chin, just a little. What would it be like to be kissed by Mitch McNaughton? For a moment Kristina felt a sense of apprehension, knowing in some instinctive way that she might not be the same afterward; but it was a pleasurable kind of trepidation, as intoxicating as it was disturbing.

At the same instant, they both leaned forward, drawn by the same mysterious attraction. Their faces were an inch apart, their hands still linked when Mitch touched Kristina's cheek with his left hand, tracing her delicate bone structure with his thumb.

"I knew your skin would be as soft as satin," he whispered, stroking her face. He lifted her captured left hand to his lips and brushed a kiss on the inside of her wrist, smiling to himself when her pulse jumped, just as his had done moments before when she'd touched his hand.

Kristina buried her face in his chest and felt his arms close about her. It was wonderful to be held like this. She felt the lightening of her burden, at least for this moment, in the comfort of Mitch's arms. His fingers played across the bare skin of her shoulders, stroking and smoothing as he whispered unintelligible sounds against her ear. Her arms crept upward and locked around his neck, pulling his face closer to hers.

"I need to be held," she whispered. "Please, Mitch,

hold me. It's been so hard . . . I need someone . . ." Her words trailed away as she buried her face in his neck.

He held her so tightly she could scarcely breathe and didn't care. She welcomed the fierce strength of his embrace because it was real, it was alive, and it made her know she was alive, too. Death had stalked too closely these past few days, and she needed the fire of human companionship to drive it back into the darkness.

His chin nuzzled her neck and she felt his warm breath at her ear. Her skin tingled as his fingers caressed her shoulder, slid underneath her dress strap and lowered it until it dangled against the firm skin of her upper arm. His breathing was ragged now as his lips bent to her shoulder, kissed its rounded corner and moved to her collarbone, trailing wildfire in its path.

Kristina twisted in his arms, searching for his mouth. Her heart was pounding wildly, her body driven by some primitive instinct that knew the release offered by human passion could forestall the dark terrors of the night.

Mitch felt the desperation that made Kristina cling to him and understood its source. The long days of anxiety over her sister had taken a terrible toll and driven Kristina to the edge of panic. It was comfort she needed tonight, not sex. Though he would later curse himself for his gentlemanly instincts, he removed his hand from her shoulder and gripped the steering wheel so hard the pain brought his own desire under control. "Kristina, please, don't," he whispered, reluctantly pushing her away from him.

"Kiss me," she insisted, trying to find his mouth.

"Not tonight," he said firmly. "I'm not the kind of guy to take advantage of a damsel in distress." Gently he began to stroke her hair and speak softly, as one would to a troubled child, rocking her against his powerful chest in a way that stopped her sensual movements. "Now, then, it's all right," he crooned. "You've pushed yourself too hard. You can't fight the whole world by yourself, you know."

"Do you have a handkerchief?" she asked. "I'm afraid I'm going to cry."

"Go ahead," he answered, taking a clean square of cotton from his hip pocket. "It'll be good for you." He held her close against his chest while she wept into the handkerchief, great, racking sobs that brought release of an entirely different sort from what she originally had in mind.

Mitch held her in his arms for a long time before she finally cried herself out, her sobs dissolving into hiccoughs. "I'm so embarrassed," she lamented, holding the tear-soaked handkerchief.

"Don't be. Tears are nature's way to relieve distress, and God knows you've had plenty of that lately." He gave her a brotherly sort of squeeze and tried to coax a smile from her.

"It's not just the crying. I practically tried to seduce you—right here in the Brackenridge Hospital parking lot!" Sensible again, Kristina was aghast. Where was that icy Scandinavian reserve people were always talking about? She'd been as hot-blooded as the most notorious Latin stereotype.

Mitch grinned. "I was flattered. Maybe you'll do it again sometime." She was too abashed to meet his eyes and kept her gaze on the floorboard. His big hand came out and tilted her chin so he could drop a casual kiss on the tip of her nose. "But if you do, Kristina, I'm giving you fair warning. If it happens again, you're on."

"It won't happen again," she muttered.

"Don't be too sure about that."

"Ha!"

He circled her wrist with his fingers. Her pulse was still fluttering like a bird's. Mitch directed his attention to the digital clock on the dash. "There," he said smugly when the clock had marked the passing of exactly sixty seconds. "Your pulse rate is ninety-six and I haven't even kissed you yet. You'll be back, Neilsen, you'll be back."

"Awfully sure of yourself, aren't you?"

"Yup."

"Well, don't be so sure of *me*, because you might be wrong." She wanted to toss her head arrogantly, but something made her give Mitch a close look instead. That damned twinkle was back in his eye, and it was irresistible. "On the other hand—" She opened the car door and fished for the keys to her Volkswagen, then turned and gave Mitch her most dazzling, most devastating smile. "On the other hand—"

"Yeah." Mitch contemplated going home alone to his well-equipped bachelor quarters and cursed himself for his chivalry. He was going to have to go home

43

and fill the hot tub with ice cubes. A mere cold shower could never extinguish the fires that had been roused in him. Giving Kristina a jaunty salute as she climbed into her car and started the ignition, Mitch then rolled down his window and shouted over her noisy engine, "I'll call you soon."

She blew him a kiss. "Yeah."

They were both smiling as they went their separate ways into the night.

CHAPTER THREE

Kristina hurried across the campus lawn to her classroom. She was running late because she'd overslept, of all things, and then she'd dawdled, her mind preoccupied with thoughts of Mitch McNaughton.

She'd tried to convince herself it was because Mitch had given her sister some peace of mind at the hospital last night, but self-honesty forced Kristina to admit that Valerie's face was absent from her daydreams. Kristina's mind pictured only the rugged good looks of Mitch NcNaughton as she experienced, anew in her imagination, the brush of his lips at her throat, the strength of his arms as he held her close.

Kristina felt a sudden churning of her emotions as her body responded to the stimulus provided by her imagination. Her pulse quickened, and heat made color rise in her cheeks. *What's happening to me, anyway?* she wondered. *I haven't felt like this since my last teenage crush. Mitch McNaughton is just an ordinary man, and it's silly to be daydreaming about him. I'll probably never see him again, anyway.* But the last thought gave her such a bleak feeling that she quickly squelched it. *Of course you'll see him again. He said he'd call, didn't he?*

Yes, he said he'd call. Her spirits brightened. One thing Kristina was sure of: Mitch McNaughton was a man of his word.

She lifted her eyes, aware for the first time of the hustle and bustle around her as everyone hurried to eight o'clock classes. There were more than 44,000 students at the University of Texas, and sometimes Kristina thought that at least 39,000 of them were board-certified, card-carrying preppies. They were nice kids, bright and enthusiastic, but it seemed to Kristina that the most serious question they ever pondered was which designer label was the most trendy. What an irony! Kristina had seen the tag end of a generation of students intent on the big social issues of their day, who had considered themselves well dressed when they'd gone off to college with two pairs of faded jeans and six T-shirts emblazoned with political slogans. Nowadays it was crisp khakis for the guys, madras skirts for the girls, and oxford button-downs for everybody.

Well, Kristina didn't care about the externals. They could wear whatever they wanted. What mattered to her was what went on inside their heads. She pulled her lecture notes from her batik bag and went over them one last time, then grinned. She'd picked one of the most controversial subjects she could think of to provoke her students out of their mental lethargy. Today's class discussion should be very interesting.

Her auditorium-style classroom, with 125 seats tiered in a semicircle on seven levels, soon became the site for howls of outrage. Kristina had begun the class by picking two students at random, one who espoused the view that "mercy killing" was always wrong, the other a student who said she'd rather be dead than live a vegetablelike existence on a life-support system. Kristina called the students to the front of the classroom, but rather than let them debate their personal views, she put them in a role-playing situation. The student who was opposed to euthanasia had to take the part of a victim of a motorcycle accident who was hopelessly brain-damaged and living in an irreversible coma. The pro-euthanasic was assigned the part of an infant born with heart and lung defects who could survive only by use of respirators and an artificial heart.

When the turmoil reached a crescendo, Kristina stopped the role-playing and sent the student participants back to their seats.

"How did you feel when you were put in the part of the victim of a motorcycle accident?" Kristina asked the student who'd assumed that role.

"I don't know," responded the young man. "I didn't feel like myself at all. I tried to imagine what it would be like to be *him*, not knowing or hearing anything, having them rotate my body on machines every half hour. Maybe being in pain, too. And my family having to watch that, maybe for years and years. My folks would be worried, and desperate, and they'd go bankrupt trying to pay the hospital bills. I've never imagined that anything like that could happen to *me*."

47

"What if it did?"

"I guess I might have a different attitude about euthanasia. I might want my family to go ahead and pull the plug, because I wouldn't really be alive myself anymore, except to cause pain and suffering for other people."

"Bravo!" said Kristina, applauding. "It's not my purpose to change your beliefs, only to get you to examine them. What I'm trying to do is help you to see that other people can have an opposite belief and be justified in it. What about you?" she asked, turning to the other student. "You said at the beginning of class that you thought people have a right to die and if they can't pull the plug themselves, their family should be able to do it for them, no questions asked. Now how do you feel?"

"I still feel the same," the student answered. "But when I was playing the part, I realized it was more complicated than I'd thought and that I ought to be ashamed of myself."

"Ought to?" Kristina was moving in, forcing the student to intellectual honesty.

"Ought to be ashamed, yes, because there's more to it than what's convenient, or expedient, or economical. Before today I didn't think it was anybody else's business what a family decided to do in a situation like that."

"What do you think now?"

"I guess I can see that euthanasia-on-demand is going too far. The person I was playing was a tiny little baby who'd never even had a chance to live, and she wanted to. I was surprised at how much I was fighting to live when I was playing her part. But I could hear all those voices from the foot of my hospital crib saying how much they loved me and didn't want me to suffer, so they thought it was best to let me die. I wanted to cry out to them to give me a chance, that someday medical science would find an answer for my birth defects, but I was too weak and nobody could hear me. And while they were letting me die, I thought how selfish they were being. They weren't thinking about *me,* they were thinking about themselves, about *their* pain and suffering." The student looked down at her hands, locked tightly together on the desktop. Her palms were sweaty.

Kristina turned to the two students who'd given such an able performance. "Thank you both. I know I put you on the spot, but neither of you is as complacent in your views now as you were when class started at eight this morning. That's a real achievement. Congratulations."

The other students looked at their two colleagues in envy. The difficulty of winning praise from Dr. Kristina Neilsen was legendary, and these lucky classmates had managed to do it. Tension crackled in the classroom. A healthy sense of competition had been aroused, and other students were now keen to earn Dr. Neilsen's respect.

Kristina turned to the class. "Now, class, do you see what hard work it is to put yourself in somebody else's position? It's easier not to think at all than have to put out so much effort. But intellectual inertia is what you must fight against for the rest of your lives. That's what you're here for, to learn how to learn. And you

49

can never learn anything until you face the darkness of your own ignorance." She flipped through her class notes. "Now, a painful topic. Term papers."

The class groaned in unison, but good-naturedly. They'd known when they signed up for this class that Dr. Neilsen would work their buns off.

"How long does the term paper have to be?" queried a brave soul at the back of the room.

"Long enough to prove to me that you've learned something."

"How many sources?"

"As many as it takes." Kristina paused, though she knew campus gossip had already told them her requirements. "But here's the kicker. I don't want secondary sources from the library. I want primary sources. You've got to go out in the community and find out what's going on. You've got to get involved."

Another groan from the class, but only because they thought it was expected.

"Just don't get yourselves arrested."

Everybody laughed. Last semester one of Kristina's students had done a term project on the subject of prostitution and had been arrested while interviewing a hooker at a local massage parlor. The mistake had been quickly rectified, but it had become part of the folklore and mystique of Kristina's class.

"Why can't we just write a paper like we do for other classes?" asked a bored, querulous student at the back who hated eight o'clock classes in general and this one in particular. He was there only because of a computer foul-up at registration, and all his later efforts to get his schedule changed and get himself out of Kristina's class had been futile.

"Why? Because this is a democratic society and the system won't work unless everybody pitches in and gets involved. Don't you understand that political participation is what it's all about? Listen up, Mr. Snodgrass." Kristina paused for dramatic effect. "There's more to life than an M.B.A. from a top-ten university followed by a vice-presidency at a big bank in Dallas. You've got to give a damn." Kristina slammed shut her notebook and thrust it into her bag. "Class dismissed."

There was a line of students waiting at her office by the time Kristina got there. It had been pure coincidence that the lazy Mr. Snodgrass had played right into Kristina's hands. Thus on the same morning, two students had won her public praise, a third her public scorn. The rest of the class had been given two examples, and there was little doubt that they wanted Kristina's praise, even if they had to *think* to get it. She was deluged with questions about possible term projects, and when everybody had finally cleared out, she felt a real glow of satisfaction. There was still hope for these adorable preppies! Spurred to succeed, they'd come up with the most challenging projects of any class she'd ever taught. *Watch out, Austin,* she thought, *there's no telling what'll happen when these kids start rocking your boat.*

There was a short rap, immediately followed by a friendly face peeking around the door. "It's Friday,"

51

said Bud Thomas, a political science teacher whose office was next door to Kristina's.

"Thank God." This was their ritual conversation every Friday.

"Are you going to wrap it up early today?" Bud was long and lanky, and an aberration among college professors because the long grind of earning his Ph.D. had failed to make him cynical. Kristina had always considered his company a refreshing change from their other colleagues.

"I've got another class at eleven. If it's anything like my eight o'clock class, I'll have another line of students wanting to talk about term papers afterward."

Bud chuckled. "You must have had quite a morning. All the kids were talking about it while they were waiting to see you. I couldn't help overhearing. Snodgrass supposedly made a beeline for the registrar's office and said if the registrar wouldn't let him out of your class, he was going to file a complaint."

Kristina pursed her lips. "Good riddance."

"Now, Kristina, where's your dedication to the teaching profession? Do you really want to let Snodgrass transfer to Dr. Kyle's class and sleep his way through PolySci 201? You're the only hope for that guy to break through his apathy."

Kristina tried to think of a sharp retort to let Bud know he was giving her an undeserved guilt trip, but then she realized that he was kidding. They both knew that teaching was a two-way street, and the student had to be an active participant in the process. She smiled at Bud. "It'll serve him right to wind up with Dr. Kyle. Maybe he'll die of boredom."

"Want to join a group of us for a swim and a six-pack at Barton Springs this afternoon?"

"I don't think I can. I've got to go to the hospital at two and check on my sister." Kristina stuffed some papers in a folder and didn't look up. Bud was a friend, but still she didn't want him to see the pain in her eyes. It was always there when she thought of Valerie.

"Say, how's she doing? Better, I hope." Bud knew only that her sister was in the hospital. Kristina had told no one about Valerie's children being taken from her and her ensuing suicide attempt. Kristina believed that personal matters should be kept personal and not become a topic of conversation on the job.

"Yes, she's better, thanks. But I need to visit her as often as I can. The hours pass so slowly for her in the hospital."

"Well, if your afternoon is taken, what about tonight? How about a movie?"

Kristina hesitated. What if Mitch should call? *Don't be foolish,* she scolded herself. *He's not going to call and ask you out at the last minute, not on a Friday night.* Anyway, she'd be too restless, sitting there waiting for the phone to ring. "I'd like that," she said to Bud. "I'm in the mood for a good comedy."

"Comedy?" Bud pretended to be hurt. "I thought I'd take you to see Richard Gere and get you in the mood for romance."

Kristina arched an eyebrow. "This is so sudden. We hardly know each other."

"That's true. We're only going on our second year of daily contact." After two years, Bud still kept trying in vain to rouse a spark of something besides friendship in Kristina.

"As I said, we're practically strangers."

"Yeah, and you've had that awful old-fashioned Scandinavian upbringing. A stranger doesn't have a chance with you."

Bud returned to his own office, the hall echoing with his merrily whistled strains from "Strangers in the Night." From his side of the partition, Bud couldn't see the bright patches of color that rose in Kristina's cheeks as she remembered the dark, handsome stranger who'd held her in his arms last night.

Kristina made an afternoon visit to the hospital and found Valerie much improved. Sometime during the morning a florist had delivered to Valerie's room a lovely bouquet with a note reading "Best wishes for a speedy recovery. Mitch McNaughton." It was obvious that Mitch had had a positive effect on Valerie's condition, and her doctors indicated that she might be released from the hospital in a few more days.

Kristina was grateful for the improvement, but she felt uncomfortable when Valerie talked earnestly of how Mitch would be able to use his legal skill to get her children back. Kristina didn't want Valerie to harbor false hopes, and Mitch had been adamant in his refusal to take on her case. Yet Kristina couldn't bring herself to tell Valerie the truth. It might cause a setback. Instead she said as little as possible and cut her visit short. There would be time for painful realities later, when Valerie was stronger.

Kristina returned home, but when she realized that

she was constantly listening for the telephone, she made herself go outside and work in the rose beds. Gardening had always been therapeutic for her because she saw the nurturing of plants as a way of nurturing life. This afternoon, though, it was nothing more than a way to occupy herself and kill time while she avoided the telephone. She would not sit in her living room and listen for the telephone to ring. She would not. That was the behavior of an adolescent. Besides, she already had a date. Why should she care whether Mitch McNaughton called her or not?

But I do care. The inner voice came unbidden and would not be stilled.

Kristina went inside, climbed into the shower, and didn't emerge until she'd used up a whole tank of hot water. But the roar of the shower had finally silenced the plaintive cry of her heart.

It was early Sunday morning when Kristina answered the telephone and finally heard Mitch's voice at the other end of the line.

"Look, I know it's ill-mannered to call at the last minute," he said, "but I wondered if you'd like to play some tennis this afternoon?" Mitch didn't tell Kristina that he'd fought a losing battle with himself all weekend, trying to keep from telephoning her. He wanted to see her again, but he didn't want to get involved in her sister's problem. It was a thorny dilemma, and finally he'd decided that a fast-paced game of tennis with Kristina should be safe enough. Not much time for talking, and all your concentration went into hitting the ball.

"Tennis? Sounds good to me." Kristina tried to sound casual. "What time?"

"I've reserved a court for two at the country club. I'll pick you up about one-thirty, if that's okay with you."

"Fine." Already her adrenaline was flowing, but Mitch would never suspect from her matter-of-fact tone. "See you then." She gave him her address, then hung up the telephone and jumped out of bed. She had a million things to do before one-thirty.

"Wow!" shouted Mitch, as the tennis ball sailed over his head, giving Kristina the set at 6–3. Mitch ran back and caught the bright-yellow ball with one hand, then started toward the net, shaking his head. "I thought you were going to drive the ball, not lob it."

"Old trick I learned from my tennis coach in college. That backhand of yours was just asking for it. Besides, I had to redeem myself after letting you win the first two sets." They met at the net and shook hands.

"*Let* me win?" Mitch was bigger and stronger than Kristina, and naturally played a more powerful game.

"You're pretty good," Kristina admitted. They walked to the sidelines and got towels to wipe the sweat from their faces.

"So are you. You gave me a better game than most women do. I guess it's because you're so tall." He grinned down at her and hurriedly added, "And of course, you play smart. I had to work at it to beat you."

Kristina nudged him in the ribs with her racket.

"You're damned right you did. I saw that surprised look on your face the first time I spun my second serve at you."

"Sorry. I didn't mean to sound condescending." Mitch reached with his towel and blotted her upper lip. "Let me make amends by buying you a drink, okay?"

"So you think I won because I'm tall," Kristina muttered under her breath, but in jest. They'd given each other a good game, and their rivalry had been both friendly and fun. They were well matched.

"Quit grumbling and go take a shower," Mitch said, dropping the tennis balls back into the can. "When you're finished, I'll meet you on the patio with a long, cold drink to soothe your ruffled feathers."

Kristina joined Mitch a half hour later, her silvery blond hair pulled up into a knot at the top of her head with a ribbon. The hairstyle exposed her slim neck and tanned shoulders, left bare by a mint-green tanktop that hugged her gentle curves. Her starched white shorts were cuffed and contrasted with the dark, golden tan of her legs.

Mitch whistled when she joined him at the table.

"Thank you," she said, smiling at him.

He handed her a frozen Margarita in a stemmed glass garnished with a wedge of fresh lime. "To the most gorgeous woman in Austin this Sunday afternoon," he said, tilting his glass in a toast.

Her lips twisted in a mock frown. "I thought you'd drink a toast to the best female tennis player in Austin."

57

"That, too. I'm easy."

Kristina looked at him in astonishment, then broke into laughter. "Oh, you're *easy,* all right." She laughed again, remembering the intensity in his game of tennis, the firmness of his refusal to take Valerie's case. "A real pushover." She took a sip of her drink and peered at Mitch over the rim of her glass. "You're blushing."

Mitch turned his head and looked out across the lush green of the golf course, edged with stately live-oak trees beside a brook cascading into a natural waterfall. "It's cooler this afternoon, don't you think?"

"Umm. A little, maybe. September is always warm in Austin." She reached for his hand. "You're funny."

Mitch ran a finger around the open neck of his blue striped polo shirt. The collar seemed loose enough, but for some reason his throat felt constricted. Though Mitch had a sense of humor and could laugh at himself, it was disquieting to be teased by a woman like Kristina. From the first moment he'd met her, she'd stirred the whole range of his emotions and left him so confused, he couldn't decide whether to run *from* her or *toward* her. He felt the gentle pressure of her fingers against the palm of his hand and lifted his eyes to hers. God, that smile of hers. It was beautiful. He wasn't going to start running from her just yet. "How about some dinner?"

Kristina glanced at her watch. "I'd love to, but there isn't time. I've got to be at the hospital at seven to see Valerie. I didn't get there to visit her this afternoon, and she'll be lonely."

Mitch leaned back in his chair, his eyelids narrowed in thought. The subject he'd hoped to avoid had now reared its ugly head. Could he head it off, or should he let it take its course and let the chips fall where they might? He'd been at war with himself for four days, no nearer a solution now than he'd been on Thursday afternoon when Kristina first walked into his office. He decided to stall for time. "How's Valerie doing? Any better?"

"Yes, quite a lot—thanks to you."

"Me?" Mitch had meant to keep his eyes on the golf course, but surprise made him turn to face Kristina. It was a mistake. For when he turned, there was something so soft and vulnerable in her expression that it touched him and undermined his stern resolve.

"She has such trust in you, you know. Just seeing you gave her new hope." Kristina sighed. "I hardly knew what to do yesterday when she started talking about all you'd be able to do for her. I didn't want her to have false hopes and then be crushed later when it didn't work out. But if I told her the truth now, when she's just beginning to rally, I was afraid it might be too much for her." Kristina twirled the stem of her empty glass.

"Another drink? I'll call the waiter."

"Better not. I have to be careful with tequila. It goes to my head."

Mitch grinned at her. "I'll remember that." He signaled the waiter across the patio, holding up two fingers. "Both for you," he said to Kristina.

"I thought you weren't the kind of guy to take advantage of a woman."

Mitch's tan seemed to deepen in the glow of sunset. They were both remembering that moment in his car on Thursday night when Mitch had stopped himself from kissing Kristina and started rocking her like a child. "I hadn't expected you to be the kind of woman to remind a man of his past mistakes."

Kristina's eyelids swept downward while she carefully examined the lacy pattern of the wrought-iron tabletop. "You didn't make a mistake," she said softly. "I'm glad you protected me from myself. I don't think many men would've done that."

"Yeah . . . well," he said, squirming a little. "I have to admit I was tempted."

"Well, thank goodness!" Kristina smiled at the perplexed look on Mitch's face. "Well, wouldn't it hurt your ego if you threw yourself into someone's arms and he *wasn't* tempted?"

"I don't know. Let me try it and see." Mitch lifted his hand, which had been loosely clasping hers on the table, and brought her wrist to his lips. Her skin had the fresh scent of soap and sunshine. He kissed the throbbing pulse at her wrist, then kissed the hollow of her palm.

"Mitch, don't," Kristina whispered. It was her turn to squirm on the chair. "People will notice—"

"Notice what? That we're holding hands?" His lips moved to her fingertips, brushing a kiss on each, then gently nipping one of them with his teeth. "I think the folks at Lakeway Country Club are sophisticated enough not to be shocked by a little innocent handholding." He turned her hand over and began to massage her knuckles.

"Mitch, this isn't *innocent* hand-holding," she scolded, trying to remove her hand from his.

Tiny laugh lines crinkled at the corners of his blue eyes. "You're right, sweetheart. I think they call this foreplay. Are you tempted?"

"Mitch, stop it." Goosebumps were marching up and down her spine.

The waiter interrupted with the arrival of their drinks, and Mitch had to let go of Kristina's hand to sign the check. When the waiter had retreated beyond earshot, Mitch grumbled, "No tip for you, my man. Worst timing I ever saw."

"I'm going to sneak him ten dollars myself. I thought his timing was perfect."

Mitch gave her a steady gaze. "I can still see a little flush along those high cheekbones of yours, and your eyes are still sparkling. Maybe it's not too late—" He reached for her hand again.

Kristina gripped the cold stem of her glass with both hands. "That's enough, Mr. McNaughton."

"Want to join me in a cold shower?" He began to trace ovals on the warm flesh of her upper arm, working his way up to her shoulder.

Kristina took a long sip of her drink to cool the heat that was spreading upward through her body. Almost immediately she felt light-headed and pushed the drink away from her. "I have to hurry so I can get to the hospital by seven."

"What are you scared of, Kristina? There's no need to hurry." Mitch had been watching with keen interest as Kristina's pupils had enlarged, turning her eyes a sexy, smoky green. "We've got plenty of time to finish our drinks." He leaned forward and casually draped an arm across the back of her chair, then grinned to

61

himself when she sat rigidly upright to distance her bare shoulders from his exploring hand.

"I've had plenty to drink, Mitch. Really, let's go."

"Okay if I finish my Margarita?" He propped himself on one elbow, then reached forward with the other hand and traced the outline of her lips.

"You're stalling."

"Sure I am."

"Why?"

"To see whether I can tempt you." His thumb moved to her cheek and traced her delicate bone structure, then brushed against her earlobe.

"Well, of course you can. You have." She turned and gazed at the sunset beyond the wooded hills. She swallowed past a lump in her throat. "Now what?"

"Now I'll leave you alone." His arm came around her shoulders with a light hug. His expression was one of total innocence.

She turned and glared at him. "Then what was that all about?"

"So you'd know I won't always be as gentlemanly as I was the other night. And so you'd know how hard it was for me to stop." He gave her a lazy grin. "And because I wanted to."

"Are you playing games with me?"

"Yep. Fun games. For grown-ups." There was a bantering note in his voice as he whispered, "And you liked it just as much as I did, didn't you, Kristina?"

Her eyes were still smoldering, though she'd never admit how much his slightest touch had aroused her, or how disappointed she'd been when he stopped.

"You get me all confused," she replied. "I'm not sure how I feel when I'm with you."

"That's certainly mutual." There was a droll tilt to his eyebrow.

"You're confused? By *me?"* Kristina was astounded.

"Sure. I don't know whether to haul you off to my bed or run in the opposite direction as fast as I can go."

"Why would you want to run away?"

Mitch hesitated. Might as well get it out in the open. Sooner or later they were going to have to deal with it—if they were ever going to have a future relationship. "Because you demand too much."

"What do you mean?"

"You know what I mean." He didn't flinch from her level gaze. "You think I should rush to your sister's rescue, no matter whether I want to or not and no matter what the consequences might be."

"Mitch, she's in trouble. Somebody's got to help her."

"Why me?"

"Because you're a lawyer and because she trusts you." It was so simple to Kristina. Why couldn't he see it? "That's part of the price of being human, the duty to help other people when they're in trouble."

"Do you have any idea what it cost me to help Valerie before, when I was practicing law in Gilbert?" Mitch couldn't help it. There was a crack in his voice. "For a while it looked like my whole career had gone down the tubes. It's a miracle that I was able to pull out of it."

Kristina fastened onto his words and turned them

to her own advantage. "But don't you see, Mitch, you got your miracle? You helped her before, and you were rewarded for it. Life evens out, it always does, and when you help people, it comes back home to you."

"I'm sorry, Kristina, but I don't agree with your philosophy. You're being very naive." Mitch sipped his drink. "I didn't get rewarded in Gilbert, I got *punished* for helping your sister."

"All's well that ends well." Her smile was pure sunshine.

"That's a Pollyanna attitude if I ever heard one." He shifted his glass and made a series of overlapping circles where moisture had collected on the base. He sighed. "I know what you want me to do. And maybe I'll give in and do it. But listen, Kristina." He let go of his glass and gripped her wrist. "Don't ask me to do it without at least thinking about the consequences. It doesn't take courage to charge into battle when you haven't given a thought to what might happen. That's a fool's courage. Real bravery is risking everything when you know exactly what you're doing."

Kristina was unconvinced, but there was no doubting Mitch's earnestness. "Go ahead and tell me the possible consequences. What would you be risking?"

"First of all, the little things: Time lost from my regular practice. That's going to cost me money in lost fees."

"We'll pay you somehow. Valerie can get a job when she gets better."

"Kristina, don't be difficult. I can afford to take the loss. What I'm trying to tell you is that you ought to be aware of what you're asking of me."

She mumbled an apology and tried not to feel defensive.

"And then she's going to need a private investigator. My law practice is too heavy for me to go chasing off on trips to Gilbert hunting for clues. Private investigators charge about two hundred fifty dollars a day, so it's going to cost plenty for that."

"She can't afford that kind of expense. Do you think I could do some of the investigating? Nobody in Gilbert knows me."

"Maybe you can. That's a possibility I hadn't thought about." Mitch made a mental note. Kristina was bright and trained in research, even if it was research of a different kind. And her university schedule gave her some flexibility. Maybe it would work.

"What other costs are involved?" Kristina asked.

"The human costs. For one thing, custody cases are traumatic, and the lawyers experience almost as much emotional wear and tear as the parents do."

"I don't guess there's much I can do about that."

"No, there isn't. I'll have plenty of sleepless nights before this thing is over and probably end up with an ulcer. That's why I swore I'd never practice family law again." He took another sip of his drink. "Then there's the big problem—the Winston family. They're powerful, evil people who'll stop at nothing to crush their enemies. They aren't going to take kindly to my going after their darling John Ed again."

"But there isn't really any way they can hurt you now, is there? I mean, you're in Austin now, not in Gilbert."

"People like that always have connections. I don't

know what they can do to me. All I know is that they'll try. They'll get me if they can." He set down his glass with a thump. "That's part of the risk that can't be measured. It's also the part that makes me wonder whether it's worth it."

"I guess I wouldn't blame you if you said no. After all, they're not your kids."

They tried not to look at each other. This was a private moment of reckoning.

"It wouldn't be so bad if I thought there was a good chance of getting them back. It's one thing to pay the price when you get something to show for it. In this case, the risk may be for nothing. This is a big country, and Valerie's kids could be anywhere by now."

Kristina laid her hand across Mitch's. "It's okay, Mitch. I may not agree with everything you've said, but I understand. I won't ask your help with this. It's asking too much."

Mitch leaned over and brushed her lips with his. "Thanks." But oddly, he felt no sense of relief to be let off the hook. "Oh, hell," he said, kissing Kristina again. "She was one of my first clients. How can I let her down now?"

"You mean you'll do it?" Kristina thought she must be suffering from emotional whiplash.

"Yes, I'll do it. I don't know why, but I'll do it." He slumped into his chair, amazed himself at his unexpected capitulation. He shook his head in wonderment. "But I think you'd better tote up one more cost."

"What's that?"

"The cost to us." Mitch tried to smile but didn't

quite make it. His lips formed a lopsided grimace. "To you and me."

"What are you talking about?"

"The lawsuit. Your sister will be my client, and you'll be helping with the investigation."

"So?" Her mind was darting ahead, but she couldn't figure out what Mitch was talking about.

"So our relationship will have to be strictly professional. This case is going to be tough, and I've got to be sharp-eyed and clear-headed."

"Of course, I understand."

"But don't you understand the ramifications, Kristina? I want you, but if we get involved, I won't have my mind on your sister's case. And neither will you."

Their eyes met in dismay.

"But—"

"No *buts*. I told you before, Kristina, I don't like to lose. I'm going into this case to win, and that means I've got to have all my concentration on the lawsuit. For the time being, well, there just isn't any other choice. Our personal relationship has got to be put on hold."

Suddenly the word *consequences* took on new meaning. But Kristina desperately wanted Mitch to take her sister's case. It just hadn't occurred to her that her own loss would take effect immediately. She turned to Mitch. "You're sure?"

"Quite sure."

She nodded. "I suppose you're right." Her fingers gripped his. "In that case, I want you to kiss me now, just once."

Mitch looked across the patio. No one was watching except the waiter. "What about the waiter?" he asked.

"To hell with the waiter," she murmured, and lifted her lips for his kiss.

CHAPTER FOUR

Kristina diverted her attention from Highway 290 long enough to check her reflection in the rearview mirror. She couldn't help smiling at the image that returned her steady gaze. It had been nearly three weeks since she had volunteered to help Mitch McNaughton with her sister's case, and she was now on her way to Gilbert, in disguise, for her first experience as an amateur sleuth. Though Kristina herself was unknown to anyone in Gilbert, she bore a certain family resemblance to her sister, who'd lived there for many years. Since someone who knew Valerie might notice their resemblance and stymie Kristina's investigation, it had seemed prudent to forestall the possibility with a disguise.

Nobody will ever guess who you are, Kristina thought, chuckling at her thick, curly mane of auburn hair. The wig she'd borrowed from a friend in the drama department had totally changed her appearance. It had also required a complete change of makeup. The natural, fresh-scrubbed look she favored had seemed washed out against the vibrant color of her wig, so she'd experimented with pots of color until she found the right combination of cinnamon-brown eyeshadow and sienna blush. It had taken plenty of each, and more mascara than she'd ever worn in her life, but she now appeared such a natural redhead that she could've posed for Titian. To emphasize her new tawny complexion she wore a silky rust-color blouse, open at the throat to reveal more creamy flesh than she normally allowed. She'd borrowed some clunky gold jewelry from her theatrical friend as well as a pair of skinny, sand-colored pants. No one who met Kristina today for the first time would detect the slightest trace of Scandinavian heritage or temperament. *I believe you could pass for a passionate Irish colleen,* Kristina thought, wrinkling her nose at her reflection.

Her foot impatiently stomped on the accelerator. She was ready to get this show on the road.

Kristina stopped at a gas station on the edge of town and looked in the telephone directory to locate the addresses of all the members of the Winston family. She wouldn't talk to them in person, but she wanted to drive past their houses and try to catch a glimpse of them. She also planned to drive past John Ed's house and see whether there was any sign of life there.

She finally located the residence of John Ed's aunt and uncle, Rose Ellen and Chester Bayless, at the end of a graveled country lane. It was a large, two-story house in the early Texas settlement style of architecture, with a veranda across the front. The house was surrounded with a forbidding barbed-wire fence and several snarling watchdogs, so Kristina had to settle for a less-than-satisfactory view through binoculars. When a stout man in blue overalls came from the barn to see why the dogs were barking, Kristina quickly hid the binoculars and put the car into reverse. There hadn't been anything unusual about the place and there was no need to attract attention. Maybe there'd be better clues elsewhere.

She drove next to John Ed's house. It was within the town of Gilbert, on a quiet tree-shaded street. It was a perfectly ordinary house of yellow brick, probably forty or fifty years old but well kept. The shades were drawn, and the front lawn hadn't been mowed in several weeks. But there were no old newspapers or milk cartons collecting on the front porch. Had John Ed cancelled those services before he left with the children, or had his parents done it later? Kristina made a mental note to try to find out.

There was a detached garage behind John Ed's house, but the doors were tightly closed and presumably locked. Kristina pulled her car into the driveway for a closer look. Near the back door she saw a girl's red bicycle chained to a metal pipe, and for a moment tears sprang to her eyes. That must be her niece Shelley's bicycle. Kristina's jaw squared. *Damn you, John Ed Winston. I'll find you if it's the last thing I ever do.*

She slowly backed out of the driveway, ready to say to any curious neighbor that she'd only pulled into the drive in order to turn around. But no one appeared. It was a sleepy Friday afternoon in early October. Nobody in Gilbert was anticipating a spy in their midst.

Kristina's third stop was at the residence of John Ed's parents, Mr. and Mrs. W. Harold Winston, who

71

lived in an imposing Victorian mansion in the heart of town. *That quarried stone makes it look like a fortress,* Kristina thought. *Especially with that tower and the turrets.* She remembered that John Ed's father had been the eldest son and had inherited much of the family wealth. The family power he'd simply assumed, like a royal mantle. Valerie had always said her former father-in-law ran the Winston family the way he ran the corporation, with a tight fist and total control. John Ed never made a move without his father's permission. Kristina had never understood how John Ed could be so domineering with his wife yet so cowering with his own father. Looking at the menacing stone structure, Kristina thought she could now comprehend the source of John Ed's fear. This edifice could never be called a home. Its very mortar emanated the ooze of evil. Somehow there was a connection between this citadel and Valerie's missing children, but what? And how was Kristina to find it? She lifted the binoculars to her eyes and scanned the Winston mansion, but everything seemed in order. It was time to move on.

Kristina sat in a booth, sipping coffee and watching the other customers in the café near the Gilbert courthouse. Her disguise as an alluring redhead attracted numerous glances and finally what she'd hoped for, an offer to buy her another cup of coffee.

"Well, thanks, that would be real fine," she said in an engaging down-home drawl to the middle-aged pharmacist from the drugstore down the street. "But only if you'll join me. It's too lonesome sitting here all by myself."

The man beamed and hastily smoothed some of the wrinkles from his white surgical jacket. He sat down across from Kristina and eagerly leaned in her direction. "New in town? Or just passing through?" Thanks to a jovial smile and chubby round cheeks, brightly flushed from chronic high blood pressure, the pharmacist resembled a merry Santa Claus. Only his faded blue eyes revealed his surrender to the monotonous futility of life.

"Oh, I'm just here to do an errand for my boss," Kristina answered with a bubbly laugh. "Or I should say, I'm trying to get up my nerve to do an errand for my boss." She waved toward the courthouse, visible through the plate-glass window of the café. "He's a leasehound—I think that's what you call those fellows who sniff around and find land where there might be oil. Anyway, my boss sent me over here to the courthouse and told me to find out who owns this land."

The pharmacist nodded. This sort of thing happened all the time in Gilbert because there was still oil in the area. When the price of oil was high, there might be twenty or more of those leasehounds haunting the county clerk's office. They brought a little business with them, though, so the town put up with it.

Kristina reached in her purse and dug around until she found the piece of paper Mitch had given her for this very purpose, to establish her pretext for being in Gilbert today. "I declare, I don't know what all these ol' numbers mean. My boss told me to take this paper to the courthouse where they have the deed records. But do you know," she said, wrinkling her nose, "I thought I just better have myself a cup of coffee before

73

I go over there." Her eyelids fluttered. "My goodness, I wish I was smart like my little ol' boss so I'd know what to do."

The pharmacist looked at the notations written on the slip of paper, then fished his reading glasses from his breast pocket and popped them on his nose. The paper still didn't make sense, and he scratched his head. "I'll tell you what, we'll finish our coffee, and then I'll take you over to the courthouse and introduce you to Belva June. She knows all about deeds and stuff, and she'll know just how to find what you need." He beamed at Kristina. "We wouldn't want you to go back to your boss empty-handed, now, would we?"

"Well, if you aren't just the sweetest thing. I never knew when I stepped in here this afternoon I'd find myself a knight in shining armor." Her eyelashes fluttered again. She reached across the table and patted his hand.

He cleared his throat. "Now, now, that's the way folks are in a small town. Anybody here'd be glad to help you out. All you have to do is ask." He signaled the waitress for more coffee.

"Oh, my, this is the prettiest little town I ever saw," Kristina agreed. "I never saw so many interesting houses in my whole life. Why, I noticed one house when I drove into town that looked like a *castle!* My goodness, I almost expected to see knights on horses come charging through the gate."

"That must be the old Winston place you're talking about. There's usually a guard at the gate, all right. They're mighty particular who goes in and out."

Kristina's eyes widened. "Really? Are they rich and scared someone will try to steal their money?"

"Oh, I reckon their money is safe. They own almost everything in town. No, they're just that way, kind of strange, you know." The pharmacist was so engrossed with Kristina's company that he didn't realize he was talking too much.

"My goodness, I'd love to be rich and live in a big ol' house like that. I don't suppose they have a bachelor son about my age, do they?"

There was a momentary flicker in the blue eyes, and the pharmacist became guarded. "Nope, 'fraid not," he said.

"Wouldn't you just know it? Well, can't blame a girl for hoping, can you?" Kristina smiled and tried once again to steer the conversation in the direction of the Winstons, but it was a lost cause. The pharmacist had buttoned up and wouldn't budge. After some idle conversation about the weather and how it affected people's ailments, a subject dear to the heart of the pharmacist, Kristina rose to go. "Now, you don't have to go over to the courthouse with me if you need to get back to work," she said.

"Nonsense, it'll be my pleasure," the pharmacist protested. He paid the check and left a 50-cent tip for the waitress. Wouldn't want this pretty redhead to think he was cheap. He held the door open for Kristina and they started across the street. To her left she could see the sign over the pharmacy shop. "WINSTON DRUGSTORE AND SUNDRIES" read the sign. Next to it was a sign reading "WINSTON HARDWARE STORE."

The pharmacist was right. The Winstons owned everything in town.

The pharmacist left Kristina in the capable hands of Belva June Blasingame, who hunted through musty record books until she located the requested deed. She was a gold mine of gossip, but unfortunately none of it had anything to do with the Winston family or the strange disappearance of John Ed Winston. A young deputy sheriff wandered down the hall to the county clerk's office, having heard there was a good-looking stranger there, and he was more talkative than Belva June until he was shushed by a warning look from someone behind the counter.

Kristina left the courthouse with the feeling that she'd gained little from her journey to Gilbert unless Mitch could figure out some way to put the bits and pieces together. She'd planned to go by the children's school to talk to their principal and also to the newspaper office to see whether there'd been any write-ups concerning the disappearance of Valerie's children. The Gilbert *Gazette* was a purely local newspaper, not circulated in Austin, so Kris had intended to check recent issues for small-town gossip. On second thought, however, Kristina decided that she'd better save those trips for other days and other disguises. In a small town like Gilbert, people were bound to talk, and if they figured out why she'd come, the Winstons would be forewarned that something was afoot. *Next time I think I'll disguise myself as a brunette,* Kristina thought. *From Boston.* She spoke aloud, practicing broad *a*'s, and decided that if she ever quit the teaching profession, she'd go into acting.

Kristina glanced at her watch. It was four o'clock. She'd have to hurry to catch Mitch while he was still at the office. The Volkswagen shuddered when Kristina shoved the accelerator to the floorboard. She could hardly wait to tell Mitch everything that had happened. All in all, it had been quite a day.

Mitch's astonishment at Kristina's altered appearance was second only to that of his secretary, who'd been unable to hold back a gasp when the sexy redhead breezed in the office and announced in a strangely familiar voice that she was Kristina Neilsen.

"What on earth!" Mitch cried, those words quickly followed by, "Man, oh, man, what a dish!" He walked around Kristina three times, trying to assimilate the changes, then cracked up when she began to repeat the day's conversations in the heavy drawl she'd used during her conversations in Gilbert.

"And then, Mr. McNaughton, why, would you ever believe, that little ol' deputy sheriff was only too happy to tell me how hard they'd worked in the sheriff's office to track down those poor missin' Winston children. Why, bless my soul, there just weren't any clues at all, nothin' to explain the mysterious circumstances, except, of course, that the children's daddy *did* disappear by coincidence at the same time as the children."

"Pure coincidence, of course," Mitch said in a dry voice, leaning back in his chair to watch Kristina cavort around his office in fine mettle.

"And, of course, there were some nasty ol' rumors," she continued, "seein' as how's some folks don't have much use for the Winstons, but that's only 'cause they're jealous of all that money. But none of those nasty ol' rumors panned out, even though all the deputies worked days and days on the matter because Mr. and Mrs. W. Harold Winston called the sheriff's office every hour on the hour askin' if everything possible was being done to find their grandchildren. And, of course, the sheriff, he kept the Winstons right up to the minute on everything, even tellin' them all that gossip about someone leavin' Gilbert with a travel trailer and comin' back without it."

Mitch's ears perked up. "A travel trailer? Now that's odd. Did he have any explanation?"

"Well, of course not, there just wasn't any. Why, the Winstons hired off-duty deputies to look into the matter, but no one could find a single clue. Must've been a big, fat lie."

"But who would make up such a crazy story? It doesn't make sense."

"I know." Kristina jerked off the auburn wig and plopped herself down in a chair across from Mitch. "That wig is hot." She sighed. "I've been thinking about it for fifty miles, and there just isn't any explanation. Why are you looking at me so funny?"

"What's that on your face?"

Kristina's fingers reached up and touched her cheeks. "Did I get something on myself?"

"No. It's all that warpaint. I've never seen you decked out like that before."

Kristina laughed. "You didn't even notice it when I had the wig on."

"Well, I certainly notice it now. I prefer your gorgeous fresh-scrubbed look."

78

Kristina reached in her purse and located a small mirror. "I think the makeup looks pretty good, myself." She put the wig back on her head and straightened it. "Looks better with red hair, though. It's a little too much for a blonde."

Mitch watched her endearing female mannerisms, patting her hair, tilting her head and smiling at her reflection. "Is what my father always used to tell me true, that inside every woman is a little girl playing grown-up?" The smile he gave her was pure affection.

"What makes you say that?" Kristina grumbled. She felt like a child with her hand caught in the cookie jar.

"Because it's hard for me to square the picture of you sitting here today primping with the tough, aggressive woman who stormed into this office a few weeks ago demanding help for her sister. Which one of you is the real Kristina Neilsen?"

Her arm lifted imperiously. "Both of those and many others. For I, sir, am a woman of many facets. I'll not be pigeonholed."

Mitch propped his chin on his hands and gazed glumly across the desk at her. "Heaven help me." He sighed. "Acting has gone to her head. She thinks she's died and gone to Hollywood." Mitch waited for her smile. "That's better. If you're going to play another role today, let it be Lois Lane, girl reporter. What else did you find out in Gilbert?"

For the next half hour they went over Kristina's information from every angle, but there were still things that didn't add up. "For example," Kristina said, "why did the pharmacist lie and tell me the Winstons didn't have an unmarried son about my age? It seems as if that would be a harmless admission to make, especially since the deputy sheriff mentioned John Ed."

"But you said someone at the courthouse tried to muzzle the deputy."

"Not until he brought up the subject of the travel trailer." Kristina doodled on a scratchpad, her brow furrowed in thought as she tried to remember the exact sequence of the conversation.

"So what we have is a pharmacist who denies there's a Winston son, a deputy sheriff who admits there is one and seems willing to tell everything he knows, and a court clerk who silences the deputy when he mentions the unexplained travel trailer." Mitch drew boxes around the points he'd listed on a yellow legal tablet. "What's the court clerk's name?"

"Belva June Blasingame. But she's not the one who got the deputy to shut up, that was someone else behind the counter."

"What did Belva June have to say about the Winstons?" Mitch tapped his pencil against the desk.

"Nothing. She talked about the weather and how many babies had been born in September and that kind of stuff."

"So she didn't contribute to the conversation about John Ed but she didn't try to stop it either?"

"What are you driving at?"

"I'm trying to figure out whether there's a pattern to who'll talk and who won't. Your Belva June doesn't seem to fit into either group."

Kristina leaned forward, her head in her hands, and

rubbed her eyes, trying to bring the entire scene back to her conscious memory. "I think she'd stepped out of the room when the deputy was talking about John Ed. She had to go down to the basement to get some old deed records." Kristina's expression was puzzled. "By the time she got back, the deputy was bragging about the high school football team."

Mitch's eyelids narrowed. "So the pharmacist won't talk, and he works in a drugstore owned by the Winstons. One court clerk says nothing, and another one gets nervous when certain aspects of the case are discussed. And the deputy sheriff blabs his head off." Mitch tossed down the pencil in frustration. "At first I thought we ought to try to find out if there's any connection between the court clerks and the Winstons, but if the deputy who's been working the case doesn't have anything to hide, then why would anybody else? The women at the courthouse don't work for the Winstons."

"Maybe their husbands do."

A slow smile began to work its way across Mitch's face. "Kristina, I think you're on to something." He jotted something new at the bottom of his legal tablet, then lined through it. "No, that doesn't solve it either. Didn't you say the Winstons called the sheriff's office every day to see if everything possible was being done to find their grandchildren?"

"Every hour on the hour. That's what the deputy said. And they hired off-duty deputies to work overtime on the case, hunting for leads about the travel trailer."

Mitch stood up and began to pace the floor of his

office, his big frame casting shadows as he moved. "Why would they do anything that would bring the sheriff any closer to finding their son?"

"That's it!" Kristina and Mitch spoke simultaneously, then grinned at each other.

"Are you thinking what I'm thinking?" Mitch asked.

"What better way to throw law enforcement officials off the trail? The Winstons telephoned constantly so it would look like they wanted to help, and then they planted a false clue with the travel trailer and wasted the deputies' time until they finally gave up the search." Kristina's doodles were no longer aimless circles but began to take on the shape of a west Texas tornado.

"Very clever." Mitch moved to the window and looked at the tiny waves rippling in the Colorado River below.

"So they must know exactly what's going on. Maybe they even helped John Ed plan the kidnapping."

Mitch leaned his head against the window casement, one arm uplifted for support. He'd been so intent on trying to untangle the facts that he hadn't been thinking about the law. It now occurred to him that this might not be a simple, garden-variety "child-snatching" case that could be resolved by kidnap and custody laws. There might be a more complicated legal issue at stake. The Winstons were an evil, powerful family and they always stuck together against the world. Had they planned the abduction of Valerie's children in concert with their son? If so . . .

Mitch went to the bookshelves and thoughtfully ran his finger across the titles of his lawbooks until he found a good starting place. He removed a volume of *Texas Jurisprudence* from the shelf and flipped through the pages until he found the topic he wanted, then quickly scanned the printed columns. He lifted his eyes from the page and found Kristina watching him. "Sorry. I just had an idea." He placed the book on his desk and took another, totally absorbed in what he was doing.

"Should I leave?" Kristina asked. "You're trying to concentrate."

"No, no, don't go." Mitch motioned her back into her chair. "This won't take long." He brought another book to the desk with him, sat down and lifted his long legs onto his desktop while he continued to read. He made a few notes on his legal tablet, then reached for the telephone and dialed a number. "Is Walt gone for the day?" he asked. "How long ago did he leave?" He glanced at his watch, then told the answering service he'd catch his friend at home later and hung up the receiver.

"Look, are you sure you don't want me to leave?" Kristina had begun to feel like excess baggage. Mitch didn't seem to remember she was in the room with him.

He looked at her in surprise. "I told you to stay, didn't I?"

"You're trying to work on something and I'm in the way."

"I'm working on your case, Kristina. All at once it seems to have a new wrinkle in it. I was trying to call my friend Walt Biggers, who's board-certified in family law. I need some information from an expert before I go off on a wild-goose chase." Mitch took the lawbook back to its place on the shelf, then turned to Kristina. "If we haven't made a mistake in piecing this thing together, then it looks like the whole Winston family may be engaged in a conspiracy to help John Ed maintain wrongful possession of the children."

"What does that mean?"

"It's something a whole lot different from when one parent snatches the kids from the other parent. If the Winstons helped John Ed plan the abduction, or if they're still helping him carry it out, why, they're in this thing up to their necks. Including the damage it's done to your sister, driving her to a desperate suicide attempt." An angry note had begun to creep into Mitch's voice. "Those rotten creeps."

"My, my." Kristina couldn't keep a little sarcasm from showing.

"Why do you say that?"

"It's taken three weeks, but you're finally beginning to sound the way I did the day I first came to see you. What made you change?" Kristina leaned back in her chair and fixed her gaze on Mitch. "The situation is exactly the same now as it was then. The kids are still gone, Valerie is still desperate, and John Ed is still in control. The only difference is that now you're getting agitated about it and then you weren't."

"Are you trying to pick a fight?" Mitch was totally mystified at this sudden attack on his motives.

"No, I'm not. I'm just curious. From the beginning I simply couldn't understand why you wouldn't get involved when someone needed you. And I don't understand what's made you ready to fight now."

Mitch left his position at the bookshelves and wandered to the window. "I didn't want to take Valerie's case because in the first place, I don't like child custody cases, and in the second place, I don't like losing lawsuits and I've learned to pick my battles." The river below had darkened as the sun dropped toward the western horizon. It seemed to Mitch that his relationship with Kristina was darkening in the same way. They were two different kinds of people, and they simply didn't have the same outlook on life. He was beginning to think they'd never be able to understand each other, but he wasn't going to pretend to be something he wasn't just to try to please her. "I'm not going to grab a jousting lance and go tilting at every opponent that comes along. You lose too much hide that way, and I've got all the scars I want." Mitch turned to face Kristina. "Sorry to disappoint you, but I'm not cut out to be a gung-ho idealist like you are. Call it cowardice if you want to, but people who mind their own business usually live longer."

Kristina rose impatiently from her chair. He hadn't really answered her question and told her why he was finally getting upset with the Winstons. Instead, he'd gotten all defensive and started taking potshots at Kristina's idealism. Lawyers! They were all alike, grabbing whatever was at hand to win an argument. She looked directly at Mitch, even more handsome with sunlight and shadows emphasizing his features. *You're not just a lawyer,* she thought, *you're also a man, and a pretty sexy one at that. And if we don't*

85

watch out, we're getting ready to have one heck of a fight. Why spoil everything?

"Oh, for heaven's sake," Kristina said. "I've never thought of you as a coward. Pig-headed, maybe, but not a coward." She glared at him in such an exaggerated way that she made him laugh, and for the moment, the tension was broken.

He left the window and came to her, his chin resting against her temple. "You sure make one hell of a redhead, you know that?"

"They say blondes have more fun." She stepped a little closer into his embrace and lifted her face to his.

Mitch bent his head, pulling her soft, pliant body against his. His mouth was halfway to hers when he realized that if he started kissing her, he wasn't going to be able to stop. Her body was having a powerful effect upon him. Instead, he dropped a quick kiss on the top of her head and stepped back to a safe distance. "When this case is over, we'll have to check that out, won't we?"

"That's what I mean by pig-headed," Kristina said, disappointed by his sudden withdrawal. "You keep saying we have to wait until Valerie's case is finished, but we may be drawing our social security checks before that happens. We're no closer to a solution today than we were three weeks ago."

Mitch grinned at her, trying to quench their ardor by being playful. "Then maybe we'll have to find out whether little old silver-haired ladies have more fun than blondes."

"I bet they have just as much fun as little old silver-haired men."

86

Mitch patted his thick head of hair. "Is my gray beginning to show?"

"Bend down here and let me check."

Mitch leaned forward, only to realize too late that his cheek was close to the soft swell of Kristina's breast. Summoning all his will-power, he resisted the urge to bury his face and cursed his body for its reaction to her femininity. No matter how much he desired her, she was forbidden to him by his legal duty to his client. He swallowed hard and forced his voice to sound normal. "Find any gray?" he asked.

With the movement of her fingers through his hair, Kristina's torso twisted, causing her other breast to brush against Mitch. In another moment, passion would take over and consume them.

"Not yet," Kristina answered breathlessly. "Come closer."

Something in Kristina's dreamy expression alerted Mitch that they were nearing the point of no return. "Not on your sweet life," he protested, reluctantly pulling away from her. "You might try to ravish me."

"No doubt I would," she said with a soft sigh. Her body was aroused by his nearness and clamoring for satisfaction. And no matter how Mitch might deny it, he was equally stimulated. There was no way he could hide from Kristina the response of his body when he'd held her close. But since Mitch was determined that nothing should happen between them, she might as well accept the inevitable with as much grace as possible. She'd follow his example and try to camouflage her desire with playful banter. "Does it matter, or are you saving yourself for marriage?"

"Kristina Neilsen—" Mitch sputtered, at a loss for words.

"Shall I go wash my mind out with soap?" She grinned at Mitch, who was still strangling for breath. "You're turning purple. Should I administer mouth-to-mouth resuscitation?"

"Do you see that lawbook on my desk? Go sit down and read the discussion on 'Conspiracy.' That should give you something besides me to feast your lecherous mind on. Read the whole thing and then I'm going to give you a pop quiz."

"Yes, sir," Kristina said meekly, promptly sitting down and opening the lawbook. Just before she looked at the printed page, she gave Mitch an ornery smile. "You know, you're really cute when you get mad."

CHAPTER FIVE

The setting sun had turned the western sky crimson, bathing the city of Austin in a warm twilight glow. Kristina's Volkswagen followed Mitch's Nissan 300-ZX west to the blue-green hills of Rob Roy overlooking Lake Austin. The community had been developed on the periphery of Austin within the past ten years for people with wealth enough to afford its natural beauty. Each custom-built home was situated on a large wooded plot to capture the soaring views. Various types of architecture, from traditional to contemporary, Victorian to eclectic, marked the development as a trend-setter, fresh and unique.

As Kristina followed Mitch, she found herself wondering which of the lavish homes they passed would be his. When his car turned into his driveway, she gave keen attention to the split-level native stone and redwood home built on the slope of a hill. She had to admit that the exterior of the house suited him, despite its contemporary design. Maybe it was because it was built of strong, natural materials that seemed timeless and indomitable.

Kristina hopped out of her car before Mitch got

there to help her with the door. "Well, I'm impressed."

Mitch shrugged. "What can I say? It's crass materialism, but it's home." Because Mitch liked the location but had no interest in building from scratch, he'd bought an existing house from a bachelor transferred to another city. Mitch liked most of the things about it, especially its masculine sense of comfort, but there were changes he'd make if he ever built a place himself. "Come on in and I'll show you around."

"I don't know how you can spend any time indoors when you're surrounded by this gorgeous view." She eyed a redwood lounge chair on the front deck. "Or maybe you spend all your time out here."

"There's another deck out back. That's where I spend my time. People can see you here in front." They'd talked while they were climbing up the steps to the front door, which Mitch now unlocked. "Let me start the fire in the grill and then I'll give you a tour."

He led her inside through the atrium-style entry and down a short hall to a bright, airy kitchen with a stovetop island in its center and a floor of glazed red brick pavers. The cabinets, countertops, and appliances were all a gleaming white, and pine accent pieces on the walls and several large green plants added color and warmth to the room. Mitch opened the freezer and removed two packages marked "rib eye steak," then placed them on a nearby counter. "Hope you like yours rare in the middle, since we'll have to cook them frozen. I hadn't planned on company tonight."

"I always eat my beef rare," Kristina said in a seductive voice.

The laugh lines crinkled at the corner of Mitch's eyes. "From the way you're looking at me, I almost believe you'd eat it *raw.*"

"Raw beefcake. Sounds good to me."

"Beef*steak,* sweetie, not beef*cake.* There's a difference."

"Really? Why don't you show me?" Her lips puckered in a 1920s pout.

"Why don't you wash this lettuce so we can have a salad? Or better yet, I'll wash the lettuce and you go take off that wig and wash your face."

"Oh, you don't like my disguise." She pouted her lips again.

"No more, vamp. We're here to talk business, remember? Me, lawyer. You, snoop." He beat his chest Tarzan-style. "This is my jungle and I say we're here to *work.* Nothing more."

Kristina laughed. "We already agreed on that when we left your office. So who are you trying to convince, me or yourself?"

Mitch muttered something unintelligible and probably profane. "I'm going to go light the grill. Why don't you come sit on the deck while I get supper started?"

Kristina leaned toward Mitch and put her fingers on his chest, stroking his hard-muscled flesh through his shirt. "Why don't you let me light the grill? I'm good at starting fires." Her lips brushed his ear and gently nibbled.

He shoved his hands in his pockets. Kristina was having a devastating effect on his body, which was about to embarrass him with its betrayal. *Mind over matter, in a pig's eye,* he chastised himself. *Flesh and blood win out every time.* He felt the heat rising and knew his face was beginning to burn. "Kristina, please, don't."

"I thought that was the woman's line. To say *please, don't* in a breathless voice all the time she's melting against someone."

Kristina gave him a closer look. Poor dear, he really was looking uncomfortable. And he'd shoved his hands in his pockets so he wouldn't be tempted to put his arms around her. It was naughty of her to tease him this way. It must be this get-up she had on and a day of acting like a sex siren. She sighed. She supposed she'd have to stop. And she'd been having so much fun too. She patted his shoulder in a very sisterly fashion. "Okay, okay. Point me to a bathroom and I'll go turn myself back into a prim-and-proper Scandinavian. You'll just have to cook our supper without any help from me."

Mitch breathed a sigh of relief. "I think I can manage. The bathroom is down the hall and to your right."

Kristina had to go through Mitch's bedroom to get to the skylighted master bath. His bedroom was simple, carpeted in leaf-green with a king-size bed and several pieces of heavy pine furniture. The walls were wainscoted with pine paneling and papered with a blue-green grasscloth. There were glass doors opening onto the deck, so that the bedroom merged with the visible expanse of blue sky and cedar-blanketed hills to create the effect of being a natural, secluded clearing in a forest. There was a sense of serenity and harmony, as though the owner of the room had found peace with himself and the world.

And I guess he has, Kristina thought. *I think that's part of what attracts me to him. He knows exactly who he is and doesn't have to prove anything to anybody. He doesn't churn inside the way I do, trying to take on the whole world.* She noted that everything was in its place and wondered about the legends she'd always heard about messy bachelors. Even if Mitch had a house-keeper, you'd think *something* would be thrown on a chair. She peeked in the closet. Perfect. How disgust-ing!

Kristina went into the bathroom, its color scheme repeating the blues and greens of the bedroom and brightened with the use of plenty of white. She pulled off her auburn wig and chuckled wryly at her own bedraggled hair underneath. She might as well take a shower and shampoo it. There was no hope of salvag-ing her hairdo after a full day of wearing the wig.

She found a supply of clean towels, located the soap and shampoo, and stripped off her clothes. A shower would certainly be refreshing.

When she rejoined Mitch, her silver-blond hair was sleek and shining, her face fresh-scrubbed. She'd had pressed powder and lipstick in her purse, but nothing more.

"Yiminy!" Mitch said, in a feeble attempt at a Scan-dinavian dialect. "Ay tank you bane Hilde from Nor-way. You bane gude vork."

93

"No, by yiminy, Ay bane Kristina from Sweden . . . by way of Austin, Texas. And I smell something cooking. Umm, smells delicious."

"It's that beefcake you ordered." He handed her a bite of avocado from the salad he was tossing. "You smell pretty good yourself."

"It's that Brut soap of yours."

"Smells different on you." He took another sniff and hastily turned back to the salad bowl. It wasn't the scent of soap he'd noticed. It was the scent of female, and it was disturbing. Pleasantly disturbing. He'd have to be careful. "I fixed you a Bloody Mary. It's in the refrigerator."

"No Margarita this time?" She got her drink and took a sip. It was mixed perfectly.

"You said you couldn't handle tequila."

Kristina came and peeked over his shoulder. "I think you didn't fix Margaritas because you can't handle me when I can't handle the tequila." She reached for a bit of romaine and took a nibble. She'd managed to press him into the corner where the two rows of cabinets met. She lifted her eyes to his and gave him a saucy grin. "I've got a little secret for you. I can't handle vodka either."

Mitch's hands shot out, took Kristina by the shoulders, and pushed her to arm's length. "The steaks are burning."

She stood on tiptoe and flicked her tongue across his bottom lip. "That's not all that's burning."

Mitch reached for a dishtowel and whacked her across the fanny. "You behave yourself or you're going

94

home. You promised me you'd come back out here a prim-and-proper Scandinavian."

"List the famous Scandinavians you know."

Mitch looked at her in surprise.

"There's Ann-Margaret, Liv Ullman, Britt Eklund," Kristina said, answering her own question. "I'm acting the way Scandinavians are *supposed* to act. After all, forebears who came from the land of the midnight sun had to find ways to occupy themselves during the times when the night was twenty-four hours long." She glanced out the window to view the lingering sunset. "Gee, isn't it ever going to get dark?"

Mitch handed her a plate. "Go get the steaks." His jaw was clenched so hard he could hardly get the words out. He might as well have invited the devil himself home for dinner. The temptation he was suffering couldn't possibly be any worse.

They ate their steaks on the deck while they watched the sun sink behind the hills in a fiery red ball. Crickets chirped, and nearby they could hear a mockingbird's last song of the day. A gentle breeze riffled the leaves in the trees and the taller grasses. The changing light played across Kristina's features, emphasizing her fine bone structure and long, slim neck. Mitch asked her about her work at the university, and she was animated as she talked about this year's crop of students and their good response to her challenge to get involved.

"Good lord, you must be giving them the same lecture you've given me."

"At least I'm consistent."

"Fanatics are consistent."

Her fingers reached across the table and touched his hand. "It's been a beautiful evening, Mitch. Let's not spoil it by arguing, okay?"

He shrugged. "I didn't know I was. I was enjoying what you said about your classes. The kids must be a lot different now from the way they were when I was in college. Nobody had to make assignments to get students involved back then."

"Times change." She swatted a mosquito. "You'd think we'd be rid of these pests by October."

"It's still warm. They'll be around for a few more weeks. Let's go inside." He pushed back his chair and helped Kristina with hers, then started gathering up their plates. "I need to call Walt Biggers at home. I have to talk to him so we can decide what to do next about Valerie's case."

Kristina took their glasses and silverware and followed Mitch back indoors, then went to the kitchen and started filling the dishwasher while he was on the telephone.

When Mitch returned, the kitchen was all in order and the dishwasher was running. "Hey, you didn't need to do that. You're my guest."

She smiled at him. He was thoughtful with excellent manners—a gracious host. If Mitch was any example, Texas A&M couldn't be all bad, no matter what people at U.T. said. Mitch was a little conservative, maybe, but there was something about his straight-arrow approach to things that was solid and comforting. "Don't you remember how it was at summer camp? If you were on Preparation, you didn't have to do Clean-Up. Well, you did the preparation all by yourself tonight. The least I could do was take care of the clean-up." She hung up the dishcloth she'd been using and followed Mitch into the dimly lighted den, their hands loosely clasped. "You can tip me with a kiss if you want to, though." Her green eyes were sparkling, daring him to kiss her.

Like most people who keep their emotions under a tight rein, every now and then Mitch would let go and do something a little crazy. This was going to be one of those times, he could feel it coming. "Do you think I can stop with just one?"

Kristina cocked her head. He wasn't running from her dare. This might prove interesting. Her tongue slipped through her parted teeth and began to trace her lips in a provocative gesture. "I think you're scared you won't be able to stop at all." She took one slow step toward him, then another. Her fingers moved to the top buttonhole of her blouse and unbuttoned it. She could feel her heart pounding in her breast.

"One kiss, Kristina, one *kiss*. Don't unbutton any more buttons." Mitch was mesmerized by the sight of her hand moving to the second button. For a moment it didn't seem that she would stop, but finally she did.

"You can unbutton the second button," she said, her voice breathless as he closed the distance between them and took her in his arms.

He held her tightly against him, and she could feel the rapid thud of his heart. "One kiss," he murmured, "and that's all. So let's make it last." His hands came up and took her face, holding her so he could see each feature. One finger traced the delicate arch of her eyebrows, then her eyelids. "Your eyes aren't green now, they're smoky," he said, brushing each eyelid with his lips. He traced her nose, then rubbed his against it. "There's an Eskimo kiss for you," he said, "but it doesn't count." His hands caught her golden hair and tangled his fingers in the shimmering mass of it.

Her hands moved up his back, tightening her grip, and as she arched herself against him, her body melded to his. She felt his body spring to life, responding to hers, and as it did so, he moaned and buried his lips in her neck. He kissed her in all the secret hollows of her neck until she sighed with pleasure. She shifted sideways, then reached for his hand and lifted it to her breast.

He shuddered, gripped by a convulsion of yearning desire, and moved his hand away from the seductive softness she'd offered him. "No, Kris, don't, or I really won't be able to stop."

"Please, I want you to." She twisted, so that his head trailed lower on her neck and he could see the soft swell of her breasts in the open V of her blouse. His breath quickened as a sweet ache coursed through him. Against his will, his hand came back to her breast, caressing its softness through the silky fabric of her blouse. He felt the hardening of her nipple, and in imagination he could see its rosy tip responding to his hand. He reached to stroke her other breast and found its nipple already erect from the whirlpool of sensation he'd created in her body.

Mitch unbuttoned the second button, and the third.

Then he sank to his knees on the carpeted floor of the den, pulling Kristina down beside him.

He unbuttoned the fourth and last button. The blouse fell open, and he reached behind her to unclasp the bra that kept her bosom hidden from his view.

In one fluid gesture she slipped off the blouse and the lacy bra. She was bare from the waist up, her blond hair flowing loose against her shoulders. She knelt facing him, her shoulders straight and chin high while he gazed at her proud, full breasts.

"Oh, God, Kristina." His finger reached out to trace a circle around the soft flesh, then brushed the hardened tip of each breast. "Oh, God, you're so beautiful. . . ."

The telephone shrilled.

"What the hell . . ." Mitch shook his head in anger.

The telephone shrilled again.

Kristina's eyes met Mitch's. She wanted to say *Don't answer it,* but the damage was already done. The mood was broken.

The phone shrilled for a third time.

"It's okay, Mitch. Go ahead and answer it."

His expression was bleak. "Don't go away. I'll be right back." He hurried across the room, calling over his shoulder. "Don't move. Don't even breathe."

"Sure," Kristina muttered under her breath. She sank on the floor cross-legged and buried her head in her hands. Disappointed, she reached for her clothes and put them back on.

Mitch came back into the room. "It's for you," he said.

"For *me?* Nobody knows I'm here." She reached for Mitch's hand and let him pull her lightly to her feet.

"It's Valerie. She says she's been calling all over town looking for you."

"Oh, for crying out loud." Kristina stomped behind Mitch as he led the way to his study, and she was none too gracious when she heard her sister's voice on the line. "What is it, Valerie?" They had a short conversation, ending with Kristina's assurance that she would be home soon to tell Valerie everything she'd learned in Gilbert. "Go on to bed, Valerie. I'll wake you when I get there." She slammed the receiver back on its cradle, muttering, "Damn, damn, damn," to the world in general.

"Anything wrong?" Mitch lounged against the door frame, wondering if there were some new crisis with Valerie.

"With Valerie or with me?"

"I think I know what's the matter with you. Same thing that's the matter with me. What about Valerie?"

"Oh, damn Valerie. She can be such a big baby sometimes. You know that she's been staying with me since she got out of the hospital. She knew I left for Gilbert at noon today, and she figured something terrible must've happened to me or I'd be home by now."

Mitch smiled. "You'll have to let her know that thanks to her timely telephone call, nothing terrible happened to you after all."

"Mitch, don't you dare joke about this!" Kristina wailed and threw herself into Mitch's arms, pounding her fist against his chest in sheer frustration.

Fortunately the roaring in his head had stopped and

he had himself back under control. He rocked Kristina in his arms until she quieted. Then he took her face between his hands and kissed the tip of her nose. "Someday soon, Kris, this case will be behind us, and I'll take you away someplace where there aren't any telephones and nobody will bother us. We'll have all the privacy we want, and I'll make love to you from the top of your head to the tips of your toes."

"Is that a promise?"

"It's a promise." Mitch allowed himself the luxury of crushing her against his chest before he took a deep breath and told himself he had no other choice but to give up this moment. He flipped on all the lights in the study and waved Kristina into a leather recliner, handed her a legal pad and a pencil, then sat behind his desk. "Now let me tell you all about Walt Biggers and what he thinks about Valerie's case."

It was with increasing zest that Mitch began to outline a different approach to Valerie's problem. "Walt agrees with me," Mitch explained, "that this isn't a run-of-the-mill case. What we have here may well be a rich, powerful family helping their son carry out an illegal act. They may have involved some of the townspeople in what they're doing, possibly even have tried to circumvent and sabotage an investigation by law enforcement officials."

"That's the feeling I have after spending a day in Gilbert, but how do we go about proving hunches and suspicions?"

"By filing a lawsuit and using what lawyers call discovery methods. When we talk about *subpoenas* and *depositions* and *motions to produce documents,* it sounds awfully boring. But when those discovery tools can help us get our hands on the information that shows what the Winstons are doing and how, it can be very exciting. In fact, Walt's really interested in this case. He says it presents an intriguing legal issue that's never been presented to the courts before."

"What's that?" Kristina glanced down at her legal pad and noticed in the process that she'd missed buttoning one of her buttons when she'd put her blouse back on. She avoided Mitch's eyes and rebuttoned it, wondering how long it would be before her breasts forgot the touch of his hand. She still felt an exquisite tenderness there.

"Can you hold family members accountable for helping with an abduction? That's the issue here. I'm not talking about *criminal* liability, I'm talking about *civil* liability. Because if Valerie can sue the Winston *family* in addition to John Ed, she can make them pay for the suffering she's been through."

"Pay? You mean, with money? All Valerie wants is her kids back."

"Of course. But what better way to get them back than to stick the Winstons with a damage award? When they find themselves looking down the barrel of a big, fat judgment, they may take it upon themselves to see that John Ed brings those children back to their mother."

Kristina gave Mitch a smile of pure delight. "Way to go, McNaughton! I knew you wouldn't let me down."

"Now, don't get your hopes up," Mitch cautioned.

"This is something brand new, and I'll have to do some research to be sure it's feasible."

"But if it is, then what?"

"Then we'll sue the Winstons, the whole bunch of them. There's no way we can get service on John Ed, since we don't know where he is, but we can damned sure find the rest of them. We'll haul them into court and force them to turn over documents to show how they've helped John Ed, and then we'll take the case to a jury and show how Valerie has been harmed by their wrongdoing. Valerie just might be lucky and become a rich divorcée."

Kristina had never been around a lawyer who was in the midst of unsnarling a complex legal problem, and she was surprised at the transformation in Mitch. His adrenaline was flowing, and he projected an aura of energy and power. He was talking rapidly, words trying desperately to keep up with his fast-moving brain while he explained the various possibilities to Kristina.

"How long do you think this is going to take?"

Mitch began to tick off the steps. "First, the research. I can finish that within a week, I think. Then we file the lawsuit and wait for the Winstons to file an answer. That's about a month. Then we file our motions for discovery and start tracking down the leads. Several more months for that. Then when everything is ready and our case is airtight, we set it for trial and wait for the court to schedule it. That may be another six months. The trial will take only a few days. If Valerie wins, it should be only a matter of time until the Winstons put enough pressure on John Ed to get the kids back home."

"Mitch, do you realize what you're saying?" Kristina had a stricken expression on her face.

"What's wrong?" Mitch was so caught up in the legal possibilities that he couldn't understand why Kristina looked so unhappy.

"All this is going to take nearly a year. A year, Mitch!"

The truth hit Mitch like a kick in the stomach.

"What are we going to do, Mitch? Look what happened tonight. How can we wait a whole damned *year?*"

Even though the straight-back chair wasn't built for such an action, Mitch sagged in it, his whole bearing desolate.

"You're just going to have to give up some of your high-minded principles," Kristina said. "You're wrong about them, anyway. You said if you had your mind on me, you wouldn't be able to do justice to Valerie's case. But that isn't true. I think you had quite a bit of your attention on me tonight, and you've still managed to come up with a legal theory that would never occur to most lawyers."

Mitch tried to make light of the situation. "Maybe most lawyers need your special kind of inspiration."

"So what's the harm?"

"It's more complicated than that."

"That's what you say about everything."

"Kristina, it's the legal code of ethics. A lawyer must avoid even the *appearance* of impropriety. Now,

104

if I went to bed with a client's sister, don't you think someone might think it *appeared* to be improper?"

"I'm sure the world is full of puritanical people who'd think it was improper for us to go to bed together, whether Valerie was your client or not. I don't see that the legal code of ethics has anything to do with it."

"Kristina, please don't be difficult."

"So what's the big deal about appearances? If nobody knows about it, there's no appearance of impropriety. And I won't tell anybody if you won't."

"You're being awfully glib for someone who's always so determined that people do the right thing. I'm just trying to do what I think is right."

He had her. It was central to her belief system that people obey their personal moral code. "Damn your legal code of ethics, anyway," she muttered, but the starch had gone out of her determination.

"I have to obey that code, Krissie. I've given my oath."

Tears sparkled in her lashes, but she tried to smile. "So what are you doing about this time next year?"

Mitch wadded up a sheet of paper and playfully tossed it at her. "I think I'll be starting at your toes and working my way up. What about you?"

"Oh, I think I'll be enjoying that very much."

Mitch squirmed uncomfortably in his chair. "Come on, Kris, let me show you to the door," he said, rising. "Valerie is waiting up for you."

"I never did get a tour of the house." She was feeling contrary. He didn't have to be so eager to get rid of her.

105

"Next time."

She sighed with relief. Then at least there was going to be a next time. "You never did give me that kiss you promised me."

"I'll save it for you."

"Do I get it next time, too, along with the tour?"

"Probably not. But I won't let anybody else have it."

"You'd better not." The enormity of waiting a year hit Kristina all over again. What was Mitch going to do during that year? Austin was full of attractive, available women who were unencumbered by sisters with legal problems.

Mitch could read jealousy in the dark expression that clouded Kristina's face and was surprised at his reaction. He actually liked it that she felt possessive of him. What was happening to him, anyway? He stretched out his hand and pulled her to her feet. "Come on, sweetheart, let me walk you to your car. I promise to save all my lovin' for you."

"Just like the song says?"

"Just like the song says."

"Even if it takes a year?"

There was a pained expression on his face. "I'll try to hurry things along."

Kristina managed to brush her body against his. She felt him stiffen and draw away, but she stood on tiptoe and flicked her tongue against his ear, then nibbled at the lobe. "Oh, well, it's only for a year or less," she whispered. Her breast pressed against his bare arm. "What's a year when you're in the prime of life?"

She laughed and ran down the steps to her car, waving merrily.

"Damn, damn, damn," she could hear him mutter from his front porch as she slammed the car door and headed back to town.

CHAPTER SIX

Kristina walked across the campus to her classroom, enjoying the beautiful Indian summer afternoon. October was her favorite month in Austin. The sun was bright, the sky incredibly blue, and the air cool and dry compared to the sweltering heat of late summer. She nodded to students, said hello to faculty friends, and felt a surge of joy to be alive. The world had never seemed so bright and beautiful.

A squirrel scampered across the walk in front of her and darted up a live-oak tree, his puffed cheeks carrying a pecan. *You think it's a beautiful world, too, don't you?* Kristina thought as she watched the gray furry animal. The squirrel made happy noises as it consumed the nut and seemed totally oblivious to a scolding blue jay in an adjacent tree.

Kristina stopped by the political science department to pick up her mail and messages, then leafed through them on the way to her office. There was a note to call Mitch McNaughton at his law office, and Kristina smiled when she saw his name on the pink message slip. She hadn't heard from him for several days, but by now she knew that was his pattern. Any time they became the least bit intimate, he retreated to let things cool down before calling her again. It was the way he kept himself under control.

You really ought not to be such a tease with him, she chided herself. *Even if he's being super-conscientious, it's because he thinks he should be. Yet there you go, throwing yourself at him, just to see whether he can hang on to his resolve.* Kris remembered the way she'd felt when she'd knelt on the floor beside Mitch and his finger had reached out to touch her bare breast. *You weren't teasing then,* she admitted to herself. *You wanted him. Desperately.* That moment had dominated her thoughts ever since it happened, and even now she felt warm and tingly remembering it. She glanced down and was glad she'd worn a loose-fitting hopsacking jacket over her dress. She was sure her nipples were puckered.

She stepped inside her own office and pushed the door shut behind her, then leaned against it with a dreamy expression on her face. *Oh, Mitch, what's happening to us?*

Someone tapped on the door, interrupting her reverie.

"Dr. Neilsen?"

Kristina opened the door to find a young male student with longish brown hair and an intelligent face. He was dressed in blue jeans and a T-shirt and had a small backpack for his books slung over his shoulder. Kristina didn't remember seeing him before. She didn't think he was one of her students.

"I'm Dr. Neilsen," Kris answered.

He looked a little surprised. When the journalism

office gave him this assignment, no one had told him he was being sent to interview a professor who was as beautiful as she was controversial. "I'm Burke Williams, from the *Daily Texan*. We'd like to do a story on your innovative term projects. Do you have time to give me an interview?" His smile was ingratiating. He was a senior journalism major and had learned to make the most of his boyish charm to get a story.

Kristina hesitated. The *Daily Texan* was the student newspaper and ran everything from human-interest features to investigative reports. She wasn't in the mood to give an interview right now, not with her mind on Mitch, but she couldn't refuse. "Have a seat outside my office, Burke, and I'll be with you in a few minutes. I have to go through this mail first."

By the time she'd finished reading her mail, Kristina's mind was no longer on Mitch McNaughton. "Come on in, Burke," she called. "I have half an hour before I have to go to class."

The *Daily Texan* gave its students good training, and Burke scribbled Kristina's answers to his incisive questions, making the most of their limited time. Sometimes he prearranged interviews, but usually he preferred to catch his subjects without warning and get spontaneous comments from them. Especially when he was dealing with faculty members. They were always so preoccupied with tenure and with what the administration might say that self-censorship made their comments dull reading. Caught off-guard, they'd sometimes say something worth quoting.

"One last question," he said. "Some of your stu-

110

dents have gotten involved in controversial issues. You're a new teacher here, without tenure. Do you think the controversy will have any impact on your own career here at U.T.?"

"In what way?"

"Well, for example, on whether you get tenure or not. Or whether you win a faculty excellence award."

Kristina leaned back and met Burke's intense scrutiny. "I'd like to say no to that question," she said quietly. "After all, academic freedom is very precious to all teachers. I'd like to think, in a university setting, teachers would be free to challenge their students without fear of reprisal."

"So your answer is no? You don't think you have anything to worry about when your students do things that make the headlines?"

Kristina grinned. "I said I'd *like* to be able to say no to that question."

Burke scribbled furiously. He could see the captioned inset already: "U.T. PROF QUESTIONS SANCTITY OF ACADEMIC FREEDOM."

"But don't you dare misquote me," she said sternly, wagging her index finger at him. "So far as I can tell, academic freedom is alive and well on this campus." She reached for one of the letters lying on top of her desk. It had arrived in this morning's mail. "I think the administration expects us to challenge our students, and they can take it in stride when sparks fly. But it can be a different matter with *parents.*"

Burke quit writing to listen attentively. What he wouldn't give to get a look at that letter in her hand! "But this isn't a high school," he said. "Surely you

111

don't get calls and letters from parents of university students."

"Not often. But this one is typical of what sometimes happens. This letter is from the father of a woman who did some role-playing in one of my classes. The subject was euthanasia, and she played the part of an infant with birth defects." Kristina paused, remembering that day in her classroom, the glow of pride the student had worn. "This isn't for publication, Burke. I'm telling you about it as an example, but you can't use it in your story. Do I have your word on that?"

He sighed. "Yes, ma'am. I won't use it." Why did interview subjects always do that to journalists? The most juicy part of the story was always off-the-record.

"The student who participated in the activity was pushed to think in a new way," Kristina continued, "and she was excited about it. Apparently she told her folks, but instead of being pleased that she's using her own mind, they've gotten all upset. This letter accuses me of brainwashing my students and indoctrinating them with my own values." Kristina tossed aside the letter. "I suppose tomorrow I'll get a letter from the parents of the other student, the one who left class leaning in the opposite direction."

"What happens to you when parents get mad at you? Do you get called on the carpet?"

"Not so far. Nobody's ever been this irate before, though." She shrugged. *"C'est la vie.* I'm not going to change my approach just because somebody's angry. I've got a job to do, and I happen to think it's an important job. The world is full of people who won't

112

think because it takes too much effort. They waste their God-given ability, and the world is a sadder place because of it. I don't intend to contribute to that waste: I intend to combat it."

"Even if you die trying?" It had been a long time since Burke had seen a teacher so fired up.

"Even if I die trying."

By God, she meant it. Burke stood and shook her hand. "Thanks for your time, Dr. Neilsen. I'll let you get to your next class."

Kristina picked up the folder with her lesson plans and stuck it in her bag. "I probably said too much. Try not to get me in any more hot water than I'm already in, okay?"

Burke circled his thumb and forefinger in a respectful salute. "I wouldn't do anything to hurt you," he said. "We need more teachers like you around this place."

Kristina was about to shut the door behind them when she remembered the telephone message from Mitch. "You go ahead, Burke. I just remembered I have to make a phone call before I go to class."

She dialed Mitch's office, then felt a smile work its way all the way down to her toes when she heard his voice on the line. "I'm on my way to class, Mitch," she said. "I've just got a minute. What's up?" The smile spread and became so warm she felt a melting sensation in her midsection. "Canoeing on Lake Austin? Sounds great. Unless you'd rather go skinny-dipping at Hippie Hollow." Her laughter bubbled over. "I'll be ready."

As she bolted upstairs to her classroom, her mind

was far from the day's lesson on the effect of grass-roots pressure on local governments. Instead, she was wondering whether she dared wear her white bikini.

She ended up taking the conservative approach and wore a green maillot cut low in front and very high on the sides, with a green-and-white print cover-up. Mitch arrived wearing a light-blue shirt the same color as his eyes and white swim trunks that emphasized his tan. For a moment Kristina almost wished she'd worn her bikini, but a quick glance at Mitch's expression told her that the cut of her one-piece suit was just as sexy.

"Hi, stranger," she said, lightly brushing his lips with hers.

"Nothing strange about me," he said, a smile crinkling his eyes. "My reaction to that swimsuit is perfectly normal, believe me." He came inside long enough to greet Valerie, lying on the sofa with a magazine, and to inquire about her physical progress. Then he picked up Kristina's canvas bag, asked about suntan lotion, and put one hand on Kristina's shoulder to steer her out the door before Valerie could ask any questions about the custody case. He wasn't ready to talk to Valerie just yet, not until he'd talked to Kristina.

They enjoyed the winding drive through the hills to Lake Austin, chatting about nothing in particular. Kristina found a cassette tape and put it in the deck so they could sing off-key to country ballads. They both wanted to keep the mood light for the present and enjoy the day. They were highly involved in the mating ritual, with its delicate series of advances and retreats whetting their desire. Would-be lovers might know their final destination full well, yet part of the excitement was the anticipation of how and when they were going to get there.

Kristina stole a glance at Mitch's profile. *I hate to disillusion you, fellow, but we're never going to last a year,* she thought. She watched the play of muscle in his biceps as he steered the car around a curve, noted the indentation in his cheek that had probably been a cute, round dimple when he was a little boy.

He felt her gaze on him and turned. "We're almost there," he said, lifting her hand to his lips for a kiss. "Your fingers are going to be calloused before the afternoon is over."

"I thought I was coming along for the ride."

"Nope. You were invited to lend a little shoulder muscle." Mitch pulled his car into a graveled driveway beside a small cottage and parked, then led her around back to a dock. "Friend of mine lets me borrow his canoe." He handed her a lifejacket. "Put this on."

"I can swim."

"So can I. But we have to wear a lifejacket. My friend insists. He doesn't want to be responsible if the canoe capsizes and we get into the current."

"How likely are we to capsize?"

"Not very." Mitch stripped off his shirt, revealing broad shoulders and a heavily muscled chest. He fastened the front straps to his lifejacket and turned to Kristina. "Am I going to have to do that for you?"

"If I didn't know you better, I'd swear that's a leer on your face."

115

"By now you ought to know me well enough to know it *is* a leer." Mitch stretched out his arms and straightened Kristina's lifejacket, then worked with the buckles and straps, deliberately letting his fingers brush her bare skin.

Kristina stood very still, her eyes straight ahead. A blush crept up her cheeks as he continued to touch her. She had the feeling that the tables had been turned, and that now Mitch was the aggressor, teasing her as she'd earlier teased him. The rhythm of their mating ritual had just shifted again, and the huntress had now become the prey. Kristina's breath came a little faster. She had a hunch there would be nothing trivial about this particular pursuit.

Mitch dropped his hands and gave her a steady gaze. "There, that's a good start," he said. He waded out to the deckhouse and pushed the canoe to the end of the dock. "Hop in." When Kristina clambered in, he waved her to the other end of the canoe. "You get in front," he said. "I'll be doing the steering today."

They paddled slowly for the next hour, enjoying the combination of wet breeze and sun against their skin, the rippling water, and the play of sunlight on the tree-covered hills lining the river. Mitch had brought along a portable cassette player, and the sound of light classical jazz echoed across the water. From time to time a motorboat towing a waterskier would cross their path, churning the water until their canoe rocked gently. There were sailboats all up and down the river, sails taut against the breeze. The river was a friendly place, and people waved as they passed by.

When their shoulders began to tire, they stopped rowing to let the canoe drift with the current. Mitch spread fresh suntan lotion on his thighs, which were burning from the glare of the late-afternoon sun, then tossed the container to Kristina. "We're just going to drift for a while," he said. "Turn around and talk to me."

The canoe swayed as she edged her body around on the seat to face Mitch, probably five or six feet away from her. She smeared suntan lotion on her face and shoulders, then put an extra dab on her nose. Her skin was fair and burned easily, but she'd spent the summer building up her tan. She hoped her nose wouldn't blister and peel this late in the season.

While Kristina applied the lotion, Mitch opened the picnic satchel he'd brought and pulled out a bottle of white wine and two clear plastic tumblers. "I popped the cork on this at home," he said. "Here, see whether you like the taste of this wine." He poured a glass of California Chardonnay and handed it to her, then poured one for himself. "To victory," he said, toasting her.

"To victory." She wasn't exactly sure what kind of victory they were toasting, but she had a hunch Mitch meant something more than Valerie's lawsuit. She sipped the wine. "Mmm, this is delicious."

"How about a turkey sandwich?"

"You think of everything, don't you?"

He gave her a lopsided grin. "I try to."

Kristina peeked into the satchel. He'd also brought along some fresh fruit and sugar cookies. "When did you have time to bake?" she said, teasing.

"My housekeeper packed this supper for us. I told her to fix us something simple that we could manage with one hand."

Mitch arranged the food on the empty seat between them. When the tape ended, he flipped it out and inserted a new one, jazz with a sexy, low-moaning trumpet.

A motorboat passed, churning a frothy wake that gently tilted the canoe and sent waves rippling in ever-widening circles. Kristina reached for the side of the canoe to steady herself, splashing some of her wine in the process. Mitch refilled the glass, then leaned forward and offered her a bite from his raw carrot stick.

They munched in unison, enjoying the extra flavor food always has when it's consumed outdoors in a beautiful, natural setting with an attractive companion. The trumpet wailed a long, quavering note, richly erotic with the complex rhythm of its piano and bass accompaniment. Kristina became aware that Mitch had stopped eating and was propped on one elbow, watching her while he sipped his wine. The lifejacket concealed her breasts, but she realized that his eyes were roaming below the lifejacket to the exposed flesh of her upper thighs and down her long legs.

Mitch felt her gaze on him and lifted his head. When their eyes met, he didn't smile. She noticed the movement of his Adam's apple as he swallowed hard, and then his eyes began to make a slow assault on her body, moving from her hair to her arms and hands, then back to her shoulders and chest burdened with the lifejacket, on down her hips and legs and back to the gentle swell of her abdomen.

118

"Don't, Mitch," she whispered.

"Don't what?" His voice was husky.

"Don't look at me like that."

His glance fell to the V between her legs where the spandex of her swimsuit clung like a second skin. "Take off your lifejacket," he commanded.

"But you said—"

"Take it off. I'll rescue you if anything happens."

Kristina's fingers fumbled with the clasp. The lifejacket fell free into the bottom of the canoe. She sat, head high, while his eyes raked her breasts. She dared not glance down. She knew if she did, she'd see her nipples visibly erect underneath the clinging fabric.

"Mitch—" Words could hardly escape the constriction of her throat.

His breathing was ragged. "What?"

"You're making me nervous."

"Why?" His eyes lingered on the soft rise of her breasts above the top of her swimsuit, then to the pointed tips.

"Because even if you're six feet away and haven't put a hand on me, you're making love to me with your eyes."

"You're right about that. Right here in broad daylight, surrounded by people, and with all our clothes on." He grinned. "Of course, I have to keep my hands in my pockets to keep from being embarrassed."

Curious, Kristina glanced in the general vicinity of his pockets and found herself taken by surprise. Even his fists couldn't conceal the hardened bulge of his groin. A liquid warmth coursed through her, making delicious prickles dance up and down in her midsection. She took a deep breath and swallowed hard.

"Do you suppose we ought to jump into the water and cool off?" Mitch asked.

"Whatever you say. You're steering today, remember?"

His lifejacket joined hers on the floor of the canoe. He held her hand and eased her over the side, then climbed out beside her. The water was cool and bracing against their skin, but did nothing to quench the passion that had begun to rage between them. They took long, lazy breaststrokes, side by side, their bodies barely touching, then swam back to the canoe. They kissed, and someone on a nearby boat applauded.

"I forgot about our audience," Mitch grumbled as he pulled away. They swam back out in the other direction, then floated and let the current carry them along. When the canoe seemed to be fading into the distance, they swam back. As they pulled up beside it, shaking water from their faces, the strap fell loose from Kristina's shoulder. Mitch reached out to trace the outline of her collarbone, and Kristina shifted beside him to take his hand in hers. As she did so, her swimsuit lowered on her breast, exposing a tiny bit of rosy aureola.

Mitch groaned, then turned to see where the other boat had gone. It was too close. He mustn't touch her. "Let's get back into the canoe," he said. "I want to talk to you about something important, and then we're going to find ourselves some privacy."

He put his hand on Kristina's waist to lift her into the canoe. Her wet, silky thighs came up through the water, and somehow one of them slid between his legs in an unintentional stroking that made him tremble with ecstasy.

Kristina's hand caught around his neck for balance, and as she pulled herself into the canoe with her other hand, she let her breast graze his lips in a seductive, deliberate gesture. She paused for such a split second that casual observers on the neighboring boat didn't notice the break in her rhythm. But Mitch was acutely aware that during that split second, he'd been able to bury his face between her breasts and savor the mossy scent and salty taste of her skin.

As Kristina came over the side and up into the boat, her fingers trailed in the water. Mitch pulled himself up beside her and she stroked him underneath the water where no one could see. His breath came faster, and Kristina's eyes widened in excitement.

"Krissie, no more," he said, and pushed her hand away. She leaned over the side of the canoe, making it sway dizzily for a moment, then balanced herself and kissed him before helping him into the canoe.

Mitch sprawled on the floor of the canoe, his head thrown back against the seat, one arm flung over his eyes.

"What can I say? I almost lost control of myself."

She blew him a kiss. "With a little help from me, I hope?"

Mitch met Kristina's gaze, "I give you all the credit." He grinned at her. "Come here, woman, and let me ravish you."

"Don't you think this canoe has seen enough gymnastics for one day? Besides, we still have our audience."

"I don't want you to be shortchanged. What you began back there was pretty tempting." Mitch mustered his strength to pull himself onto the seat.

"You're right." There was a rosy tint to Kristina's cheeks.

"Come here, darlin'. I owe you one." He stretched out his arms and leaned back.

The canoe capsized.

They fell laughing into the water, bobbing their heads. Nearby other people joined in the laughter. Everybody had heard the splash and drew their own conclusions as to why the canoe had overturned.

"Where's that lifejacket?" Mitch called. He scrambled until he found both jackets, then flipped the canoe back onto its bottom and climbed back inside. "Let me help you," he said to Kristina, extending his hand.

"I think the wine bottle just sank," she said.

"Along with the tape deck and cassettes," Mitch answered.

Kristina fished until she caught the picnic satchel and their towels, now soaked. The suntan lotion had floated out of reach. She crawled back into the canoe. "Home, James."

"Do you know how far we are from the dock?"

Kristina looked around. They'd come a long way, and the sun was now low on the western horizon. "How far?"

"Four or five miles. Against the current."

"I'll tell you what," Kris said. "I'll catch a ride with the next motorboat, and meet you back at the car."

122

Mitch reached for her hand. "You don't have any calluses yet. Heave ho, woman. We've got a lot to talk about while we're paddling this canoe back up the river."

"Obviously there's something on your mind," Kristina said, breaking the long silence. They'd paddled at least a mile without saying a word.

"It's hard to talk to your back."

"Oh, go ahead. I'm a teacher, remember. I have eyes in the back of my head."

"I want you to be serious." They paddled in unison, making soft lapping noises in the water.

"I'm always serious."

He chuckled wryly. "Even when you're teasing a man to death?"

"I only do it because you like it."

Mitch scooped up a handful of river water and splashed it against Kristina's back. "Okay, I like it. Now let's have a serious talk. And hear me out before you start yelling, okay?"

"I never yell."

"Do I have your word on that?"

"Mitch, come on. Tell me what's going on inside that head of yours before I drive myself crazy trying to figure it out."

"It's about Valerie's case."

She sighed with relief. "Thank goodness. I didn't know what to expect."

"Kris, I've been researching the case all week and talking to Walt Biggers about it. The pleadings are drafted, and the case is ready to be filed in court."

"Mitch, that's wonderful. Valerie will be excited that things are moving along so fast. Why didn't you tell her while we were at my house?"

He rowed several strokes before he said anything. "Because I wanted to talk to you first."

"Oh. What about?"

"I want to turn the case over to Walt Biggers and let him handle it. I don't want to be Valerie's lawyer."

"Mitch!" Kristina was too stunned to say anything else.

"You promised not to yell."

"You ought to know better than to tease about serious matters."

"I'm not teasing, Kris. I don't want to be involved in Valerie's case any longer. Walt is better qualified than I am, and he'll do a good job for Valerie."

"Your mind is made up?" Kristina's voice held disbelief.

"Yes, it is. I've given it a lot of thought, and this is my decision."

Kristina could sense the steel in his words and manner. She quit rowing and propped her head between her hands. "So we're right back where we started. No matter how much Valerie needs you, you don't want to get involved with real people who have real problems. You want a nice, safe law practice where you don't have to think about anything but oil wells and drilling applications. What's the matter with you, anyway? How can you stand aloof when people are hurting?" Words poured out of her in a torrent. "How can you let us down this way, Mitch? We need *you*, not Walt Biggers."

"Krissie, please don't talk this way. I know you're disappointed, but try to understand, won't you?"

"Understand what? That you're cold and selfish with a rock in your chest for a heart? Why did you lead me on this way? Damn it, Mitch, it killed me to have to beg you to take this case in the first place, and here I am having to do it all over again. Why do you want to hurt my pride and make me plead with you this way?" Tears began to flow down Kristina's cheeks but she was too far gone to get control of herself. "Does it give you a feeling of power, knowing that I'd do anything for Valerie? And what about her? She's just now getting back on her feet and looking like a human being instead of a corpse. This is going to do her in. And all because you're too chicken-hearted to get involved."

The deluge of words had done its damage. Mitch was stung by Kristina's disdain and her utter refusal to hear him out. Angrily he retorted, "I told you before. Cowards live longer. People who get involved always end up getting hurt." *Just like I am right now,* he thought, surprised that her words could cause him so much pain. Like a wounded animal, he struck back. "You wouldn't even give me a chance to tell you why I wanted to farm out the case."

Kris continued to cry, her tears spilling through her fingers onto the canoe bottom. "Does it matter?"

"Apparently not, but I was stupid enough to think it did." He was taking long strokes with the oar. Would they never get back to the dock and put an end to this ugly scene? God, how he hated a woman's tears. They always had a way of making a guy feel all wrong, even when it wasn't his fault. He'd brought Walt into the case for Kris, for *them,* and she'd gotten things all mixed up and blown out of proportion until even a saint couldn't straighten it out. Mitch had never felt so bitter . . . or so self-righteous. "Maybe it doesn't matter to you, but it damned sure did to me. I wanted another lawyer to take the case so I wouldn't have to keep worrying about whether I was violating the legal code of ethics. Damn it, Kris, I wanted to get sexually involved with you, and I knew we couldn't keep going on the way we were. Either I had to stay away from that beautiful body of yours or else get rid of the case. I decided to get rid of the case."

Kristina was so upset about Valerie's case being farmed out to another lawyer that she couldn't think clearly and nothing seemed to make sense to her. All her lingering fears about Valerie's attempted suicide surfaced in a nightmare blast of terror. Kristina knew that Valerie was still too emotionally unstable to accept another lawyer at this point and was totally dependent on Mitch. If he walked out on Valerie . . .

Kristina's teeth began to chatter from fear. What was it Mitch had said, his reason for turning the case over to Walt Biggers? Kristina tried to remember, but the only thing that came back to her consciousness was his last statement: "Either I had to stay away from that beautiful body of yours or else get rid of the case." It was her own fault, then. She'd fired Mitch's passion without realizing that she was pushing him to choose between sexual desire and Valerie's lawsuit. How could she have been so reckless, jeopardizing her sister's happiness for a few stolen moments of bliss?

Kristina cried harder, her shoulders shaking with the effort to keep the sobs inside. Somehow she managed to speak without breaking down. "So you ended up getting rid of both."

"Kris, for God's sake, won't you be reasonable? You're not listening to a word I'm saying."

"To the contrary, I've heard every rotten word. Including how you wanted to be sexually involved with my body." Kristina's anger at herself spilled over, and she transferred it to Mitch. After all, he was to blame, too. He was the one who'd decided to abandon his client in order to have an affair—no, damn it, to have *sex*—with his client's sister. "Is that all I am to you, a *body*? Are you such a robot that you can't even think of me as a person? I've never been so insulted in all my life! I threw myself at you, sure, but I was offering you myself, Mitch, everything I am. And all I am to you is a *body*. You might as well say *receptacle,* because that's all you want, a place to deposit your lust, with no strings, no questions asked, nothing personal!"

"Kris, please, I'm sure people can hear you halfway down the river. You've made your point."

"I certainly hope so," Kristina answered, retreating into cold Scandinavian reserve. Her every word dripped ice.

Mitch was not only confused, he was furious. He never allowed himself the luxury of anger, and here it had foisted itself upon him in full bloom. He thought he could probably strangle Kristina with his bare hands, a smile on his face. She deserved it. How dare she talk to him this way! "I don't believe we have anything left to say to each other," he continued. "If

127

you'll help me row, I'll get you home just as soon as I can."

"Help you row? Not on your sweet life," Kristina answered, tossing her oar overboard. It hit the river with a loud splash.

Mitch found himself muttering obscenities he'd never said in his life. Strangling was too good for Kristina. She deserved to be buried alive in a red-ant bed. Slow torture, to punish her for the terrible, untrue things she'd said to him. His shoulder ached from rowing, but he welcomed the pain. He rowed harder. Maybe his shoulder would eventually hurt enough to obliterate this other pain, deep inside him.

CHAPTER SEVEN

Kristina was in misery for the next several days. She could hardly keep her mind on anything, and most of her time was spent in mental dialogues with Mitch. Sometimes in her mind she'd call him ugly names, and at other times she'd plead with him as she alternated between anger and despair. She couldn't eat and couldn't sleep and became a bundle of nerves. The only peace she knew was when she was in her classroom with all her energy concentrated on her students. Twice a day, for fifty minutes each, Mitch McNaughton was driven from her mind. Surprisingly enough, she did the best teaching of her career.

Mitch suffered his own special brand of torment. Basically an easygoing person, he seldom experienced anger and certainly never vented it. Yet Kristina Neilsen had driven him to such a state of fury that he'd lost control of himself. It was maddening to find that the emotions he'd kept in a zip-locked container had burst free, destroying the careful equilibrium of his life. Unlike Kristina, he found it impossible to do his work, and after misplacing his fourth drilling application, he told his secretary he was leaving for the day.

His secretary was glad to see him go. His constant pacing had begun to get on her nerves. The elevator button chimed, just as she noticed the file on her desk.

"Mr. McNaughton," the secretary cried, running down the hall behind Mitch. "You told me to remind you that this case had to be filed today. Do you want me to take it to the courthouse for you?"

Mitch stopped in his tracks. He didn't have to look at the label to know which file she had in her hand. "Give it to me, Betty. I'll take it myself."

"Don't forget that it hasn't been signed. I left a signature blank because you never did tell me who was going to handle the case, you or Mr. Biggers." She gave him a questioning glance but quickly averted her head. He looked ill.

Mitch shoved the file under his arm and punched the elevator button. "See you tomorrow, Betty." *If I don't self-destruct in the meantime,* he thought with a vengeance.

Mitch climbed into his sports car and buried his face against the steering wheel. The dilemma could no longer be avoided. The noose had tightened around his neck and any moment now his body would start to swing. Thanks to Kristina Neilsen, he was trapped. Because of that ugly fight they'd had, he hadn't been able to talk to Valerie about letting Walt Biggers take over her case. Mitch certainly couldn't turn over the case to another attorney without his client's permission. He glanced at his watch. It was still early. Kristina probably wouldn't be home from her classes yet.

He'd drop by and talk to Valerie. Maybe she'd be more reasonable than her sister.

Mitch discovered, to his dismay, that Kristina had been an absolute stoic compared to Valerie. There had always been a character weakness in Valerie, making her utterly dependent on other people for emotional ballast. She'd spent her life leaning first on her parents, then on her husband, and finally on her children. When she'd lost the children, she'd become suicidal until she was able to turn her problems over to Mitch. Now Mitch was deserting her, too, and Valerie came close to hysteria when he tried to explain that another lawyer could do a better job with her case.

"No, Mitch!" she cried. "I need someone who'll be my friend too. I don't want some stranger working on my case." She dissolved into noisy tears, and Mitch was unable to quiet her.

Kristina returned from campus to find Mitch pacing her living room and Valerie slumped in a corner of the sofa crying her eyes out. Kristina gave Mitch an I-told-you-so look and wondered what on earth to do for Valerie before her sister came completely unglued. Kris marched across the room without a word, went to the bathroom and got a wet cloth, then found one of Valerie's prescription bottles and shook out a pill.

"Here, Valerie," she said, handing her sister a glass of water with the pill. "The doctor doesn't want you to get upset like this." Valerie tried to push away Kristina's hand, but Kris was steadfast. "Now, then," she murmured, wiping Valerie's face with the wet cloth, "you'll feel better in a few minutes."

"Kris, I'm sorry." Mitch stood near the window not knowing whether to go or stay. "I didn't mean to upset her."

Valerie burst into a new round of tears at the sound of his voice. "Kristina, he's going to send me to another lawyer," she said brokenly, clinging to her sister's hand. "What's going to happen to me now?"

Kristina drew a deep breath. She must be calm. The rest of the world had gone mad, and if she didn't maintain her composure, she'd go mad along with it. "Now, now, Valerie," she said slowly, distinctly, as though the measured tones of her voice could drive away her sister's panic. "Let's quiet down and think about this, okay? Mitch is our friend, and he wants only the best for you. Isn't that right, Mitch?"

He nodded.

"Isn't that right, Mitch?" Kristina turned her head in his direction and whispered *sotto voce*, "She didn't hear you."

He cleared his throat. "That's right. I want Valerie to have the best lawyer in Austin to handle her case."

"But, Mitch," Valerie protested, "you're the one who knows how to beat the Winstons. You did it before. A stranger isn't going to know how to deal with that family." Like most weak people, Valerie had an amazing tenacity when it came to getting her own way.

Mitch swore silently. "Well, of course I'll coach Walt Biggers on the Winston family. That's no problem."

"You see, Valerie, everything is going to be just fine." Kristina stroked her sister's hair and wiped her face again. Valerie seemed to be calmer. The pill must be helping her relax. Kristina turned her attention to Mitch. He looked ghastly. There were dark hollows under his eyes, as if he hadn't slept for a week. Kristina fingered the circles under her own eyes. She hadn't slept for a week either.

Valerie drew a long, shuddering breath and sat upright. "Mitch, why don't you want to work on my case?" she asked.

He stopped pacing and turned to look at the two beautiful sisters, arm in arm at one end of the sofa: Valerie, the weak one, the one who needed him; Kristina, the strong one, the one he wanted. God, how he wanted her! Seeing Kristina again, he knew their fight had made no difference at all. His feelings for her were as strong as ever. He had to be with her.

But the look in her eye told him he wasn't going to get her, not this way, not at Valerie's expense. His eyes pleaded with her, but this time it was Kristina who was made of steel. If he touched her now, she'd be as cold and unyielding as a . . . robot. The irony of the predicament was almost laughable. If he dropped Valerie's case, Kristina would drop him. And if he took Valerie's case, Kristina was off limits. He, Mitch McNaughton, the man who hated to lose, was in a no-win situation. A mocking grin twisted his lips. What was it they'd said in law school? *If you know you can't win, at least lose with dignity.*

His shoulders straightened. Valerie was waiting for an answer to her question. "Oh, I do want to work on your case," he said, lying through his teeth with a glibness he'd never have thought himself capable of. "I thought it would be better for you to have someone with Walt Biggers's expertise. Naturally, the important thing is that we win the lawsuit, and not *who* wins it. If you really want me to stay on the case, of course I'll do it. It'll be my pleasure."

Mitch hardly noticed the radiant smile Valerie gave him. It was meaningless next to the confusion on Kristina's face, a peculiar mix of triumph and anguish. The trap door had sprung on Mitch, the noose had jerked. Now all he could do was wonder how long he'd have to twist in the wind.

The next few days required intense planning. Although Valerie's lawsuit was ready to file, Mitch realized that once the sheriff received a copy and served it on the Winstons, the town of Gilbert would be in an uproar and it would be difficult to get any further information. He had several strategy sessions with Kristina over the telephone, and they decided she should make one more trip to Gilbert before the suit was filed. Mitch knew the Winstons would immediately try to get the suit dismissed, and Valerie would need something more definite than a hunch to keep the case alive.

"You're sure you can handle this?" Mitch asked on the telephone from his office in the Petroleum Building.

"Sure, I can. I'll get Bud Thomas to help me. He's got an old pickup truck."

"Who's Bud Thomas?"

"He's a teacher, one of my colleagues in the political science department. We've been friends a long time. He won't mind." Kristina spoke from her office on the U.T. campus and felt a strange kind of emptiness. Since their terrible fight, her relationship with Mitch had entered a new phase. There was never anything personal between them now; they saw each other as seldom as possible and tried to confine themselves to the telephone. Even then, they talked only of Valerie's case. Things were simpler that way.

"Call me after you get back to Austin and let me know what you find out."

"Yeah." She was about to replace the receiver on the hook.

"Krissie?" The affectionate nickname slipped unawares from Mitch's lips, but Kristina noticed and felt tears spring to her eyes. "Be careful," Mitch added.

"Sure." The line went dead.

Kristina swore Bud Thomas to secrecy, then enlisted his help for her new assignment. Bud was a nice guy with a sense of humor and rather enjoyed the notion of going on a lark with Kristina. On the road to Gilbert in his pickup truck, they rehearsed for her grand performance.

"You certainly look different with black hair," he said, still finding it hard to believe that underneath Kristina's wig reposed the same Scandinavian snowball he'd known for two years.

"Ha! You should've seen me when I was a redhead. That was really fun."

"You don't think anybody will realize you're the same person?"

"You've known me for two years, but you said you

135

wouldn't recognize me with dark hair. I don't think anybody will catch on. Besides, I'm going to a different place today, so maybe I won't run into the pharmacist again. Or the deputy sheriff." Kristina tossed her head, practicing. Her black wig, made of long, straight hair, hung almost to her waist. "Maybe they'll think I'm Crystal Gayle," she said.

"With that hat?" Bud laughed. "Crystal Gayle wouldn't be caught dead with that thing on her head."

Kristina wore a broad-brimmed straw hat, lavender in color and trimmed with an ivory silk rose. Her dress had a long ruffled skirt and full sleeves, designed in the "country" style with tiny purple flowers on a lilac-color background. She'd decided to wear plenty of lilac tones because her eyes picked up color from her clothing. Usually she emphasized the green, but today's purples turned her irises almost blue. Instead of dressing as a sex siren as she'd done in her previous disguise, today she looked like a fresh-faced country lass. She would abandon the thick drawl she'd assumed earlier, using her normal speech patterns but a light, breathless voice. No one would ever suspect her.

"Stop here and let me telephone Mitch," she said as they came upon the gas station at the edge of town where she'd stopped on her previous trip to Gilbert. She hopped out of the truck and made a quick telephone call to Austin. "We're here," she said when Mitch's voice came on the line. "Let's get this show on the road."

"It's going to take thirty minutes. Can you manage for that long?" Mitch asked.

"I'll be fine. Let's do it." She hung up the phone and

got back in the truck. "We're on," she said to Bud Thomas. "Let's go find those bright city lights and ring up the curtain."

Bud turned the pickup onto Gilbert's main street and headed toward the Western Union office. "Nervous?" he asked.

"A little," she admitted.

"Good luck." He parked the truck and held up his crossed fingers.

Kristina opened the door and climbed down. "Don't you go away."

"I'll be right here waiting for you. Holler if you need me."

"Thanks." Kristina drew a deep breath. It was time to make her entrance.

The Western Union office was tiny and cluttered. Not much light made its way through the old-fashioned Venetian blinds in the front window, and it took a minute for Kristina's eyes to adjust to the gloom. She heard a movement before she saw the man who swiveled in his chair to face her.

"Howdy," he said. He was a man in his late thirties, slightly built and balding on top. His tan wash-and-wear shirt had never seen an iron, and its open collar collapsed around his skinny neck. He peered at her through wire-rimmed spectacles and quickly got to his feet. Who was this pretty stranger? "Can I help you with anything, ma'am?" he asked.

"Goodness, I hope so," Kristina answered in a breathless flutter. "I'm just having the worst luck today."

The man put aside his dog-eared magazine. "What's wrong?" he asked with genuine concern.

"Oh, my goodness, I hardly know where to start," Kristina answered. Her plan was to confuse the man by prattling endlessly so it would be difficult for him to follow her conversation.

She went into a long, meandering story about how she was on her way from Plum Grove, near Liberty, Texas, to Austin, following a horrible fight with her father over a boyfriend. She claimed to have an old friend in Austin who'd let her visit for a while until things cooled down in Plum Grove, so she'd just upped and gone, with $18.47 in her purse.

And then, Kristina continued with her story, of all the bad luck, she'd had a blowout on her old car. A nice man had stopped and offered to change it for her, but she'd forgotten that she didn't have a spare tire—you didn't need a spare in Plum Grove; the town was so small you could walk home from any point. And now here she was, stranded on the road with no money to buy a new tire, and even though the nice man had offered to lend her the money, she couldn't be beholden to a stranger, so she'd let him bring her into the closest town to use the telephone and call her friend in Austin.

Kristina was truly breathless by the time she got to the end of her concocted tale. "So here I am," she said, spreading her arms wide and noting with satisfaction that the man's eyes had gone completely out of focus.

He shook his head to clear it. "Yes, ma'am, here you

are." He peered at her over the top of his glasses. "Now what?"

"Oh, I thought I told you at the beginning." Kristina twirled the sash on her bonnet. "Now, where was I? Oh, yes, well, it's so simple, you see. I just telephoned my friend in Austin—collect, of course—and told her I needed to buy a new tire. The nice man is waiting out there in his pickup truck—" Kristina turned and pointed vaguely out the window, though it was difficult to see the truck between the slats of the Venetian blinds. "And when you give me the money, he'll take me to the gas station to buy a new tire, and then he'll take me back to my car out yonder on the highway and change the blowout." She stopped and took a deep breath, then plunged on. "And then I'll drive on to Austin where my friend lives, and she'll help me find a job, and then I'll pay her back." She lifted her shoulders and smiled brightly. "So everything will have a happy ending. Can I have my money?" She extended her hand, palm-up.

The man sank back onto his chair. "Now, let me get this straight," he said, scratching his head. He got a pencil and started to write something, then gave it up. "You want me to give you money?"

"Why, yes. That's why I'm here." Kristina's face took on a saint-like expression of patience.

"How much money?"

"Why, enough to buy a new tire, of course."

"How much is that?"

"About fifty dollars."

The man had started to reach in his hip pocket for

139

his wallet, but stopped midway. "I don't have fifty dollars."

Kristina laughed merrily. "Oh, you're talking about *your* money. I'm talking about *my* money." She stroked the long, silky dark hair that hung over her shoulders and waited.

"Oh, *your* money." The man slapped his forehead in relief. "You mean your friend in Austin is sending it to you by wire?"

Kristina nodded.

"For you to pick up here in Gilbert?"

She nodded again.

The man's laugh could only be described as a titter. "I've worked here almost two years and no one's ever wired money *to* Gilbert before. We've only had money wired *out* of Gilbert."

Kristina stepped a little closer to the counter, toying with the strand of hair at her breast. Her smile was quite captivating. "My goodness, this must be a rich town, if money always goes out and never comes in."

"Actually, it's what you might call a sleepy town, because it's not even all that often that money goes out, not more'n once or twice a month. In fact, I'd worked here a long time before I ever had to learn how to do it. First time was only a couple of months ago."

"Is that so?" Kristina asked, letting the pink tip of her tongue glide over her lips. "My goodness, this must be an interesting job, if you can still learn something new after two whole years."

The man wore an embarrassed, aw-shucks grin. "Naw," he said modestly. "You just take the cash from the people here in Gilbert, and send a message to the Western Union in the other town telling them that the money's here. Then they give it to the folks at the other end of the line. Just like's going to happen to you today. They'll telegraph a message from Austin that your friend has deposited fifty dollars cash, and I'll type you out a money order."

"Well, my goodness, is that all there is to it? That doesn't sound so bad. Do you ever have any problems?"

The man was compelled to do some embroidery. Mustn't let this pretty miss think his job was simple. "Oh, once or twice. Like, for instance, if there's no Western Union in a town, then you have to send it to the town closest by and get word to the person who's waiting for the money."

"How do you do that?" Kristina wrinkled her nose. "It sounds hard to me."

"Not if you have a telephone number. You just call up the people and tell them to go on to the next town —say, for instance, if they're in Granite Falls, Washington, you send them on in to Everett to get their money."

Kristina perked up her ears. Names like Granite Falls and Everett weren't exactly household words in this part of Texas. And John Ed's last known whereabouts with the children had been Disneyland. He might've driven right up the Pacific coast with those kids. "Is Granite Falls a small town?"

"Oh, real small. Not near as big as Gilbert."

"I just love small towns, don't you?" Kristina thought it was time to distract the man again, lest he

141

realize that he was revealing information of great importance. She talked at length of her imaginary life in Plum Grove and her impossible-to-please father and too-good-to-be-true boyfriend. By the time she'd finished, the man's head was once again spinning. Fortunately, a flashing light told him he'd received a telegraph message.

"Well, well," he said, beaming at her. "This must be for you." He went to a rickety old typewriter and pecked out a few letters and numbers on a blank money order, then pressed it in a machine to validate it. He came back to the counter, waving the money order in her direction.

Kristina gave him a simpering smile that was a perfect match for her straw bonnet. She stretched out her hand. "Why, thank you."

"I'll need to see your identification first."

Kristina froze. It was the one thing she hadn't thought of. Her purse was lying on the seat of Bud's pickup, but all her identification showed her name as Dr. Kristina Neilsen, address Austin, Texas. If he saw her driver's license, the man would know she'd told him a whopper about driving here from Plum Grove. He might figure out that her entire story had been sheer fabrication, and the Winstons would be onto her immediately.

They heard the sound of the door opening and turned to see who else had business with Western Union today.

"Well, hello, there," Kristina said to Bud.

"Wondered what was taking you so long," he said, nodding at the man behind the counter.

"Why, we've just been visiting while we waited for the money to arrive," Kristina answered. She used the same little-girl breathless voice she'd been using, but Bud had known her long enough to recognize an extra dimension of nervousness. Something must've gone wrong.

"Maybe your friend had trouble raising the cash," he said, hoping she'd cue him.

"Oh, no, the money just arrived, just this minute," she said.

"Little lady needs her I.D.," said the man behind the counter.

"I was just going out to the truck to get my purse," Kristina said.

"Well, now," Bud said, hemming and hawing while he tried to think. "Guess it's a good thing I saved you some steps, then. You didn't have a purse."

"I didn't? Didn't I put it on the seat of your truck when you so kindly stopped and brought me into town?"

"Why, no. You didn't have a thing in your hands. Remember, you were trying to jack up your car when I came along?"

Kristina gasped. "Oh, no. You mean I left my purse in my own car, back there on the highway?" Her hands fluttered in helpless consternation.

The man behind the desk turned from first one, then to the other of them. Company policy required verification of identity before money could be released. "Hmmmm." He contorted his mouth as though somehow he could think better that way. Then he clapped his brow with the ball of his hand. "I know what we'll do," he said, brightening at once. He turned to Bud and smiled. *"You* give me her name to verify her identity, and then you can show me *your* driver's license. That ought to fix everything up all good and proper." He handed Bud a sheet of paper. "Just write down there something like *I verify this person is named*— whatever it is, and sign your name."

Bud swallowed hard. What was the name Kristina had said she was going to use? And even if he could remember, had she actually used it? He wanted to bend down and let her whisper in his ear, but they'd never get away with a stunt like that. He dared not look at her. He took the sheet of paper from the man. *I verify this person is named*—, he wrote slowly, trying desperately to remember. He smiled. It had suddenly come to him.—*Amanda Tucker. Signed, Robert "Bud" Thomas, Jr.*

The man behind the counter took the sheet of paper and tilted his head back, comparing the name on the paper with the message that had come in on the telegraph wire. "Amanda Tucker. That's a nice name."

"Sorry, I forgot to introduce myself," Kristina said, offering her hand for a handshake. "I'm Amanda, and this fellow here is named Bud, that's the only name I know for him."

"Bud Thomas," Bud said, offering his hand.

"Pleased to meet you," the man said. "I'm Troy Blasingame."

Kristina wanted to jump up and down with joy. *Blasingame!* That was the name of the woman who worked at the county clerk's office! "Could I have my money now?" she asked. She knew if they didn't hurry and get out of here, she was going to burst out laughing.

"Oh, sure thing. Just as soon as Bud lets me see his driver's license."

Kristina held her breath while Bud pulled out a well-worn license and passed it over the counter. Fortunately, Bud had never bothered to put in for a change of address after he'd moved to Austin. His driver's license still showed the address of his family's farm in Lufkin, the address he'd used since he left home as a college student. He and Kristina were going to be able to make their escape from Gilbert without leaving a single clue behind.

CHAPTER EIGHT

Flushed with triumph from their trip to the Western Union office in Gilbert, Kristina and Bud stopped at Mitch's office as they returned to Austin.

"We had to pass right by your building anyway, so we decided to report in person," Kristina said, removing her straw hat and trailing a finger through the long, dark tresses of her wig as she made the necessary introductions.

Mitch offered his hand, sizing up the other man. Bud was tall and lanky, not quite as tall as Mitch and not so solidly built, but Mitch knew at once that Bud Thomas would never have to worry about getting beefy around the waistline. Bud also had a headful of curly brown hair and an impish dimple that gave him the look women usually described as "cute." Worst of all, Bud had an easy camaraderie with Kristina that was born of their two years of friendship and working together. Mitch disliked the man on sight.

"Have a seat," Mitch said, indicating. "Can I get you a cup of coffee?"

"We really ought to have a glass of champagne to

celebrate," Kristina answered, "but I guess we'll settle for coffee."

Mitch wanted to growl. He remembered all too well the exhilaration Kristina had demonstrated upon her return from her previous successful mission to Gilbert. That was the night Mitch had taken her home with him to grill steaks—

Damn, damn, damn. Would Bud Thomas be the lucky recipient of today's jubilation? *Over my dead body!* Mitch swore to himself as he passed out steaming mugs of coffee.

He spent the next half hour staring out the window at the Austin skyline while he listened to Kristina's enthusiastic recital of their day's adventure. Any time Mitch removed his eyes from the window to look at Kristina, he found her smiling at Bud, who was obviously enamored with her. Mitch felt like an intruder in his own office, odd man out to the dynamic duo. An angry muscle twitched in his jaw.

"So where are we now?" he asked, when Kristina's bubbly laughter ended the tale.

"Well, we know that the Winstons have been sending John Ed money once or twice a month, and that he's probably driving up the Pacific coast, hiding out in small towns where there aren't any police bulletins about the missing children."

"You mean we *suspect* that's what's happening." There was an edge to Mitch's voice that had nothing to do with the content of Kristina's conversation.

"Okay, we *suspect.* Isn't there any way we can prove it?"

"It sounds as though John Ed's been in Washington

147

state recently. I think I'd better try to get an investigator to track them down before he gets to Canada."

"Canada!" The ramifications of John Ed's movements hit Kristina. She remembered that draft evaders from the sixties had gone to Canada so they couldn't be prosecuted. "Oh, Mitch, if he takes the kids to Canada, Valerie will never get them back!"

It was some small comfort to Mitch that Kristina looked to him for reassurance rather than to Bud Thomas. "I think I've got a map around here someplace," Mitch said. He rummaged on a shelf until he located a map of the United States and spread it across his desk. "There's Everett, Washington," he said, pointing. "But this map isn't big enough to show Granite Falls."

"Mitch, look! It can't be more than a hundred miles from Everett to the Canadian border."

Mitch rubbed his chin. "We may already be too late."

Kristina slumped in her chair. Mitch was annoyed when Bud Thomas leaned over to pat her hand. He involuntarily curled his fingers into a fist, but fortunately nobody noticed.

Mitch buzzed the intercom. "Betty, put in a call to Marc Stanley in Dallas."

Kristina lifted her head in a questioning glance.

"Marc's an old friend of mine from law school. He's in a big Dallas firm with contacts all over the country. Someone there should know how we can locate a good private investigator in Seattle." Mitch took the telephone call when his secretary put it through and swapped a few ribald insults before telling his friend what he needed, then hung up the telephone. "He'll call me back as soon as he can," Mitch said to Kristina. "I told him it was urgent."

While they waited for the return call, Mitch made notes on a legal pad and buzzed his secretary to get some long-distance telephone numbers for him. From time to time he made a cryptic remark, but nobody asked for an explanation. He was too intent on what he was doing.

The intercom buzzed. "Marc?" Mitch scribbled furiously. "Thanks, friend." He chuckled. "Fair enough, a steak dinner. I'll pay off the next time you're in town. Say hello to your beautiful wife for me."

Mitch replaced the receiver and glanced at his watch. There was two hours' difference between the Pacific and Central time zones. He still had plenty of time to make his calls to Washington. While Kristina and Bud waited, chatting occasionally but mostly listening, Mitch placed telephone calls to a private investigator in Seattle, to the Everett and Bellingham police stations, and to the Border Patrol. "If John Ed hasn't already gotten across the border to Canada," he said when he'd finished his calls, "that should make it a little more difficult for him."

"What next?" Kristina asked. "I don't know what to tell Valerie when I go home."

"Soft-pedal it as much as you can. Tell her a private investigator is hot on John Ed's trail this very minute. In the meantime, I'm going to get this lawsuit filed tomorrow so I can subpoena the Western Union and telephone records. I don't think we'll have any problem connecting the Winstons with John Ed's disap-

149

pearance. When they realize how much trouble they're in, they'll make him bring the kids back, even if he's already gone to Canada. At least, I hope they will," he muttered in an undertone. More firmly he added, "Tell Valerie not to lose hope." Mitch stared glumly across his desk at Kristina and her companion until jealousy gave him a sudden inspiration. Maybe he could slow the tempo of their duet *presto*. "This is a critical point in the lawsuit, so you'd better spend as much time with Valerie as you can for a few days. The pressure is going to build, and she may not be able to handle it very well."

Kristina was too preoccupied with the possibility that John Ed might already have escaped into Canada with the children to notice any mischief in Mitch's suggestion. "You're right. I don't want Valerie to collapse on me again. I'll stay with her at all times except when I'm at work."

"What about the Halloween party tomorrow night?" Bud had finally wangled a date with Kristina for their department's annual party, and he wasn't about to surrender it without a struggle. Halloween was the biggest social occasion of the year in Austin, an even more festive holiday than New Year's Eve. It was unthinkable to spend the evening alone.

"Oh, Bud, I'm sorry." Kristina was stricken with guilt. She'd accepted the date in exchange for Bud's help on the mission to Gilbert today, and it wasn't fair for her to renege. She turned to her friend with a furrowed brow. "Would you mind if Valerie goes to the party with us?"

Bud shrugged. He'd never even met Kristina's sis-

150

ter. It wasn't what he'd had in mind, but he supposed it was better than nothing.

Kristina sensed Bud's disapproval and was caught in a dilemma. Should she disappoint her friend or abandon her sister? Either choice was unpleasant. She glanced in Mitch's direction and caught him smugly observing the scene he'd engineered, obviously pleased that Valerie was going to be an unwitting chaperone.

He wasn't quick enough to erase the self-satisfied expression from his face, but at least he had the grace to blush. Kristina took pleasure in the reddening at the tips of his ears. She took even greater pleasure in the thought of the embarrassing torment it would cause this conservative Aggie lawyer to have to stuff himself into a Halloween costume. "I know what we'll do," Kristina said with real enthusiasm. "Mitch and Valerie can both go with us. Won't that be fun? A double date, just like when we were in high school!"

Mitch tried to decline, claiming every excuse short of infectious mononucleosis, but Kristina would have none of it. "Be at my house tomorrow night at eight," she commanded. Then she stood to make her departure. "I can hardly wait to see your costume."

Mitch decided to beat Kristina at her own little game. She obviously thought he was dull and stuffy, with too little imagination and too much reserve to come up with an appropriate costume. He hied himself off to the theatrical shop, and after trying on every costume big enough for his towering physique, he narrowed his choices to a swashbuckling pirate and a dashing Southern gentleman.

151

"Which one do you like best?" Mitch asked the pretty college student who'd turned the task of finding the right costume into an entertaining adventure.

"I think the frockcoat," she said at last, pondering. "Your Rhett Butler is every bit as handsome as Clark Gable's." Her silent survey of Mitch's tall frame was full of admiration. And he cut a splendid figure indeed, dressed in a sapphire-blue velvet frockcoat, black trousers that hugged his muscular thighs, and a crisp white shirt with a touch of lace ruffling at the collar and sleeves. She handed Mitch a sky-blue silk jacquard cravat that exactly matched his eyes and hunted until she found a faux diamond stickpin to go with it. "Now if I can find you a pair of black Wellington boots—"

"No spats?" Mitch asked in amusement when she handed him a shoe box containing shiny black boots.

"Heavens, no." She gave him her intense scrutiny. "My, you *are* a big man, aren't you?" The clerk was of average height, and Mitch loomed above her in a way that she found quite irresistible. "I suggest you stop at the florist shop and have them make you a small boutonniere of lilies of the valley." Her eyes swept over Mitch in another admiring glance. "You'll definitely sweep her off her feet."

"Who?"

"Why, the woman you're going to all this trouble for." She gave him a conspirator's smile.

Am I that obvious? Mitch wondered, then realized that he didn't even care. He turned to look at himself in the three-way mirror, adjusting his top hat to a rakish angle. He'd never looked better in his life. *You'd better watch out, Neilsen, because I'm definitely going to sweep you off your feet, just as this young lady has predicted.* "How much?" he asked the clerk, reaching for his wallet.

"You really don't want to know," she answered, chuckling. "Just sign the ticket with your eyes closed and know that it was worth every penny."

When Mitch knocked on Kristina's door promptly at eight o'clock the following evening, it was Valerie who opened it for him.

"Why, Mitch, how handsome you look!" she said. "And isn't it a nice coincidence that our costumes match?" Valerie swept aside her full taffeta skirts to let Mitch enter. She was quite beautiful in a soft, vulnerable way, with her blond hair parted in the center and twisted around her ears in ringlets. She wore an off-the-shoulder dress of rose-petal pink trimmed with lace and ribbons, a true Southern belle.

But she doesn't have the fire of a Scarlett O'Hara, Mitch thought. He bowed gallantly and lifted Valerie's outstretched hand to his lips. "You look very beautiful this evening," he said to her. "I'm glad to find you doing so well."

She took him into the living room, where Kristina and Bud were engaged in shop-talk about their students. Bud hadn't put much effort into a Halloween costume, taking the easy way out by dressing as a cowboy. But Kristina nearly took Mitch's breath away. She was dressed as a 1940s tap-dancer à la Ann Miller, wearing a short black tuxedo jacket over a glittery vest. What made Mitch's eyes bulge in their sockets,

153

though, was her legs. She wore black satin shorts, and her long, long, sexy legs were covered with nothing more than black mesh stockings and well-placed sequins that sparkled with every movement. And boy, did she move!

Kristina felt Mitch's eyes on her, and before she turned to look at him, she stretched sensuously and lifted herself from the sofa to greet him. Halfway up, she caught her first glimpse of him and gasped in surprise. "Why, Mitch, you look—"

He preened himself in an exaggerated manner, turning for her inspection. "Will I do?" he asked with feigned cockiness.

Kristina swallowed hard. Her mouth was too dry to speak, so she nodded. *Fool*, she scolded herself. *Why did you have to taunt him into getting himself decked out like that and then toss him into Valerie's waiting arms?*

"You and Valerie are perfect together," she said when she could finally get her breath. *And Valerie, if you so much as lay a finger on my man, you're going to have me to deal with, sister or not.* Kristina gave her sister a simpering smile and hoped Valerie had sense enough to comprehend the unspoken message that sent jealous sparks from Kristina's green eyes. "Let me get you a glass of wine."

"I'll do it," Valerie protested. "I can't sit down anyway, without getting tangled up in all these petticoats." She poured Mitch a glass of wine and handed it to him with a warm smile. "I'm so glad you could go to the party with us tonight," she said. "I've been wanting a chance to talk to you."

154

"This is a lovely wine," Mitch said, sipping it and trying to ignore the invitation in her voice. Tonight was not the time to discuss her lawsuit. "One of my favorites, in fact."

"I guess you and Kristina must have the same taste. She insisted on it."

I'm sure she did. He thought of the pleasure it must give Kristina to twist the knife as she took her revenge on him. It would be a long time before either of them would be able to forget the last time they drank this wine—that fateful canoe trip and their ensuing argument. Mitch leaned against the doorpost while Valerie fluttered around the room, refilling glasses. She was a little keyed up, and Mitch supposed it was because she hadn't been out in a crowd for some time. After the quiet life of Gilbert, Texas, and several weeks in the hospital, a university party might seem threatening to her. He tried to draw her into a casual conversation and decided he'd better keep a watchful eye on her throughout the evening. She was too nervous and high-strung tonight.

Mitch stole glances at Kristina. She'd looked spectacular in the green bathing suit she'd worn to the river, but she was positively breathtaking tonight in those black sequined stockings. Mitch couldn't keep his eyes off her, and he seethed every time he caught Bud Thomas looking at her. *If that guy so much as touches her, I'm going to punch him in the nose,* Mitch promised himself. He grew even more frustrated when he realized that every man at the party would be staring at Kristina's legs. Between trying to keep Valerie calmed down and wanting to smash every guy who leered at Kristina, it was going to be a long evening for Mitch. They might as well get started.

"Ready to go?" Mitch asked.

Kristina glanced at the grandfather clock in the corner. "I guess so. It's about time."

Everybody stood, and there was a discussion about cars. Mitch's sports car held two passengers, Bud's pickup truck held only three, and Kristina's Volkswagen could hold four if they were squashed in.

"Not in this dress, Kristina. It'll take up the whole back seat," Valerie pointed out.

"We'll have to take two vehicles, then," Mitch said, hating the only logical alternative. Kristina was Bud's date and would have to ride with him, leaving Mitch to take Valerie in his own car. Kristina glared at Valerie and Mitch glared at Bud. But there was no other choice. "Come on, Valerie," Mitch said as graciously as possible. "I'm sorry I don't have a horse and carriage for you to ride in." He escorted Valerie to his car and watched Kristina climb into the pickup ahead of them in the drive, her long legs shimmering in the moonlight. "We'll follow Bud's truck," Mitch told Valerie. "I don't know where the party is being held."

As the pickup made its journey across town, the bright beams of Mitch's headlights illuminated the passengers in the cab. There was plenty of room for a third person in the middle of the seat, Mitch was pleased to observe. If Kristina had cuddled up against Bud, Mitch would have belted the guy for sure.

A Halloween party with university faculty members wasn't much different from any other campus party,

Mitch decided, remembering similar get-togethers from his days as a law student. There was an abundance of cheap wine and decent cheese, a tray full of homemade hot tamales, and the *de rigueur* chips, dips, and crackers. He knew without being told that there would be a keg of beer in the backyard. The behavior and conversation varied little from student parties, he also observed. Same games, different players. Only the subject matter had changed. Instead of *Hadley v. Baxendale* and *International Shoe,* the topic for law-student parties, these political scientists discussed grassroots pressure and executive privilege—with the same glazed expressions of inebriated law students as their alcohol level increased, Mitch noted.

He tried to keep an eye on Valerie and was glad when Bud Thomas took her under his wing. They found a quiet corner, and from the looks of things, Valerie was pouring out her life story to Bud's sympathetic ears. She looked a little tired but was otherwise holding her own. Mitch turned in the other direction, hunting Kristina.

Kristina, to the contrary, wasn't holding her own; she was holding court. She was surrounded by a group of admirers, swapping stories about outrageous student behavior—whether about their own student days or their current students Mitch was unable to decipher. Whichever it was, apparently it was quite hilarious, because there were constant bursts of laughter.

Mitch had never seen Kristina on her own turf before, and he was discovering still another facet of her personality. He'd known she was strong and opinionated, but here in her own milieu he could see that she

157

was also popular and outgoing, not at all a shrinking violet like her sister Valerie. He should've known, however, because a shrinking violet would never wear a waist-length tuxedo top with absolutely nothing but sheer black stockings from her fanny down. It took a dynamic personality and a dynamite figure to wear an outfit like that. And Kristina had both.

To Mitch's consternation, Kristina didn't need him or anyone else and seemed perfectly capable of taking care of herself. If it hadn't been for Valerie's legal problem, she probably wouldn't give Mitch the time of day. She obviously found him tedious and uninspired since she'd been ignoring him all evening. This was a new and humbling experience for Mitch, who'd grown accustomed to receiving a woman's undivided attention. He flicked a particle of lint from his velvet sleeve. He'd lost all interest in the party.

"Well, who are you?" inquired a sexy voice at his elbow. Mitch looked down into liquid brown eyes set in a lovely face desecrated with punk makeup.

"Is that your Halloween costume, or do you wear that stuff on your face all the time?" Mitch asked.

"I'm Sylvia, and I only dress like this on Saturday nights when I go to Club Foot," she answered. "I don't remember seeing you at any of these faculty parties before."

Mitch laughed. "You haven't. I'm a guest."

"Really? What do you do if you're not a teacher?"

"I'm an oil and gas lawyer."

Sylvia's eyes brightened. "That sounds lucrative."

"It is," interrupted a cool female voice. "He's filthy rich, Sylvia."

158

"Oh, hi, Kristina. I didn't realize he was your date."
Sylvia was a poacher, but she knew better than to tangle with Kristina.

"He's not. He's with my sister."

Mitch watched the interchange with amusement, his whole attitude markedly improved. Kristina had only been pretending to ignore him. She couldn't have gotten there so quickly if she hadn't been aware of every move he made.

"Well, it was nice meeting you," Sylvia said to Mitch and sidled away.

"And it's nice meeting *you,*" Mitch said to Kristina, brushing her cheek with his thumb. "I was beginning to think you'd forgotten me."

"I thought Valerie was looking after you."

"Liar."

"Me?" She was a specimen of offended innocence.

"You knew damned well I was standing here like some wallflower at a high school dance while you entertained the troops."

"But Valerie—"

"Don't 'Valerie' me," Mitch said, his breath warm against her temple. "I didn't spend two hundred bucks on this costume for Valerie's benefit."

Kristina's fingers stroked the velvet lapels of his frockcoat. "Two hundred dollars? Wow!"

"You think I wasted my money?" His thumb had worked its way down to the pulsepoint of her throat.

Kristina covered his hand with hers. "No," she answered with a coquettish smile. "I think it was worth every cent."

"Now that we've got that settled—" Mitch leaned forward to kiss her forehead.

"Kristina," interrupted Bud Thomas, joining them. "All this noise and smoke is getting to Valerie."

Kristina turned to the corner where Valerie was standing and waved. "I imagine she's getting bored. She doesn't know any of these people."

"I think it's too much for her to try to make conversation with a bunch of strangers," Bud agreed.

"I suppose we ought to go home, then." Kristina felt curiously dejected. The evening was ending too soon.

"Does she seem tired?" Mitch asked. From here Valerie looked okay.

"No, not really, just ready to get out of here."

"Then why don't we go down to Sixth Street to get some fresh air and watch the crowds for a while?"

"That's a good idea, Mitch," Kristina said. "She won't have to worry about making conversation, and it'll be fun to see the costumes."

"I'll go ask her." Bud hurried away, hoping Valerie would approve the change in plans. They were just beginning to get acquainted, and Bud wasn't ready to see the evening end just yet either.

Sixth Street was closed to automobile traffic during the Halloween festivities, but they managed to find parking places for the two vehicles within a reasonable walking distance. The October evening had grown cool, but Kristina insisted that her bare legs were warm enough. As they trekked down the street, she attracted plenty of attention from bystanders, mostly in the nature of catcalls and whistles, but since there were other scantily clad women in the crowds, nobody took offense.

Mitch made a point of staring at a gorgeous brunette in a belly-dancer costume, and she wiggled her hips in such an enticing way that Kristina nudged him in a different direction.

"I was just looking," he said, grinning down at her.

"So I noticed."

"It's Halloween, a night for revelry and play. Besides, this was your idea."

"Coming to Sixth Street was *your* idea."

"But getting decked out in these costumes was *your* idea. And you know how disguise affects people, Kristina. Once you hide your real self behind makeup and costume, anything can happen." Mitch expanded his chest and fingered his lapels. "When I'm in my work clothes, I'm just a dull attorney. But now that I'm all dressed up like a Southern dandy, I've got to live up to my image." He doffed his top hat to a tall, attractive ballerina in a tutu.

"Since when does a Southern dandy play ladies' man to another man?" Kristina asked, laughing. "That ballerina we just passed was a man in drag."

Mitch did a double-take, then plopped his hat back on his head and walked a little faster. "Never mind," he said, when the ballerina murmured something over his shoulder, "my mistake."

Bud and Valerie were ahead of them, strolling hand in hand with their heads together, so they didn't notice what had happened until Mitch and Kristina ducked around the corner and collapsed against each other trying to contain their laughter.

"Shh, he'll hear us," Kristina said, putting a cautioning finger against her lips.

"Is he headed back this way?" Mitch asked.

Kristina peeked around the corner of the building. "No, he's gone on down the street."

"Then let's go in this café," Mitch said, signaling Bud and Valerie to join them. "We can watch out the windows and see everybody pass by."

"We'll never get a table with this huge crowd."

"Sure we will."

"I hope so," Valerie said. "I'd like to sit down and rest for a while." She'd been standing the entire evening, trying not to wrinkle her flowing taffeta skirts, but now she was tired.

The waiter put Mitch's name on the list, then moved it near the top as Mitch handed him a folded bill with a quiet remark that his date had been ill and needed to sit down. "I'll see what I can do," the waiter said. "I think those people over in the corner are about ready to leave."

It wasn't long before they were seated at a table for four, and somehow they managed to lump Valerie's skirts underneath her chair so no one would trip over them. Mitch ordered a bottle of wine, but Valerie asked for hot spiced tea instead.

Kristina reached across the table to squeeze her sister's hand. "You look wonderful tonight and you're doing so much better," Kristina said.

Valerie smiled. "Of course I am, with Mitch to handle the lawsuit and Bud to be a friend." She stretched

162

out her arms to clasp the hands of the men on either side of her. She'd lost some of her tension and no longer made the restless, fidgety motions with her hands that had concerned Mitch earlier in the evening. Apparently Bud Thomas was having a salubrious effect on her. And gauging from the light in his eye, Valerie was having a similar effect on him.

Bud continued to hold Valerie's hand long after she'd let go of Mitch's. For two years Bud had had a futile crush on Kristina that was never going to lead to anything more than friendship. Now he'd been lucky enough to meet her sister, who was just as beautiful, though in a softer, more subdued way. Valerie's personality was far more pliable, and Bud found it appealing that Valerie was capable of leaning on someone. He'd never realized how much strength it had taken to rise to Kristina's level and how draining that had sometimes been. It was much more comfortable to be with someone like Valerie, whose expectations were less. Bud had the feeling that Valerie would blossom with a man who loved her and wanted to look after her, whereas that would never be enough for Kristina. She'd always be pushing a man to a higher level of achievement, just as she drove herself. *Takes all kinds,* Bud thought, suddenly realizing that he wasn't as aggressive as Kristina and never would be, but that he was content to be himself.

There was a subtle shift in attitude around the table. Mitch sensed that Bud had abandoned his long-running pursuit of Kristina in favor of her more docile sister and that he was no longer competing with Mitch. With the cessation of rivalries, there was a new

163

friendliness in the group, and they found themselves talking quite easily about life in Austin, their work, the university, Valerie's lawsuit. This time when Kristina and Bud described their trip to the Western Union office in Gilbert, Mitch was able to laugh heartily and to commend Bud for coming to Kristina's rescue in the nick of time.

They finished their drinks and wandered back into the street, listening to the bands that played on the streetcorners and now and then dancing a few steps down the sidewalks. They amused themselves analyzing the costumes, and decided that all the young people dressed as punk rockers were university preppies in their real lives, and that no doubt over at Club Foot, the punk nightclub, all the real punkers were dressed for Halloween in three-piece business suits like preppies. They saw every kind of costume, from the normal Halloween garb of ghosts, goblins, and vampires to astronauts, robots, sultans, and mermaids.

"Look, that guy's dressed like Willie Nelson," Valerie said, pointing to an older man with a long braid and a headband.

"That *is* Willie Nelson," someone else shouted, and several people ran in his direction to get his autograph.

They bought popcorn and candy apples from street vendors, munching as they strolled, until finally they jostled through the crowd all the way to Congress Avenue.

"Shall we walk down to the Bradford Hotel and have some breakfast?" Mitch asked.

"I'm not hungry," Kristina said. "We've been snacking all evening."

"You wouldn't even be interested in a cup of coffee?"

"Well, maybe. My legs are beginning to feel a little cold."

Mitch gave her a wicked grin. *I can warm them up for you,* said his expression.

"I'm not that cold," she retorted, reading his unspoken thought.

Valerie leaned against the brick building at the corner. "I hate to be a party-pooper, but I'm getting a little tired," she said. "It's almost one o'clock, and I haven't been out like this in months."

Mitch was instantly attentive. Officially she was still his date. "If you'll all wait right here, I'll go get my car and take Valerie home," he said.

In the glow of the streetlight, all three faces stared at Mitch in confusion. When she'd said she wanted to leave, Valerie had forgotten that Mitch was the one who'd be taking her home. What she really wanted was to go home, get out of her bulky costume, put on something comfortable, and snuggle up on the couch with Bud. He was the most congenial man she'd ever met.

Bud feigned a deep yawn. "To tell you the truth," he said, yawning again, "I'm feeling a little tired myself. Why don't *I* take Valerie home?" he asked disingenuously. "We're the ones who are tired and ready to call it a night, and that way we won't spoil things for you and Kristina."

Mitch gave Kristina a questioning glance, then shrugged as if it didn't matter to him one way or the other. He didn't intend to give anybody the impression

165

that he would be less than chivalrous to Valerie, his date of the evening.

"You two stay," Valerie said, deciding the matter. "I insist." She gathered up her full skirts so she could walk more easily and took Bud's elbow for the hike back to his pickup truck.

Mitch and Kristina had taken only a few steps toward the Bradford when Valerie came running back for Kristina's house key. While Kristina fumbled in her vest pocket for the key, Valerie whispered, "Please don't hurry home, Kris. Have a long, long breakfast, won't you, so I can have plenty of time with Bud?"

CHAPTER NINE

Somewhat surprised at the way fate had intervened to give them time alone, Mitch and Kristina walked the short block to the Bradford Hotel.

"Your sister seems to have taken quite a fancy to Bud Thomas," Mitch said, drawing Kristina closer to his side.

"Jealous?" There was mischief in Kristina's voice.

Mitch cleared his throat. He'd experienced unfamiliar pangs of jealousy over Bud's proprietary manner with Kristina, and he didn't want Kris to know how relieved he was that Bud's attention had now turned to Valerie. "Of course I'm jealous," he answered, barely concealing a grin. "I've always thought Valerie is a beautiful woman. And besides, it hurts my pride that she prefers a nondescript cowboy to a dazzling Southern buck like yours truly."

Kristina stopped in the middle of the sidewalk, one foot tapping in irritation, and turned to Mitch. "If you're so interested in Valerie, you should've taken her home yourself."

"Now who's jealous?" he asked.

"Jealous of Valerie? For heaven's sake, she's my sister. Why would I be jealous of her?"

"Just checking. I wanted to be sure you wouldn't mind if I took Valerie out again sometime."

Kristina resisted the urge to glare and was about to pretend a lack of interest one way or the other when she caught the twinkle in Mitch's eye. "You!" she said, giving him a gentle shove. "I think one Neilsen at a time is all you can handle."

Mitch's hand strayed at Kristina's waist. "True. But you've had your turn. I could confine myself to the other Neilsen sister."

Kristina maneuvered her body away from Mitch's questing hand. "So you could. And that would leave Bud available." Her fingers reached out to stroke his lapels.

Mitch gazed down at Kristina's body, shimmering in the moonlight. His hand closed over her fingers and pressed them against the velvet fabric of his frockcoat, while the other hand tilted her chin. "Touché, Kristina. I think I'll stick with the tap-dancing Neilsen!"

A noisy group emerging from the hotel jostled against them, interrupting them just as they were about to kiss.

"Come on," Mitch said, "let's go inside before something indecent happens right here in the middle of Congress Avenue." They went inside the hotel and walked across the lobby, only to discover that the dining room had already closed.

"Now what?" Kristina asked. "I can't go home yet. Valerie told me to be sure to give her plenty of time with Bud."

Mitch pondered the situation. "You're cold," he said. "You wait here in the lobby while I go get the car. Maybe we can still find some hot coffee somewhere to warm you up."

"You're spoiling me."

"I'm just trying to live up to this costume. Southern chivalry, you know." Mitch escorted Kristina to an out-of-the-way corner and turned to go. "I'll be back in a few minutes," he said. "Don't talk to any strangers while I'm gone."

Mitch pulled the car into his darkened driveway, lit by nothing more than the beams from his headlights. Because the few restaurants still open were crowded and noisy, he'd finally volunteered his own kitchen, promising himself that this visit wouldn't end up like Kristina's previous one. This time he would keep himself under strict control. They'd drink black coffee and scramble some eggs. That would be harmless enough.

He punched the button on the remote control and all the house lights came on. As he helped Kristina from the car, he realized that in the bright lights, her legs were even more tempting. He'd have to dim the lights a little.

"Aren't you going to give me that tour you promised?" she asked as they went up the steps from the garage and Mitch headed into the kitchen.

"You've already seen most of the house," he said. He went to the kitchen sink and poured water into an automatic coffee maker.

"Not what's down there," Kristina said, pointing to the stairs.

"Just rooms." He rummaged for coffee and cups. "This won't take long. We'll soon have you warmed up."

Kristina came and stood at his shoulder. He was putting roasted beans into an electric grinder. "What are you doing?"

"Grinding fresh coffee for you. Would you rather have Colombian or amaretto?"

"My, you're quite a gourmet, aren't you?" She smelled the beans. "I'll have amaretto."

"No, I'm not a gourmet. I'm a simple man with simple tastes. I just happen to like good coffee."

Kristina studied the gadgets that equipped the countertop and compared them to those of her own kitchen. Hers were mostly old and well used, handed down from her mother. His were shiny, new, and expensive.

"Can I help?" she asked.

"Do you want to scramble the eggs?"

"I thought we were just going to have some coffee."

"Might as well have some breakfast, as long as we have time to kill."

Kristina lifted herself onto the counter and dangled her crossed legs. "Time to *kill?*"

"Sorry. You know what I mean." Mitch tried not to look at the black-stockinged legs she was swinging in his direction. "I should've said time to *occupy,* so we don't get ourselves in trouble. In fact, maybe we should make pancakes and an omelette, and squeeze some fresh orange juice."

"And wax the kitchen floor and wash the windows?"

"How much time does Valerie need, anyway?"

"About as much as we do," Kristina answered, leaning forward and placing her hands behind Mitch's neck, drawing him close beside her on the cabinet.

He lifted her down from the countertop and set her firmly on the floor. "I guess I'll go ahead and give you a guided tour while the coffee is dripping," he said. "Follow me." *At a safe distance, too,* he muttered to himself.

Kristina had seen most of the upper level, including the kitchen, dining area, and study, on her previous visit to Mitch's house. She recalled that the living area and master bedroom had opened onto the redwood deck where they'd cooked their steaks in the glow of sunset. That prior evening she'd seen another redwood deck below and had wondered how many rooms the house contained, since the upper level seemed more than ample for a single occupant. On tonight's tour, she now discovered that the lower level was almost equal in size to the upper one. In an indifferent manner, Mitch indicated two bedrooms, each containing a separate bath.

"No furniture?" she asked, looking at the bare rooms.

"I never got around to buying furniture for these rooms," Mitch answered. "Nobody ever uses them anyway."

"Why buy a house with more room than you need?"

"I like the view," he said, shrugging his shoulders. He led her through one of the bedrooms to a door opening onto the lower deck, and they could see the lights of the city in the distance, the play of moonlight on the rippling Colorado River below.

"It's a beautiful view," Kristina agreed. "But it's a little too chilly to be out here tonight."

Mitch pointed to the opposite end of the deck. "There's a hot tub if you want to warm up," he said with a grin.

Their footsteps echoed on the redwood planking of the deck as they walked to the corner where the hot tub stood, steaming as its heat made contact with the cold night air. Kristina could see through the glass patio doors to an adjoining room with a wet bar, a massive stereo system, and a large-screen television set. "What's all that?" she asked.

"It's a party room. The guy who built the house designed it that way. There's a pool table and everything."

Kristina tried to slide open the glass doors to go inside for a closer look, but they were locked. "Can we go back the other way so I can see it?"

Mitch squirmed. He didn't use this part of the house very often and had never thought about how it would strike someone who'd never been there before. "You can see everything from here," he said.

"But what's behind that screen?"

"Just a sort of lounging area."

Kristina was curious and started back across the deck, intending to make her way through the vacant bedrooms to the party room.

"I'm sure the coffee is ready by now," Mitch said, trying to steer her upstairs instead of letting her proceed down the hallway.

172

"I thought I was going to get a complete tour." Kristina stalled at the foot of the stairs and didn't budge.

"You are. You did. You've seen it all."

"I haven't seen what's behind that screen."

"I told you, there's nothing there. Just a lounging area, so someone can watch TV or listen to music."

"Then why does it matter if I look at it?"

"It doesn't matter." Mitch clenched his jaw. "It's just a waste of time because there's nothing to see, and the coffee is ready."

"I think you must have something hidden there," she said, smiling. "I knew this house was too neat for a bachelor. That must be where you hide your dirty laundry."

Mitch didn't think fast enough to agree with her and thereby put the matter to rest. "I don't hide my dirty laundry," he said, offended that she would contemplate such an idea.

"Then what *do* you hide there?" Kristina asked, now quite determined to see the room. "Is it dead bodies of your former lovers? Or a few nasty skeletons in the closet?" She broke loose from the grip he had on her elbow and marched down the hall, her fanny switching with each step.

Mitch leaned against the wall and buried his face in the crook of his elbow.

"Oh, my God, what is this!" Kristina said, positively shrieking with laughter. "A French bordello if I ever saw one."

Mitch jammed his hands in the pockets of his jacket and followed her into the room. "When did you ever

173

see a French bordello?" he asked, knowing he must take the initiative or she'd never let him live this down.

"In the movies." Kristina had collapsed onto a shaggy rug on the floor and was laughing till tears streamed down her cheeks. "All you need is a mirror on the ceiling." She lifted her eyes. "Oh, I see you have one. Goes well with this fancy chandelier, doesn't it?"

Mitch reached for the light switch. The tiny flame-shaped bulbs of the chandelier dimmed, reflecting against the mirrored ceiling and turning the room into a sparkling fairyland. "Does wonders for the imagination, doesn't it?" he asked in a droll voice.

The walls were swathed in ruby-red satin to match the satin comforter and pillow shams on a huge waterbed. The entire room glimmered with reflected light in an opulent, voluptuous glow, and there was a scent of jasmine from candles strategically placed on the nightstand and at the headboard.

"Isn't there a black lace negligee somewhere?" Kristina asked, unable to get her laughter under control.

"I believe there used to be one, but he took it with him."

"Who?"

"The man who built the house," Mitch answered. "Surely you don't think *I* invented something as decadent as this room, do you?"

Kristina stopped laughing. "You mean this boudoir came furnished with the house?"

Mitch nodded. "He said it would be too much trouble to take down the waterbed, since he had it built into the paneling. He threw in the bedspread and stuff because it matched the wallpaper."

"How long have you lived here?" Kristina asked. She was still sitting on the shaggy rug.

"Almost a year."

"And you've never used this room?"

Mitch felt himself blush. "I'm not exactly the type," he said. "When I first bought the house, I promised myself to cut loose and be a hedonistic bachelor. But somehow I just never got around to it. As you're so fond of telling me, I'm a dull, conservative Aggie."

Kristina drew herself up onto her knees. The blatant sensuality of the room was overpowering. "I never said you were dull," she objected. "As a matter of fact, in that costume you look pretty damned sharp. I believe you could out-Rhett Rhett Butler." She offered her hand for Mitch to lift her to her feet. "As a matter of fact—"

She stepped lightly into Mitch's waiting arms. "Oh, Krissie," he said, his breath warm against her cheek. "I've been wanting to kiss you all night."

"I know," she answered, twining her arms around his neck. "And I've been wanting you to kiss me."

His big palms moved to her face and pressed the sides of her cheeks as he smiled into her eyes. "You're beautiful," he said. He fingered her full lower lip, then brushed it with a kiss. He found her ear and gently nipped its lobe. "And you're sexy," he added, burying his lips in her ear so that the words were warm and tickled. His tongue traced an outline in the inner hollow of her ear, then moved down the slim column

175

of her neck, nipping and licking fiery little circles that made her arch against him.

Her heart pounded in her chest, and she felt a warm, melting sensation in the center of her being. Her body was drawn to his by a magnetism too fierce to resist. She'd wanted Mitch for so long, wanted so desperately to know the joy of his lovemaking, yet been denied so often that she dared not let the moment linger lest it once again be snatched away from her. "Mitch." She spoke urgently, burying her face against the starchy lace at his collar. "Mitch, please, I want you." She lifted his hand to her breast and felt her nipple harden even before his hand made contact.

"Oh, God, Krissie." He moaned, stroking the softness underneath his hand. In the back of his mind, a warning bell rang. He'd have to be careful and not let himself get carried away. But he could kiss her just a little longer without losing control. For the moment, they were safe. His arm tightened at her waist and lifted her against him so that she felt his thrusting strength. His mouth became wildfire, searching for hers until their lips met in a passionate kiss. "Krissie, my Krissie," he breathed, over and over. His tongue plunged between her lips, forming a point to stroke the sensitive area at the roof of her mouth, then darting out to tantalize the corners of her lips.

As she responded, the warning bell rang again. He'd have to stop, and quickly, or it would be too late. He tried to pull away from her, his mind clouded with broken phrases about *she's your client's sister* and *legal code of ethics.* But the words were no match for the powerful emotions that consumed him. He couldn't

176

stop, not yet. He had to hold her just a little longer. He was near the edge, but he could still stop when he had to. "Krissie," he murmured, "just one more kiss." He buried his lips in her neck, kissing and nipping playfully, then licking in a way that wasn't playful at all.

His hands found the buttons to her vest and worked them loose, jerking the vest open. He shuddered with delight when he felt her bare breasts underneath his searching fingers. He pulled away from her long enough to look down at the warm, full globes, their tips pink and firm and glimmering in the magical light of the room. His eyes were dilated with passion now, and he tilted her backward, teasing one of her nipples with his tongue until she cried out with pleasure.

And then it was too late. Now there was no way to stop the tidal wave of desire that seized and lifted him into its roaring, majestic cascades, far beyond the reach of professional duty. "Upstairs," he murmured almost incoherently, lifting her into his arms.

"But why, Mitch? Why not here?" she asked, not caring where they were, only that they were together at last.

Without responding he carried her out of the room and down the hallway, then paused on the landing to kiss her, delicately and deliciously. "Because the first time I make love to you, I want it to be in a place that's mine, not in a place that's haunted by the ghosts of another man's lovers." In six strides he was in his own bedroom, furnished to his own taste, and he laid Kristina on the clean sheets of his own bed in a room fresh with the blues and greens of nature. "Pretend you're in a secluded forest," he whispered, dimming the light as he sat down beside her.

His hands worked with her tuxedo jacket until she shrugged free, and he tossed it on the chair beside the bed. The vest followed immediately, so that she was clad now only in her black silk stockings and the briefest of black shorts. He flung her shoes into a corner, edged the shorts down over her hips, and then simply stared as she lay alongside him, naked except for her stockings. "You're the sexiest woman I've ever seen," he said gruffly, almost unable to speak for the constriction in his throat. He lifted her head onto the pillows and leaned across her, stroking one breast until it tingled with sensation.

"Mitch," she whispered, fastening his hand with hers to stop its arousal. "Lie down with me."

"In a few minutes," he said, leaning down to kiss her neck, her ears, her eyes. She whimpered softly, and he lowered his lips to hers, kissing her now with an urgency that made her wild with pent-up desire. Their mouths bruised each other's as they plundered more deeply, and Kristina's body thrashed upward, searching for the satisfaction to be found in his hard male strength.

"Mitch," she cried, gripping his waist and trying to pull him against her.

"I'm right here," he said, smiling down at her, intoxicated by the fervor in her expression.

Her fingers worked clumsily with his shirt, but he stopped them. "In a few minutes," he said.

"But I want—"

"I know what you want," he said, tickling the side

of her waist with his chin. She wriggled to escape the delightful torture, and he nudged her back onto the mattress, burying his lips in the soft swell of her abdomen. His fingers worked their way inside her stockings, moved up and between her legs, then smoothed the skin of her inner thighs to force them apart. Beads of perspiration formed on her forehead as he searched out the pulsing core of her being and stroked her until she quivered and throbbed under the enchantment offered by his knowing hand.

"Mitch—" Her excitement was near the breaking point, and blindly she reached out for him.

"You're so beautiful, Krissie," he murmured, letting his lips trail into the soft curve of her waist, never letting his finger stop its stroking. As she thrust upward again, he moved his head to revel in her breasts. His teeth fastened onto a nipple and gently tugged, stretching and releasing until it budded to twice its normal size and knew an exquisite tenderness that demanded further exploration.

"More—" she whispered brokenly.

But his tongue only toyed with her until in desperation she seized his head to her breast. Her eyes glazed with bliss as the suction of his lips and tongue gave her the pleasure she sought, and she offered her other breast for the same delightful stimulation.

"Go ahead, my darling," he whispered into her ear, stroking her to a hot, slick vortex that exploded inside her, forcing spasms of joy outward in an irresistible whirlpool of sensation. As her breathing quickened, his lips trailed a path of molten lava over her body,

179

searching out each swell and eddy, each yearning crevice until she shuddered and cried his name aloud.

She fell back onto the bed, her hair damp, her face flushed, every inch of her body tingling. "Oh, Mitch," she whispered, turning to him with a mystic smile.

He smoothed the silver-blond strands of hair back from her face and brushed her lips with his. "God, you're beautiful when you make love," he said.

"So are you," she said softly. She moved her fingertips to her breast and slowly massaged it.

"Tender?" he asked. Her breast was lovely in the lamplight, the blue veins barely visible, the pink tip still erect. He bent and kissed it gently.

"A little," she answered, "but it's a delicious kind of tenderness."

"Delicious?" His mouth fastened on the pink bud and made tiny sucking noises.

"If you don't stop that, you're going to get yourself in trouble."

"Exactly what I had in mind," he said. He lifted her feet and began to work the black silk stockings down over her hips.

"Careful with those," she whispered. "They're very expensive."

"Then help me get them off," he said, nipping her waist with his teeth.

Kristina wiggled her hips in a manner more seductive than helpful, but somehow the stockings were stripped off and tossed onto the floor. "Your housekeeper is going to be shocked," she said, giggling into the pillow.

"She'll never know," Mitch said, grinning as he surveyed the pile of feminine plunder that destroyed the erstwhile neatness of his room. "I'll hide all the evidence."

"Not until later," Kristina said, letting her whole body wiggle in a demonstration of impatience. She was now totally naked, her hair in a tangled, abandoned mass, and she knew from the hunger in his eyes that her body, shimmering in the lamplight, was desirable to Mitch. She lifted herself from the pillows and clasped her hands around his neck. "Come here, you handsome devil, so I can ravish you," she said.

Without taking his eyes from Kristina's, Mitch fumbled with the buttons of his velvet frockcoat, unbuttoning them one by one. He shrugged off the jacket and flung it over the back of the chair, then started on the buttons of the shirt.

"Let me help you with that," Kristina said. The lace of the collar tickled her cheek, and as she undid the wrist buttons, she buried a kiss in the palm of his hand, then traced an oval with her tongue.

"Naughty, naughty," he said, trying to keep his desire under control.

The shirt was off, and he stood to remove the Wellington boots and undo the trousers. As his last garments joined the pile on the floor, his naked passion became evident. Kristina felt her throat constrict and the heat rise in her face. A new desire swept over her —to know the joining of their bodies in a bold coupling that would fill and satisfy her as nothing else could do. She reached out to touch him and felt him harden and swell against her hand.

"Careful," he said, "I'm near the edge as it is." He lowered himself onto the bed beside her, then turned and swept her into his arms. Gone now was anything tentative or tame in their lovemaking, for they were caught up in their tumultuous, unrelenting sexual urges. Their bodies twisted and writhed in the bed, seeking and giving pleasure as they sought the positions that offered the greatest sensation.

"Here," Mitch commanded, forcing Kristina on top so that her full breasts were suspended above his face and he could have them at will. When her sighs became moans, he twisted again, rolling on top so he could devour her mouth with his, their tongues thrusting in and out to foreshadow the fusion of bodies that was yet to come. Mitch lowered his mouth, once again searching out all her sensitive, secret places until her will melted and she became a living torch, a blazing fire that could not be consumed.

Just as she neared her peak, he drew himself up to mount her and paused, letting her hover at the edge of cataclysm in order to heighten the moment when he thrust himself inside her. He took her sweat-drenched face between his hands and gazed into her eyes. "I love you, Kristina Neilsen," he said in wonderment. He lowered his head and kissed her with a sweetness that surpassed anything she'd ever known.

Then their kiss deepened, moving beyond sweetness to rapture, and at that moment he entered her, plunging himself into her dark warmth with a wild, jubilant abandon that totally filled her. Her heartbeat pounded until she felt a roaring in her ears and felt herself being lifted into a whirlwind of sensation.

"Now!" he cried, and with one last thrust, he convulsed inside her. His spasms ignited hers, and together they were transported to that secret world where passion reigns supreme and where nothing exists except the sheer wonderment of one body responding to another. Suspended together in time and space, they knew ecstasy.

Kristina lay in the crook of Mitch's arm, her ear against his chest, and heard his heartbeat return to a normal, rhythmic beat. Her slim fingers stroked the glistening skin of his muscular shoulder and forearm, and she tilted her head, smiling lazily when she saw that her own skin was also burnished with sweat.

"What's so funny?" he asked, brushing her nose with a kiss.

"We are," she said, lifting her face to his. "Drenched with sweat on a cold October night."

"It's now a cold November morning," he said, lifting his wrist over her head to peer at his watch.

"What time is it?" She snuggled against him and adjusted the sheets.

"Three o'clock."

Kristina sat upright. "Oh, no. You'd better take me home right now before Valerie calls the police and reports me missing."

"Maybe Valerie has other things on her mind."

"Like Bud, you mean?"

"You'll have to admit, their friendship looked promising."

"I'm sure he's gone by now, though." She sat on the

edge of the bed and tried to summon the energy to get up and get dressed.

"Come back to bed, Krissie," Mitch said, looping an arm around her and pulling her backward. "The night is only beginning."

She giggled as he nuzzled the curve of her waist with his chin. "Don't do that," she said. "I'm ticklish there."

"Mmm, so I discovered." He gently shoved her onto the bed spread-eagled and tickled her until she doubled up with laughter.

"Let me go, Mitch. I've got to get dressed so you can take me home."

He shook his head. "No. I want to wake up in the morning with you beside me."

She reached out to trace the outline of his lips with a long fingernail. "You're sweet," she said in a soft whisper. "But I have to go. I've got to teach an eight-o'clock class in the morning."

Mitch swore under his breath. "It isn't fair," he muttered. "Anytime I have you in my arms, there's always something taking you away from me." He pulled himself into a sitting position and leaned down to kiss her. "One of these days," he said, "I'm going to take you to a beautiful deserted island and have you all to myself, with no phones, no jobs, and no responsibilities."

"Mmm, sounds heavenly to me." She buried her face in his neck.

"Sounds like a honeymoon to me." He waited in silent tension until his words registered.

"What did you say?" She sat up beside Mitch and looked directly into his eyes.

"What do you think I said?"

"I know what you *said.* What do you *mean?*"

"What do people usually mean when they talk about a honeymoon?"

"But, Mitch, we don't even know very much about each other—" Kristina was so flustered she hardly knew what to say. "We only met six weeks ago."

"Are you telling me no?"

"Well, no, of course not, only—" She felt very confused. "What do you know about me?"

"That you're a fighter, that you have principles, that you're caring and compassionate—and passionate." He grinned at her. "As we've just proved in the past hour." He nibbled her ear to remind her, then continued, "I know that you're smart, and stubborn, and a little bit of a fanatic sometimes. And even though you have the self-discipline of a true Scandinavian, there's some Italian or Irish in there somewhere that makes you pretty emotional even though you try to keep it a secret. How am I doing so far?"

She shook her head. "For a list of character traits, you're pretty much on the money. But even if you know everything there is to know about me, so what? That's what you haven't told me. That's why I'm so puzzled."

Mitch brushed her lips with the tip of his finger. "You want me to tell you what it means to me to meet a woman like you?"

She nodded and snuggled a little closer in his arms.

"I never met anyone like you before, Kris. I never

185

felt this way about anyone else. I don't know how to put it into words."

"Try."

"You make me mad, sometimes, because you're always challenging me. But you're the person I'd want at my side to face any problem or any enemy. I know I can count on you. I can trust you. And that's what marriage means to me, trust and commitment." He stroked her shoulder, his intensity communicated by the way he gripped her skin.

"Don't you think you're leaving something out?" Her hands crept up his chest and clasped behind his neck.

"That's the part that's hard to talk about." Mitch placed his chin against the top of her head and a silky strand of her hair tickled his nose. "I'm an old-fashioned guy, Krissie. I've been waiting all my life to feel the way about someone that I feel about you. You're beautiful, and I want you, but it's the most overpowering kind of desire I've ever known. When I touch your body, I feel a kind of reverence."

He pulled her into his arms and kissed her, deeply and tenderly. "I love you, Krissie. That's what I'm trying to say. I love you and I want to marry you."

Kristina was overcome with emotion, and tears sprang to her eyes. Mitch McNaughton wasn't the kind of man to offer his love lightly. "You're really incredible, do you know that?" she whispered against his chest. Butterflies were dancing in her midsection. "I think I must be the luckiest woman in the whole, wide world."

"That's quite possible," he said, teasing her.

She tossed a pillow at him. "Your sense of timing is awful. You had to crack a joke just when I was about to tell you I loved you. Now you're just going to have to wonder."

Mitch bent his elbows and propped his head against the headboard, shaking his head at her. "Do you think a cautious Aggie like me would propose marriage to a woman if he didn't know exactly how she felt about him? No way, Neilsen, no way."

"How can you be so sure of me?" He was right on target, but how did he know?

"Because sometimes I know you better than you know yourself."

"You're so smug."

"I'm so lucky." He pulled her into his arms and buried his face in the soft, creamy skin at the hollow of her throat. "Just the same, I'd like to hear you say it." There was something boyish and shy in the way he said the words, and Kristina realized that he hadn't been nearly so sure of her feelings as he'd pretended.

She leaned forward to brush his lips with hers. "My darling Mitch," she said in a voice that was suddenly breathless, "I love you more than words can ever say. You're the best thing that ever happened to me. Oh, I do love you so!"

The kiss that followed left them both shaken. As they broke apart, gasping for air, Mitch exclaimed, "Krissie, we've just solved our problem!"

"What are you talking about?" she asked in bewilderment.

"The legal code of ethics! Don't you see, Krissie, now that we're engaged to be married, there's no problem. It won't be a conflict of interests for me to handle Valerie's case if she's my sister-in-law-to-be!"

"That's wonderful, Mitch," Kristina said indulgently. At the moment, she couldn't care less. "Come here, you Southern rogue. I've decided to spend the night with you."

CHAPTER TEN

Two weeks later, when Kristina returned to Gilbert, Texas, once again disguised as a flamboyant redhead, she found the townsfolk subdued. She didn't want to jump to conclusions, but she suspected that the filing of her sister's lawsuit against the Winston family was the cause of the nervous tension in the town. Kristina's first stop was in the county clerk's office to request help in locating old deed records.

"My goodness, my boss is really going to town on these old deeds, isn't he?" she asked, trying to stir up a conversation with Belva June Blasingame, the deputy clerk she'd met on her first trip to Gilbert. "I wonder how long it's going to take to find the folks who own these oil rights?"

"Sometimes it takes months," said Belva June, who'd seen many leasehounds come and go during her years as a deputy clerk.

"Oh, my." Kristina handed over another slip of paper prepared for her by Mitch, with mysterious markings to indicate the records she needed. "I hope my ol' boss will be lucky, then," she said, wrinkling her nose, "because he promised me a nice bonus as soon as we find the person who owns this land." She'd dreamed up a new ploy to account for her unusual interest in an imaginary oil lease. She held out her hand to show off the beautiful solitaire engagement ring Mitch had given her the previous week, immediately after they'd decided to get married as soon as Valerie's case was finished. "I want that bonus as soon as I can get it so I can buy my wedding dress."

"What a beautiful ring!" Belva June exclaimed. "Is it real?" She'd never seen a ring that size in Gilbert.

Kristina looked down at the diamond ring, almost three carats of blue-white perfection. "Oh, my, I certainly do hope so!" she answered, then giggled. "Do you think I ought to have it appraised?"

"The man you're engaged to must have lots of money," said Belva June with a touch of envy. She motioned to Gladys Duffy, the other woman who worked in the office, to come to the counter to see Kristina's ring.

"Goodness, gracious," said Gladys, admiring the ring, then comparing it to the tiny stone in her own gold band. "My Wilbur could never buy me a ring like that if he saved everything he earned for ten years. What line of work is your fiancé in?"

"He's an oil man. I met him through my sweet little ol' boss."

They had an interesting discussion concerning Kristina's good luck in meeting such a man and how such a thing could never happen in a small town like Gilbert.

"No, here in Gilbert you have to take what you can get," Gladys said, recalling that she'd been an old maid until she was twenty-six and Wilbur had finally come back from his stint in the army to a job at the hardware store.

"How long ago was that?" Kristina asked.

"Almost fifteen years," Gladys answered. "I'll be forty-one next month."

"My goodness, you surely don't look it," said Kristina with sincerity. And Gladys indeed looked younger than her forty-one years, with soft pink skin that knew few wrinkles.

"Why, thank you," Gladys answered. "I guess it's because Wilbur has been such a good husband to me. We may not have had much money, but he's a good man and he's done everything he could to make me happy."

"Then you're a mighty lucky woman," Kristina said, patting the older woman's hand.

"There's not a kinder man than my Wilbur," Gladys said, wiping a tear from her eye. "He'd do anything for anybody and that's a fact." She picked up a stack of legal papers from the counter and took them over to her desk and began sorting them. She wasn't a sentimental woman, and it wasn't like her to get all choked up this way.

"Are you married?" Kristina asked Belva June, sure in her own mind that the man she'd met in the Western Union office on her last trip to Gilbert must be Belva June's husband.

"I sure am," Belva June answered proudly, wanting to give a good account of her own husband so this pretty stranger wouldn't think Gladys was the only woman in town with a man worth bragging about. "I

191

married my high-school sweetheart and we've got twin sons. Plus two dogs and a cat. And a hamster."

"How old are your children?" Kristina asked.

"They're twelve. They started junior high this fall."

Kristina did some rapid mental calculations. Her niece Shelley was twelve. Maybe she'd been a classmate of the Blasingame twins. "Is that old enough for them to have girl friends?" Kristina asked.

Belva June chuckled. "It's old enough for them to start looking around," she answered. "But my husband Troy keeps the twins so busy doing chores they don't have time to do more than look."

"Do y'all live on a farm?" Kristina asked.

"We have a little piece of land out at the edge of town," Belva June answered. "But Troy works here in Gilbert. He's the local manager of the Western Union office."

"My goodness," Kristina said, seeming to be impressed. "Does he let your sons work in the Western Union office with him?"

"Once in a while," Belva June said. "They'd rather do that than do their chores at home, of course."

"Why, of course, most boys would. Do you have a picture of them?" Kristina glanced toward Belva June's desk and saw some framed photographs.

Belva June was a proud mother, and she was pleased to show Kristina her photos. "This is their band uniforms," she said. "They both play the trombone."

In a small Texas town, playing in the marching band carries almost as much social status as playing on the football team. Kristina remembered that her niece Shelley had set her heart on being the drum majorette when she got old enough to be in the marching band and had taken twirling lessons since she was eight years old. "Do you have a picture of the entire band?" Kristina asked, looking more closely at the photographs Belva June handed her.

"Not here with me," Belva June responded. "The boys framed their band picture for their bedroom wall at home."

"When I was a little girl, I used to think it would be fun to be a twirler," Kristina said as casually as possible.

Clearing her throat, Belva June turned and put the photos back on her desk. "I'll run down to the basement and see if I can find this old deed for you," she said when she came back to the counter. "Our boss will be coming back from lunch any time now, and I wouldn't want her to catch me gabbing when I have all this work to do."

"Oh, my, I didn't mean to keep you," Kristina said, trying to alleviate any suspicions she might have aroused. "You know how it is when you first get engaged, you think you have to tell everybody in the world about it. Thank you for being so patient and listening to me." Kristina went on talking about her engagement until Belva June relaxed and went downstairs for the old records, but all meaningful conversation was at an end. *I probed too far,* Kristina thought to herself. *When I mentioned wanting to be a twirler, she got scared. She must know something about Shelley that worries her.*

Kristina left the county clerk's office and wandered down the hallway, peering in the adjacent doorways. Mitch had told Kristina that Valerie's lawsuit was filed in the district clerk's office because that was the court with jurisdiction of lawsuits seeking large damages. Only small suits were filed in the county clerk's office she'd just left, and Valerie's suit against the Winstons was a big one, seeking half a million dollars in damages.

Kristina and Valerie had been shocked when Mitch first told them how much in monetary damages he'd claimed in the lawsuit. But then he'd explained his legal theory to seek recovery from the Winstons for conspiracy and intentional infliction of emotional distress. If Valerie won her lawsuit, Mitch explained, she was entitled to financial compensation for all the pain and suffering she'd experienced over the loss of her children. Even though all Valerie wanted was her children back, the threat of a big money judgment might pressure the Winstons into being reasonable enough to see that John Ed returned the children.

Kristina found the district clerk's office and was delighted to see the same young deputy sheriff she'd met on her first trip to Gilbert. He was leaning across the counter, a bundle of papers in his hand, talking to one of the female clerks.

"Well, hello, there," Kristina said, giving him a friendly wave from the hallway.

"Well, howdy," he answered, doffing his Stetson hat. "What brings you back to Gilbert?"

"More of those musty old deeds for my boss," she answered, smiling at him. "I do declare, it's so boring

194

to dig around in boxes of old files. Those ladies in the county clerk's office have my admiration. I don't see how they put up with it." Kristina stepped inside the district clerk's office and smiled at the young woman behind the counter. "Do you have to poke around in old boxes too?" she asked.

"Once in a while," the clerk answered. "But not like they have to do down there in the county clerk's office. It's all those old deeds they have, you know, where someone is always wanting to search the chain of title for years afterward. In here, when a case is over, it's over."

"Oh, you don't have deeds in here?" Kristina asked, furrowing her brow in mock bewilderment.

"Oh, no," the clerk explained, wondering how anyone could be so dumb. "This is the *district* clerk's office. We do the big, important cases in here, not deeds and all that stuff."

The deputy sheriff riffled the pages of the legal instruments in his hand and nodded in agreement. "Like this big case right here," he said, jabbing his finger on a summons. "I had to take these papers all over town last week and serve them on the most important people in this county. Lordy, lordy, did they holler when I handed them their copies of these papers."

"Nothing boring about that, I bet," said the clerk, giggling at the deputy. She was too young to have had any dealings with the Winston family and could afford to be amused that even rich folks got put in their places once in a while.

"I was just doing my job," said the deputy sheriff, still smarting from the tongue-lashing he'd received from Mr. W. Harold Winston. "If someone files a lawsuit and pays the sheriff's fee, I have to go serve the defendants. Even if it's a trumped-up case like this one."

"Trumped up?" asked Kristina, resisting the urge to tell the deputy sheriff all about what the Winstons had done to her sister. How could he side with the Winstons? Didn't everybody know how evil they were?

"Of course it's trumped up," the deputy sheriff answered. "Why, Mr. Winston told me himself that if it took every dollar he had, he'd get even with the person who brought these scurrilous, vindictive charges against his family. It's not right for someone to darken the name of a fine, upstanding family like the Winstons."

"Who are the Winstons?" Kristina asked, trying to peek at the papers in the deputy's hand. He'd scribbled his name at the bottom of a sheet showing the date and time when he'd served the papers, and Kristina was curious. How long had it been since the Winstons were served? How many days had they known something was afoot? And what did they plan to do about it? She'd secretly hoped that when they got served with the lawsuit, the Winstons would phone John Ed and tell him to bring the children back home to Valerie. But the way this deputy sheriff was talking, the fight wasn't going to end so easily.

"Don't know as I should be talking about this lawsuit," the deputy sheriff muttered. He damned sure didn't want to cross the Winstons when they were in such a powerful bad mood.

"The lawsuit is a public record, Tommy," the clerk

said. "No harm in discussing a public record. Why, this lady could look at the whole file if she wanted to." The clerk took the papers from the deputy sheriff and inserted them in a gadget that stamped the date and time of filing. The clerk next pulled a numbered manila folder from a file drawer and stuck the papers inside. "If there was anything in here to look at, that is. But right now there's nothing but the petition. The rest of the pleadings won't be filed until later on, when the Winstons hire a lawyer and the case heats up."

"My goodness, it sounds to me like it's heated up already," Kristina said, patting the deputy sheriff's forearm. "If someone is squawking at a poor man who's just trying to do his job." Her green eyes were full of sympathy for this misunderstood hero who stood before her.

"Just part of the job," the deputy sheriff said, a bashful grin on his face. "You know what they say: 'If you can't stand the heat, stay out of the kitchen.'"

"My goodness, you must be a brave man to shrug off trouble that way," Kristina said. "Do you think it's going to get worse for you, or is it all over?"

The deputy sheriff scratched his head. "Too soon to tell," he finally decided. "I hear around town the Winstons are all up in arms over this lawsuit, and most of the folks in town don't know what to think. Some folks are afraid to say much of anything, leastwise to me."

"Maybe the next time I come over to check on some old deed records for my boss, you can tell me all about it," Kristina said. "By then you should know how it's going to end."

"How long before you come back?" the deputy sheriff asked.

"A month, maybe."

"Oh, it'll all be over but the shouting by that time. Mr. W. Harold Winston has already hired himself the best lawyer in this part of the state, and there's rumors that he's going to file some motions and get the case thrown out of court. The way that high-priced lawyer figures it, the Winstons can go after the lady who brought the suit against them and make her pay plenty. Something about libel or slander of their good name."

That same afternoon while Kristina was in Gilbert, an unexpected visitor stopped by Mitch's office.

"Show him in," Mitch said over the intercom to his secretary, wondering to himself, *Now what brings Jim Sutton to Austin to see me?* "Hello, there, Jim," he said, extending his hand for a cordial handshake as his visitor, an old-time lawyer, entered his private office.

"Been awhile, Mitch," boomed his guest.

"You haven't changed a bit," answered Mitch, sizing up the other man.

Jim Sutton was tall, almost as tall as Mitch, with a headful of wavy silver hair and a well-tanned face that looked younger than his sixty-plus years. He was dressed, as always, in an expensive, western-cut suit and cowboy boots, and carried a felt cowboy hat in his hand. His voice had lost none of its resonance, and other lawyers had learned to fear his silver-tongued eloquence. He'd grown more handsome through the years, and he made full use of the smile and charm

198

with which nature had so amply endowed him. He waved toward one of the leather chairs. "Mind if we sit down and visit for a spell?"

"Coffee?" Mitch asked, noticing that Sutton slouched comfortably in the chair, totally relaxed.

"Fine, fine," Sutton boomed, "unless you've got a drop of bourbon around here somewhere."

"I'll see what I can do," Mitch answered, buzzing his secretary to bring some ice from the kitchenette.

"Looks like you're doing all right for yourself, son," Sutton said, indicating the costly furnishings. "This is a long way from that dinky little office you had upstairs over the bank in Gilbert."

Mitch chuckled wryly. "I'm surprised you even remember that office. It was a long time ago."

"Always glad to see a young man make good." Sutton fingered his drink so that the ice tinkled against the side of the glass. "Sorry you didn't want to stick around Gilbert, though. The town needed a lawyer. Still does. The way things are now, folks have to go all over the county to get their legal work done."

Mitch was beginning to understand the reason for this visit. "Is that what brings you to Austin today, Jim? Did someone from Gilbert come to you with a legal problem?"

His guest nodded. "Yep. These folks named Winston have hired me to represent them in this lawsuit you filed against them."

"Guess I should've expected they'd get the best hired gun in the county," Mitch said. They both knew that Mitch was no equal for the other man's experience. And as for coaxing what he wanted from a jury, Jim Sutton had no peer.

"You aren't serious about this lawsuit, are you, son?" Sutton pulled a copy of the petition from his inside breast pocket and slapped it against the chair arm. "It's the most gosh-danged legal theory I ever heard of. Not a court in the country is going to let you past the starting gate with a crazy argument like this one."

"Oh, I think I'll wait and let the judge decide that question, Jim. He just might take a different view from yours. After all, you're getting paid to look at it like the Winstons do."

"But, son, you've accused the most prominent family in the town of doing something terrible. Their reputation is at stake. They can't let you get away with allegations like these." Sutton's voice dropped to a conspiratorial whisper. "Get out of it now, son, while there's still time. The Winstons don't want to have to ruin you."

Mitch lifted his eyebrow in surprise. "Ruin *me? I* haven't done anything wrong."

"Oh, but, son, look at it from their perspective. You've smeared them with a claim that they've joined together in a conspiracy against their former daughter-in-law, and there's not a bit of truth to it. If you were the Winstons, wouldn't you think the legal system was being abused?"

"Sorry, Jim, but I'd rather not think like the Winstons do. And don't you let yourself fall into that trap either. They're wicked, evil people, and you wouldn't want their stench to rub off on you."

Sutton banged his glass on the desktop. "Now, just a minute, Mitch. You used to live in Gilbert. You know what kind of people the Winstons are. Why, they practically own the town. I suppose you might say they're the First Family of Gilbert."

"Don't kid yourself, Jim. They own the town, sure. But they're rotten to the core."

"Son, I came all the way over to Austin to try to help you see reason. You're headed for a fall—a mighty big one. I'm trying to do you a favor." Sutton's expression was full of compassion for what he perceived to be a misguided attitude.

Mitch snorted. "Don't do me any favors, Jim. I've had all the favors from the Winstons I know what to do with. The biggest favor they ever did me was when they ran me out of Gilbert."

Sutton's blue eyes were alert. "I wondered if you hadn't filed this lawsuit to try to even up an old score. Son, don't you know that's an improper use of the legal system?"

"Come on, Jim, you know me better than that."

"You could lose your law license over a stunt like that."

"Is that a threat?"

Sutton leaned back against the chair. "No, son, it's not a threat. It's a promise."

Mitch felt his fist begin to clench and unclench. He'd always admired Jim Sutton, but at the moment he'd like nothing better than to punch him in his handsome square jaw. "Suppose you just tell me what you came to tell me, Jim. No need to keep beating around the bush this way."

201

"Well, son, first of all you've filed a lawsuit on a theory that won't hold water just so you can get revenge for an old grudge you have against the Winston family. Second, there's not a shred of evidence that any of this so-called conspiracy ever happened, so I'm going to file a cross-action against your client and sue her for everything she's got. She's slandering the reputation of a fine old family. And third, I'm going to take you to the grievance committee of the bar association for your unprofessional conduct and improper use of the legal system. Before this thing is over, your client is going to be up to her ears in a money judgment, and you're going to lose your law license." Sutton rose in his chair. "I guess that's all I came to tell you." He put his glass on the desk. "I'd intended to make a friendly suggestion that you dismiss your suit immediately and I'd try to talk the Winstons out of going after you and your client. But I guess I won't waste my breath. I don't think you'd recognize a friendly suggestion if it bit you on the toe."

"You really believe the Winstons, don't you?" Mitch was puzzled that a lawyer with Sutton's experience had been taken in by their protestations of innocence.

"Yes, I do." Sutton paused on his way to the door and gave Mitch a steady glance. "We've all had clients who lie to us, but I'm convinced the Winstons are telling me the truth. I'm sorry, Mitch, but these folks don't know where their grandchildren are. If they did, they'd be the first to tell you. It's just about broken their hearts to lose their babies that way. Poor Mrs. Winston sat there in my office and cried her eyes out."

202

Sutton rolled the brim of his Stetson around his fingers. "Sure wish you'd think it over, son. These poor people have suffered enough. Don't put them through any more. Please."

Mitch slowly nodded his head. "Sorry, Jim, but I think you're wrong about them."

"I've been practicing law since before you were born, son. I don't think a client can pull the wool over my eyes at this late date."

"What if I'm right?"

"You're going to have to prove it to a judge and jury," Sutton answered. "And if you push the case that hard, you're going to have to pay the price. Sorry, son, but I can't let you use the courts to punish people who aren't guilty of anything. I'll have to do everything in my power to stop you."

"You're welcome to try, Jim, you're welcome to try."

"Have you ever known me to lose any case I went after?"

"Can't say as I have." The men gave each other measured looks.

"Sure you won't change your mind and drop your case?"

"Can't do it, Jim."

The older man shoved his hands in his pockets. "Don't say I didn't warn you." He turned and left the room without another word. He'd figured this trip to see Mitch would be a waste of time, so he'd already hired the best private investigator in Austin to find out everything there was to know about Mitch McNaughton and his client, Valerie Winston.

Kristina sat in Mitch's hot tub feeling delightfully warm even though she was outside in the cold November air. "I'm scared, Mitch," she said, reaching for his hand on the bench beside her. "The Winstons are up to no good."

Mitch exhaled a raspy breath. It was hard to get his mind off today's visit from Jim Sutton. He hadn't intended to tell Kristina about Sutton's threats, but when she'd returned from Gilbert with the information from the deputy sheriff, Mitch knew he had to warn her. "I told you in the beginning, Kris. The Winstons will stop at nothing."

"I'm sorry I dragged you into this, Mitch. You tried to tell me and I wouldn't listen. Now they're threatening to take away your law license!"

"Try not to worry about it, okay?" He squeezed her hand. "Where's your engagement ring?"

"I left it on your dresser when I put on my swimsuit."

He remembered how brightly her eyes had sparkled the day he slipped the ring on her finger. "I thought you weren't ever going to take it off."

"My swimsuit?" She wriggled seductively on the seat beside him.

"Naughty, naughty," he said, catching his breath as she reached behind and unfastened the top of her bikini, then held the wisp of fabric above her head. "Come here, you gorgeous creature," he said gruffly.

Moonlight shimmered across her body, emphasizing its gentle curves and hollows. She lifted herself in the hot tub, tossing the swimsuit top onto the redwood deck, then raised her arms above her head and rotated slowly in the water like a graceful ballerina. Her body was silhouetted against the dark horizon, each perfect feature contoured by starlight. "Have you ever noticed how soaking in the hot tub relaxes you and takes away all your resistance?" Kristina reached for Mitch's hands and pulled him up beside her.

"I never had any resistance to start with, not where you're concerned," he answered, burying his face in her neck. The warm water swirled about them, chest-high like an enveloping womb, while they clung together in a passionate kiss. Behind them glowed the soft lights of the party room, casting their melded bodies into an erotic silhouette. "I love the smell of your skin," Mitch said softly when they broke apart. "And the smell of your hair." He lifted his hand and brushed a stray tendril from her cheek.

Her fingers crept up his chest, toying with the hair that covered it, then gently kneading the underlying muscle. It was thrilling to Kristina to discover this kind of feeling, something so much more than physical intimacy, a bonding of their very souls. She turned her head and gently nipped the muscle of his shoulder with her teeth.

"So you want to play games," he said, lifting her easily in the water and sinking his teeth into the firm swell of her abdomen. "Let me show you a new one."

She writhed with pleasure as his lips made a sensuous exploration of her water-slicked body. "What's it called?" she whispered.

"The mating game," he answered. "Male takes female, female takes male." His tongue traced ovals across her midriff.

"Who gets the first move?" Kristina shifted in his arms so that his tongue moved higher up her body.

"I do."

"Who gets the last move?"

"I do."

"That doesn't sound fair. When do I get my turn?"

"I'll see that you don't get cheated," Mitch said with a chuckle. "I get the first and last moves, and you make as many moves as you want in the middle." He gently tugged at her breast. "That's my first move," he said.

Her nipple tightened, and Kristina sighed with pleasure. "Oh, I thought it was *my* move," she teased.

"I think I detected some movement on your part," Mitch agreed, "but since it was my turn, it doesn't count. *Now* it's your move."

"Now, or when you've *finished* your first move?" His greedy lips had never stopped their lush assault on her nipple.

"Maybe you'd better go ahead," Mitch murmured huskily. "I can't seem to stop what I'm doing."

"In that case—" Kristina lifted her mouth to his ear and nibbled at the lobe, then darted her tongue inside to lick moist circles. When his breathing came faster, she reached underneath the water to stroke him.

"No fair," he moaned, "you're taking two moves."

"Guess you'll have to get even," Kristina said, twisting to bring his mouth to her other breast.

Mitch buried his lips in Kristina's neck, then groaned aloud as their mouths came together in a tumult of desire. "I think it's about time to end this game," he said hoarsely. "I'm ready to make my last move."

"In the hot tub?"

"I told you this was a new game." Mitch pulled her underneath the water and gave her a long, lingering kiss before they ran out of air and had to burst to the surface, laughing and splashing. Mitch's fingers slipped inside Kristina's bikini bottom to tug it loose. "Come here, sweetheart," he whispered. "Let's find out what it's like to make love in a hot tub."

Kristina dug her fingers into his hair and coiled her upper torso around his face. "You know what I really want?" she asked in a sexy whisper.

"I have some idea." Her bare, inviting breasts were against his lips.

"You won't think I'm naughty?"

He helped himself to the feast of her breasts. "I won't think you're naughty," he promised. "After all, this is an adult game we're playing."

"Mitch, let's use that French bordello of yours," she said, with a cunning smile. "I want to watch you make love to me in that mirrored ceiling."

Mitch grinned. "I think you're naughty."

"Mitch, you promised!" she squealed. "Now I'm embarrassed." She giggled and twisted out of reach.

"Come back here."

"Thought you weren't interested."

"I never said that."

There was a long silence while he held her close and ravished her mouth. When they broke apart, Kristina uttered a light, merry laugh, then let her hand slip beneath the water to stroke him again. "Something tells me you might be interested after all," she said, tugging off his swimming trunks.

In one motion, Mitch lifted her from the hot tub and scrambled out behind her. "The mirrored ceiling awaits us, my precious, naughty darling," he said, as he picked her up and carried her inside the house.

On the hillside below, a camera with a telephoto lens recorded each motion in the glassed-in room as the sparkling rays of light cast by the crystal chandelier outlined their naked, vibrant bodies.

CHAPTER ELEVEN

Mitch sat behind his desk and explained the latest developments in the lawsuit to Kristina and Valerie, who were sitting in the leather chairs across from him. A thick bundle of legal documents had been delivered in yesterday's mail, marking the newest round in the ongoing war with the Winstons.

"What does this mean?" asked Valerie, hopelessly lost in the confusing legal jargon of the page she was reading.

Kristina peered over her shoulder at a long, white typewritten document entitled *Special Exceptions*. Already spread out on the desk were other pleadings labeled *Motion for Protective Order* and *Motion to Quash*.

"In a nutshell, the instrument in your hand says that the judge should throw out your lawsuit because it doesn't have a proper legal basis. Jim Sutton claims that you can't sue the Winstons for conspiracy or anything else because they had nothing to do with your divorce or any of the problems you've had with John Ed." Mitch saw that Valerie still looked puzzled, so he added, "The Winstons say for you to go ahead and sue

John Ed if you want to, but you don't have any right to sue his family because they weren't parties to the divorce."

"Maybe not to the divorce, but I'm sure they're involved in the kidnapping of the children. Everything Kristina found out in Gilbert points in that direction." Valerie turned to her sister for reassurance.

"Mitch understands all this legal mumbo-jumbo," Kristina said, her voice projecting confidence for Valerie's benefit. "We'll let him worry about how to handle it."

"That decision is already made for us," Mitch said. "That's why I asked you to come by the office today." He gathered up the papers and put them in a manila folder labeled *Pleadings,* part of a thick, bulging red file marked *Winston v. Winston.* "Jim Sutton has filed all these pleadings and requested a court hearing. There's a notice here somewhere that says the judge will hear the motions next week."

"Next week? I thought you said it would be months before my case went to trial." Not only was Valerie feeling confused, she was suddenly frightened. She didn't know whether she was ready to face the Winstons yet.

"It will be months before the case goes to a jury trial. This is a preliminary hearing." Mitch decided not to tell Valerie that if things went badly at the hearing, the case would be dismissed and never reach a jury. She was already beginning to sound distraught. It would be best not to alarm her any further. "We'll go to the courthouse, and Jim Sutton will argue his legal position to the judge. Then we'll answer with our legal position, and the judge will decide what to do next."

"So you'll be going to Gilbert next week for the hearing?"

"You'll need to go with me, Valerie. I may have to put you on the witness stand."

Valerie reached out and gripped her sister's hand. "Kris can go too, can't she? I'll be so nervous, I won't be able to do anything without her."

"What day is the hearing?" Kristina asked.

"Tuesday morning at ten o'clock."

"That'll be okay, then. I don't have morning classes on Tuesdays, and we should be back in time for my afternoon class."

"You'd better get somebody to cover for you in case this thing runs over," Mitch said. "It may take only half an hour, or it might run all day."

There was an undercurrent of tension in Mitch's behavior that worried Kristina. There must be more to this than he was willing for Valerie to know about. "All right, I'll get Bud Thomas to take my class if we don't get back."

"Can't you get somebody else?" Valerie protested. "I want Bud to go to Gilbert with us." Bud had been her constant companion since Halloween night, and she needed his emotional support as much as she needed her sister's.

Mitch frowned. "I'm not sure how that will look, Valerie, if you waltz into the courtroom to sue your former in-laws with a new boyfriend at your side."

"He can sit in the courtroom with Kristina, can't he?"

"I suppose so." Whether Mitch liked the idea or not, he'd learned that Valerie could be mulishly stubborn about getting her own way. It would be a waste of energy to disagree.

"What if I wear my lavender hat and black wig and go in my Amanda Tucker disguise? That way if Mitch needs me to help him, I'll be able to do so." Kristina warmed to the idea of dressing in disguise again. It gave her much more freedom, and it might be helpful in case anything went wrong at the hearing. "Nobody saw Bud and me that day except the Western Union man," she continued. "We can drive over in Bud's pickup truck and nobody will connect us with you. We can pretend that we just happened along and decided to watch a trial."

Mitch gave up, shaking his head. "Whatever you say. It would take a stronger man than I am to do battle with *two* Neilsen sisters when they have their minds made up."

"You sound just like our father," said Valerie, smiling at him.

Kristina leaned back in her chair and gazed down at her diamond ring. "When it comes to dealing with *one* Neilsen sister, however, I think you do just fine."

Mitch swallowed hard. When Kristina had changed positions in the chair, the jade-green lambswool sweater she was wearing somehow tightened across her body, clinging to her breasts. Mitch couldn't seem to avert his eyes and caught himself staring, wondering whether she was wearing anything underneath the sweater. It certainly didn't look like it. He felt a flush work its way up his neck to his ears.

212

"I think I'll go fix myself a cup of coffee," Kristina said. She hadn't missed a single blinking of his eyes.

Mitch stood with her. "Need some help?" he said, clearing his throat. "What about you, Valerie? Would you like a cup of coffee?"

Valerie reached for the legal papers and bent forward to read them. "No thanks," she said. "I'll entertain myself with this fascinating reading for a few minutes." As Kristina and Mitch made their way to the adjoining kitchenette, Valerie called over her shoulder, "You two act like teenagers who've just discovered the birds and bees."

"You should talk," Kristina retorted. "Every time I come home, I have to climb over you and Bud." Kristina closed the door to the kitchenette with a firm shove and lifted her face for Mitch's kiss. "Come here, tiger," she said breathlessly, "I have something for you."

When they emerged from the kitchenette five minutes later, Mitch had splashed his face with cold water and Kristina's breasts were tingling. Mitch had the answer to his question, though: Kristina wasn't wearing anything underneath her sweater. They tried to distract themselves with the coffee cups they were carrying, but both of them felt the sweet ache of desire that has been aroused but not yet satisfied.

"Ready to go home now?" Valerie asked.

"I think I'll stay and have dinner with Mitch," Kristina answered, unable to stop a blush from staining her cheeks.

"It figures." Valerie stood and held out her hand for Kristina's car keys.

"Do me a favor, will you?" Kristina asked. "Run by my office on campus and pick up my mail on your way home. There should be some mimeographed handouts in my box, and I'll need to look them over before class tomorrow." Kris smiled at her sister. "Maybe Bud will still be in his office."

"In that case, I'll be happy to run that little errand for you."

"Thanks."

Valerie paused in the doorway. "What time will you be home tonight?" She'd be glad when she could afford a place of her own so she and Bud could have some privacy. They never knew when Kristina was going to walk in on them.

Kristina turned to Mitch with a question in her eyes.

"I'll bring Kris home in the morning on my way to my racquetball game."

"Naughty, naughty," scolded Valerie, but she was smiling. Bud Thomas was going to be very pleased with this news.

On the day of the hearing, Kristina and Bud drove to Gilbert in a heavy November mist that turned the sky a depressing pewter-gray. Leaves had been falling from the trees for several weeks, so that except for the pines and live-oak trees, the wooded areas they passed were now bleak and barren.

They found a parking place on the town square well away from Mitch's sports car and tromped across the wet leaves to the stone steps leading into the courthouse. Kristina adjusted her lavender bonnet and

214

looked around to see whether there was anybody in the corridor that she'd met on her earlier trips disguised as a redhead. Now that she was there, she was beginning to worry that she might be recognized after all. She shook her long black tresses and said a silent prayer that all would go well today.

"I wonder how Valerie is doing?" Bud pondered, hunting for the district courtroom.

"Scared to death, I'm sure. At least she was when Mitch picked her up this morning."

They went to the end of the hallway and found the imposing old courtroom. Its mahogany walls and ceiling vaulted forty feet to a peak, and the Great Seal of Texas emblazoned the east wall behind the raised bench where the judge would sit.

"I didn't know the courtroom would be so—" Kristina broke off, at a loss to describe her feelings.

"Takes your breath away, it's so intimidating," Bud answered, leading the way down the aisle but giving no sign of recognition to Mitch and Valerie, who were seated at the varnished oak counsel table near the judge's bench. The Winstons were nowhere in sight.

Kristina glanced at the large clock on the wall behind them. "It won't be long now," she said. She slid onto a bench near the aisle, leaving just room enough for Bud. "I don't want anybody else to sit down with us," she said, still nervous that she might be recognized by someone. She turned her head to glance at Mitch, but he appeared to be oblivious to their arrival. He and Valerie had their heads together, going over a stack of papers from Mitch's open briefcase.

In addition to the judge's bench and the counsel

215

table, there was a high-backed wooden armchair with a microphone attached where witnesses would give their testimony. Adjoining the witness chair was a small table for the court reporter. On the wall opposite the counsel table was the jury box, which would remain empty today. Separating that area of the courtroom from the wooden benches where Kristina sat with Bud was a carved wooden rail. Only people connected with the case could go past the rail.

Kristina felt an elbow nudge her arm. "Here they are," Bud said. Four members of the Winston family paraded down the aisle, followed by their attorney, Jim Sutton. Kristina had met the Winstons years past at her sister's wedding and at rare family gatherings in the early years of Valerie's marriage. But Kristina had been a young teenager then, and there was no reason to think the Winstons would remember her now, especially in her disguise.

Jim Sutton walked over to shake hands with Mitch, and they exchanged pleasantries in the way lawyers do, even when they're about to engage in a legal slugging match. The Winstons stared insolently at Valerie, then glanced away as though she were not worthy of their notice. Hatred seeped like a mist into the courtroom as the Winstons took chairs across the table from their former daughter-in-law.

Kristina sighed. *They're so bitter,* she thought. This had all the earmarks of a bad, bad day. She shifted on the bench and noticed that the bailiff had arrived at the back door, along with some curious spectators and someone with a notebook in hand. For the first time it occurred to Kristina that the local newspaper would be aware of the lawsuit and the person with a note-book was probably a reporter. There would probably be some juicy columns about the public mudslinging that would go on in this courtroom today. Or did the Winstons own the newspaper too? Kristina couldn't remember. In any event, with a prominent family involved, the press would have a heyday, regardless of whether the Winstons were portrayed as victims or villains.

"All rise," the bailiff shouted, and the judge, dressed in a formal black robe, entered the courtroom from a side door and hurried to the bench. "The district court is now in session, the Honorable Charles Nolan presiding," the bailiff said, indicating that everyone could now be seated again.

"The court calls the case of Valerie Winston versus Mr. and Mrs. W. Harold Winston, et al," Judge Nolan said. His voice was rich and mellow, with a trace of a drawl. "Counsel?"

"The defendants are the movants in this hearing, your honor," said Jim Sutton, standing to address the court. "Movants announce ready."

Mitch stood. "Plaintiff is present and announces ready, your honor."

"Let's list the appearance of parties for the court reporter," said the judge. If he was intimidated by the presence of the wealthiest voters in his district, he didn't show it.

Jim Sutton pointed to his clients. "Present are Mr. W. Harold Winston, Mrs. W. Harold Winston, Mr. Chester Bayless, and Mrs. Chester Bayless."

"Valerie Winston, the plaintiff, is also present, your

honor." Sitting back down, Mitch arranged his files in order and placed a yellow legal tablet beside them.

"You may proceed, counsel." The judge peered over the top of his reading glasses at Jim Sutton, who was on his feet and ready to begin. "Do you wish to make an opening statement?"

"Yes, your honor, but I'll make it brief." Sutton was better with a jury than with a judge, but nonetheless highly persuasive with either. "Defendants have filed a number of motions for the court to consider, but I think we'll start with our Special Exceptions." Sutton reached for a document and handed a copy to the judge. "Fact is, Judge, if you grant our Special Exceptions, there won't be any need to hear the rest of our motions."

"I'll bear that in mind, Mr. Sutton. You may proceed with your Special Exceptions."

"I hope the court received a copy of the brief I mailed earlier in the week," Sutton said. "I wanted you to have time to study the law before we came to this hearing today. Of course I also made a copy of my brief available to Mr. McNaughton."

The judge nodded, as did Mitch.

"Your honor, I've been over Mr. McNaughton's petition with a fine-tooth comb and spent days working in my law library, but there just isn't any law to support this claim he's making. As I pointed out in my brief, there's not a case in Texas that permits a mother to sue her in-laws because her ex-husband has run off with their children. These folks aren't parties to the divorce between Valerie and John Ed Winston. If the plaintiff has a beef, it's with John Ed. She's welcome to sue him if she can find him, but we think the law of the State of Texas is clear: She has no right to sue his parents for something he's done, and we ask the court to grant our Special Exceptions and dismiss this case."

"Do you wish to respond, Mr. McNaughton?" asked the judge.

"Yes, your honor," Mitch answered, rising immediately.

"Your honor, I'll grant that no one has ever brought a case like this in the State of Texas. I'm sure I've spent as much time searching out the law as Mr. Sutton has, and I didn't find any such case myself. But just because no one has ever done it doesn't mean that it can't be done. Your honor, if you'll study the cases I pointed out in my brief, you'll see that the law on conspiracy is very clear, and Valerie Winston is entitled to sue anybody who's conspired in defiance of a child custody agreement to keep her children from her. She's not bound by the parties to the original divorce decree."

Mitch flipped a page on his yellow legal tablet and read some notes he'd scribbled there, then continued. "Furthermore, your honor, Texas recognizes the tort of intentional infliction of emotional distress and sets out the elements that have to be proved in order for a plaintiff to recover. Of course Valerie Winston has to prove those elements to the satisfaction of a jury, but if she can prove the allegations of this petition, she's entitled to money damages. We've pled this case properly, your honor, and it would be unjust to dismiss it at this stage of the proceedings."

Mitch paused and took a drink of water. He wanted to give the judge time to think over what he'd said.

"Do you have anything further, Mr. McNaughton?"

"Just this, your honor. This is a case of first impression in the State of Texas. We're breaking new ground. Valerie Winston understands that she has to prove all the things she's alleged in her lawsuit, but if the facts bear out her claim, she's entitled to recover."

Mitch took another sip of water. He didn't want to make the judge impatient, but he had to say one more thing. "Now, you can grant Mr. Sutton's Special Exceptions and throw this case out of court today, your honor. Then Valerie Winston will have to appeal, and the higher courts will figure out what to do with it. This is a new issue, and it'll be a lot easier for the appellate courts to deal with if they know the facts. I'd like to suggest, your honor, that you give us a chance to get the facts on the record. Today we're just asking you to let us stay in court and put on our case for the jury when trial time rolls around. If we're wrong, you can instruct the jury to bring in a verdict for Mr. Sutton and the Winston family."

"Rebuttal, Mr. Sutton?" the judge asked, glancing at the other lawyer.

"Well, your honor, it just doesn't seem fair to me that this family has to go to all the expense of discovery and trial just to help Mr. McNaughton with his appellate record. The case ought to be thrown out of court today and save everybody's time and money." Sutton sat down, his entire bearing conveying disgust that his clients should be so misused.

The judge lifted his heavy eyebrows. He'd pondered the issue for several days, thanks to the briefs the lawyers had sent him. Now he had to decide. As always, he took the cautious path. "I'm not going to rule on your Special Exceptions at this time, Mr. Sutton. I'll carry them along with the case, and if I see something later on that changes my mind, I'll rule at that time. In any event, I'll announce my ruling before the case reaches trial."

"Thank you, your honor." Sutton was irritated, but there was only one way to handle judges, and he'd just done it. *Thanks, my foot,* he thought.

"Are you ready to proceed to your next motion?"

Kristina turned to Bud. "Sounds like Valerie just won the first round," she whispered.

"I think you're right," Bud agreed. "Mitch told us if the Winstons won on their Special Exceptions, Valerie was out of court, and that hasn't happened yet. They're moving on to the next item."

Kristina turned her hands palms-up. "Look at that," she whispered. "I'm all clammy."

Bud took her hand in his. "So am I. I'll be glad when this is over."

"Valerie looks white as a ghost."

"Poor kid. It must be awful for her." Bud's concern was touching.

"Mitch acts like there's nothing to it, though. How can he be so cool?" Kristina was proud of her man.

"Did you notice how the other lawyer's ears got all red when the judge didn't grant his motion?"

"It's not over yet. That Sutton has the good-old-boy

role polished to a satiny glow. He may be slick enough to pull ahead on the next round."

The bailiff frowned in their direction, and they gave their attention to the proceedings in the front of the courtroom.

"What's happening?" Bud asked, after they'd listened a few minutes and tried to pick up the thread of Jim Sutton's argument.

"It sounds like they're talking about the protective order. Mitch told us the Winstons are trying to stop him from taking their depositions and that their lawyer didn't want them to have to make all their bank records and stuff available to Mitch. Mitch also subpoenaed the Western Union and telephone records, and they're fighting that too."

The bailiff turned again and held a cautioning finger against his lips to shush their conversation. They stopped whispering and started listening. The real show was just beginning.

"We call Mrs. W. Harold Winston to the stand," said Jim Sutton.

John Ed's mother stood and held up her right hand to be sworn.

"Do you solemnly swear that the testimony you're about to give in the case now before the court will be the truth, the whole truth, and nothing but the truth, so help you God?" said Judge Nolan.

"I do."

"Please take the witness stand."

Mrs. Winston, a handsome, middle-aged woman with a proud carriage, wore a black crepe dress with a white collar, white kid gloves, and an opera-length string of pearls. In her hand she clutched a lace-bordered handkerchief.

"Mrs. Winston, what is your relationship to Valerie Winston, the plaintiff in this case?" asked Sutton.

"She used to be married to my son until their divorce seven years ago. She's the mother of my three grandchildren." Mrs. Winston dabbed her eyes with the handkerchief, as if to wipe away a tear.

"Tell the court the names and ages of your grandchildren."

"There's Shelley, who's twelve." Her voice caught. "And Michael, he's ten and looks just like his daddy." She buried her face in her hands. "And little Jason, he's not even eight yet." Tears began to flow unchecked down her wrinkled cheeks.

"How long has it been since you've seen your grandchildren?"

Mrs. Winston's shoulders shook with silent sobs. "I believe it must've been the Fourth of July weekend."

"That's four months ago?"

She nodded, unable to speak.

"I'm sorry, Mrs. Winston," said Jim Sutton in a kindly voice, "but you'll have to speak up for the court reporter. Is it your answer that it's been four months since you last saw your grandchildren?"

"Yes." The word was barely a whisper.

"Have you heard from them since that time, either by letter or telephone?"

She shook her head. "Not a word." Her voice was so low the court reporter had to strain to hear it.

"If you knew where the children were, would you tell their mother, the plaintiff in this lawsuit?"

Mrs. Winston broke into uncontrollable weeping, and her husband rose to go to her aid.

"I apologize to the court," Jim Sutton said, interrupting, "but I'm afraid Mrs. Winston can't continue to testify at this time. May she be excused until later in the hearing?"

Mitch stood to object but realized it would be a lost cause. The judge wasn't going to keep a hysterical woman on the witness stand. And this outburst had neatly forestalled any opportunity for Mitch to cross-examine Mrs. Winston. He muttered a silent oath as Mr. Winston led his wife from the courtroom.

"Let's take a short recess," said Judge Nolan. "Court will stand adjourned for fifteen minutes."

"Let's go out in the hall and see if we can sneak a word with Mitch," Kristina said, scooting across the pew.

They joined a milling group in the corridor, and Kristina managed to work her way to the water fountain where Mitch was standing. He gave her a warning look, however, and she dared not say anything to him. She looked around and saw Valerie headed toward the women's restroom.

"Psst," she whispered, trying to catch up with her sister. "Don't go in there."

"Why not?"

"That's where Mrs. Winston went. Let's go upstairs. There's bound to be another restroom up there." Kristina walked at a discreet distance behind her sister so that no one would suspect they were to-

224

gether. Upstairs they found an empty restroom and huddled at the window whispering urgently. "Are you okay?" Kristina asked. Valerie looked dreadful.

"I'm a nervous wreck. That's just the way Mrs. Winston used to act with John Ed when we were married, getting hysterical when he wouldn't do what she wanted him to. I never knew whether it was real or whether she was acting."

"It looked real enough from the audience, but I'm sure it was well rehearsed. Doesn't matter, it fooled the judge."

A courthouse employee opened the door and came into the restroom. "Excuse me," she said.

"I'm just leaving," Kristina answered, washing her hands in the porcelain sink. She left without a backward glance, not wanting to arouse any suspicion. Valerie would have to cope by herself. No one could help her now but Mitch.

Mrs. Winston did not return to the courtroom when the recess ended, and Jim Sutton explained to the judge that she'd gone home to lie down for a while but would return after lunch. "Defendants call W. Harold Winston to the stand."

Mr. Winston stood and took the oath, then seated himself at the witness stand. He was a severe man at best, and today he was at his most dour. He wore a dark business suit with a vest and a starched white shirt that could probably stand alone.

"Mr. Winston, it was your wife who testified earlier, is that correct?"

"Yes, sir." The man's teeth were clenched together so tightly that words could barely escape.

"And you agree with her testimony concerning your grandchildren?"

"Yes, sir."

"The plaintiff in this lawsuit has requested that you turn over all your bank records, credit records, telephone records, and any other documents that indicate the way you've been spending money for the past four months?"

"Yes, she has."

"And you've come to court today to ask the judge to protect you from this demand?"

"That's right."

"Why is that?"

"Because it's an unreasonable demand. My financial records are no concern of hers."

"Would it cause you any hardship to turn over these records?"

"It certainly would. If my personal financial records become a matter of public record, everybody in this county would know all about my business activities. These are matters that concern no one but myself, and it might even damage some of my business relationships." Mr. Winston turned to the judge. "I beseech this court to protect me from the vindictiveness of my former daughter-in-law."

Mitch was immediately on his feet. "Objection, your honor. That remark is inflammatory and I request that it be stricken from the record."

"There's no jury present, counsel. I'll disregard the remark." The judge gave Mr. Winston a sharp look.

226

"Please refrain from further comments of that nature."

"Yes, your honor." If Mr. Winston was cowed, he didn't show it.

"You agree with your wife's statement that you haven't seen your grandchildren in four months and have no idea where they are?" Jim Sutton used a put-upon tone of voice for his question so it would be clear to the judge that these people had no information to be gleaned from a search of their private records.

"That's correct."

"And if you turned over your personal documents to the plaintiff, she wouldn't know any more about her children's whereabouts than she does now?"

"Correct."

"But your business dealings would be revealed and possibly harmed?"

"Of course they'd be harmed. I admit that I'm a wealthy man, but the extent of my fortune is no one else's business."

"Does this demand by the plaintiff for your records constitute harassment?"

Mitch was on his feet. "Objection, your honor. That's a leading question."

The judge frowned. "I'll sustain the objection. Don't lead your witness, counsel."

"Very well, your honor. I'll rephrase the question." Sutton paused to rethink the point he wanted to make. "Why would the plaintiff demand that you turn over this information to her?"

Mitch stood again. "Objection, your honor. The

227

question calls for an opinion. This witness hasn't been qualified as an expert."

Jim Sutton reared back and let his voice boom. "Your honor, we all know the general rule that a lay witness who's not an expert can only testify as to the facts and isn't permitted to express opinions. I've been trying to keep the testimony brief by taking a shortcut in order to save the court's time and save counsel from embarrassment."

Sutton gave Mitch a warning look and paused long enough for Mitch to withdraw his objection. When Mitch remained silent, Sutton continued. "I'll be happy to lay my predicate by letting the witness testify to the primary facts and let the court draw its own conclusion as to whether the plaintiff's demand for Mr. Winston's personal business records constitutes harassment."

Mitch knew from Sutton's manner that he had a trick up his sleeve, but he had no idea what it might be. In any event, it was already too late. The judge had sustained Mitch's objection.

"Go ahead and lay your predicate, counsel," the judge said to Sutton. "I'll draw my own conclusion from the facts you put in evidence."

"Thank you, your honor." Sutton adjusted his half-rim reading glasses and scrutinized the notes on his yellow legal tablet. "Who represented Valerie Winston when she divorced your son seven years ago?" he asked.

"The same lawyer who's with her today," answered Mr. Winston.

228

"Mr. Mitchell McNaughton, who's present at the counsel table?"

"That's correct."

"Were there hard feelings between your family and Mr. McNaughton when that divorce trial ended?"

"I ran him out of town, if that's what you mean."

Mitch was halfway to his feet when the judge waved him back down. "Sustained. Instruct your witness, counsel."

There was a short pause while Sutton went to the witness stand and engaged in a whispered conversation with Mr. Winston. The witness finally gave a grudging nod of his head and Sutton returned to his seat at the counsel table. "Tell the court exactly what role you played in Mr. McNaughton's departure from Gilbert."

"I called everybody who did business with me and asked them to find themselves a new lawyer."

"And did that happen?"

"I believe my efforts were successful."

"How long did Mr. McNaughton remain in Gilbert after the divorce?"

"About two months, as I recall."

"And then he moved away?"

"That's correct. To Austin."

"And where does your former daughter-in-law now reside?"

"In Austin."

"Are there also hard feelings between your family and Valerie Winston?"

Mr. Winston had to clench his teeth before he answered. But he'd had his instructions from his lawyer, so he didn't say all the things he wanted to say. "Yes, sir. Very hard feelings."

"And now with all this old bitterness, she's filed a lawsuit against your whole family?"

"Yes, sir."

"And who is her attorney for this lawsuit?"

"The same one. Her lover, Mitchell McNaughton."

Valerie gasped, and Mitch was immediately on his feet to object. His face was flushed as he angrily said, "Objection, your honor. There are no facts in evidence to support such a flagrantly erroneous conclusion."

"We're just trying to show the court the true motives behind this lawsuit, your honor." Jim Sutton was pleased to see the reaction he'd drawn. "If the court requires, we can lay our fact predicate."

Judge Nolan didn't like the way things were going. It was embarrassing to see a personal attack on the motives of an attorney who was practicing before his court. He hesitated.

"Your honor," interjected Sutton in the pause, "Mr. McNaughton asked the court at the beginning of this hearing to get all the facts on the record so the appellate courts would be able to make a proper decision on the merits of his claim. We're trying to honor that request."

"There are no facts to support such an outlandish claim, your honor," Mitch protested with heat. "The statement made by the witness is untrue." Mitch's fist was clenching and unclenching, as it always did when he was under attack.

"Will counsel approach the bench?" Mitch and Sutton did as directed to hear the judge's off-the-record remarks. "Mr. Sutton, this testimony is on the verge of getting out of hand," the judge whispered, leaning forward so no one could hear him except the lawyers. "I'll not sit idly by and let you sully another lawyer's reputation with insinuations. You go talk to your witness and don't you proceed with anything you can't prove, do you understand me? Otherwise I'm going to hold you in contempt of court."

Mitch went back to the counsel table and tried not to show his outrage while Sutton engaged in a brief, whispered conversation with Mr. Winston.

"Are you ready to proceed, counsel?" asked the judge.

"Yes, your honor." Sutton was walking on eggshells now. He thought he had the facts he needed, but Mitch's anger warned him that he'd have to be careful. "Mr. Winston," Sutton said to his witness, "I don't want you to testify to anything except facts, is that clear?"

"Yes, sir."

"And it's a fact that Mr. McNaughton represents Valerie Winston in this lawsuit, isn't it?"

"Yes, sir."

"And that your family hired me to represent you?"

"Yes, sir."

"And in preparing for the lawsuit, we've hired a private investigator to check on various details for us?"

"Yes, sir."

"What is one of the things that investigator is supposed to find out?"

"Whether there's anything other than an attorney-client relationship between Mr. McNaughton and my daughter-in-law."

"Have they made a report to you?"

"Yes."

"What is it?"

Mr. Winston pulled an envelope from his breast pocket and fanned out a series of glossy color photographs taken at Mitch's house on the hill at Rob Roy. "Here's Mr. McNaughton naked with Valerie Winston in his arms. Here they are on the bed. This one is in the hot tub. Well, I'll let the judge draw his own conclusions. I think the facts speak for themselves."

CHAPTER TWELVE

Mr. Winston's photographs had the effect of a bomb exploding in the courtroom. The spectators gasped and leaned forward, wishing they weren't too far away to see what was in the pictures. Valerie clutched Mitch's arm, whispering, "No, no, that's not me, it's Kristina. They must've gotten us mixed up because we're the same size and coloring!"

Kristina buried her face in her hands, feeling violated because she and Mitch had somehow been spied upon in their most private moments.

And Mitch seemed to turn to stone, so much control was he exerting over himself. When Valerie kept tugging at his sleeve and insisting, "Tell them it's not me, Mitch," he responded that he wasn't going to drag Kristina into this mess if he could help it; somehow he would find another way to handle it.

Mitch stood to make a series of heated objections to the photographs. "Your honor, this is an invasion of privacy!" he said in outrage.

"No, your honor," replied Jim Sutton, rapidly rising to respond. "These photographs were taken at a location away from Mr. McNaughton's property, and as the Court can see, most of them were taken outdoors where Mr. McNaughton couldn't have had any expectation of privacy. Further, your honor, these photographs are relevant to the very heart of this lawsuit because they show the plaintiff's motive in filing it."

"Mr. Sutton," the judge answered, his face grim with disapproval, "you understand that if you fail to prove your legal argument, Mr. McNaughton may well be able to file his own lawsuit against your client for invasion of privacy?"

"Yes, your honor. I've researched this issue very carefully, and I've prepared a brief in support of my client's position." Sutton reached in a folder for a typewritten brief and handed it to the judge, then offered Mitch a copy.

"You may proceed, counsel, and I'll study your brief during the noon recess."

"Thank you, your honor."

Before Sutton could continue questioning Mr. Winston, Mitch stood to make another angry objection. "Your honor, this witness didn't take these photographs, and the person who did isn't present in the courtroom to verify the accuracy of the scenes and persons depicted."

"Did the photographer attach an affidavit to these photographs?" Jim Sutton asked Mr. Winston, in an effort to counter Mitch's objections.

"Yes, he did."

"And does it say where the photographs were taken?"

"From the hillside below Mr. McNaughton's residence at the Rob Roy development in Austin, Texas."

"Does it give the date the photographs were taken?"

"There are two dates, November thirteenth and November nineteenth."

"Does the affidavit state who the persons are in the photographs taken on November thirteenth?"

Mr. Winston polished his glasses with his handkerchief, then put them back on to continue reading from the paper in his hand. "It says that a private investigator observed Mr. McNaughton arrive at a residence on Thirty-eighth Street where the subject Valerie Winston lives with her sister, Kristina Neilsen. Miss Neilsen remained at the residence and was joined there by a man later identified as Bud Thomas, who teaches in Miss Neilsen's department at the University of Texas. The investigator followed Mr. McNaughton and Valerie Winston when they left the Thirty-eighth Street residence and drove to Mr. McNaughton's home in Rob Roy, where they remained until the following morning."

Kristina and Bud listened in stark amazement. "They have us mixed up," Kristina whispered. "They think I'm Valerie, and they followed the wrong person."

Jim Sutton continued with his questioning of his witness. "And who are the persons in the photographs taken on November nineteenth?"

"On the second date, Valerie Winston and her sister were observed entering Mr. McNaughton's office in the Petroleum Building on I-35 in Austin. Miss Neilsen departed alone and drove her Volkswagen vehicle to her office at the University of Texas, then returned to her home on Thirty-eighth Street, where she was later joined by Bud Thomas. The investigator followed Valerie Winston and Mr. McNaughton when they departed from his office and once again drove to his house in Rob Roy and remained throughout the night."

Mitch stood again. "Your honor, it doesn't matter how many affidavits are attached to these photographs because the affidavits are hearsay. The witness is not the person who observed these scenes and took the photographs. Therefore he isn't able to state under oath in this courtroom that this is an accurate portrayal of what he observed. Only the photographer can do that, and he isn't here today. Plaintiff objects to the admissibility into evidence of these exhibits under the hearsay rule."

"I believe counsel is correct," the judge responded. "I'm not going to permit these photographs to be put into evidence at this time. If you want to use them at trial, Mr. Sutton, you'll have to bring your photographer to prove them up."

"Very well, your honor." Sutton walked to the witness stand and took the photographs from Mr. Winston, then placed them on the edge of the counsel table. At this point, it really didn't matter whether the pictures were officially admitted into evidence or not. They'd done their damage. "I don't believe I have anything further from this witness at this time. Mr. Winston has laid out the facts, and the court can draw its own conclusion as to why Valerie Winston, the plaintiff, is demanding Mr. Winston's personal financial

236

records and why Mr. Winston needs the court's protection."

"Counsel?" The judge turned to Mitch to see if he wished to cross-examine.

"No questions, your honor." Mitch wasn't about to give Mr. W. Harold Winston a chance to do any more damage.

"You may step down."

Mr. Winston walked behind Valerie's chair on his way to his own seat, and she shuddered visibly. Mitch reached out to grip her hand and whispered, "It's okay, Valerie. This is their show. We'll get our chance later today. Just hold on."

"We call Mrs. Chester Bayless to the stand," said Jim Sutton.

Mrs. Bayless, sister of W. Harold Winston, got up from the counsel table, took the oath, and went to the witness stand. She glared once at Valerie and then shifted in the witness chair so Valerie would no longer be in her line of sight.

"What is your relationship to the plaintiff?" asked Sutton.

"She *used* to be married to my nephew, John Ed Winston," Mrs. Bayless answered with heavy sarcasm.

"When was the last time you saw your nephew and his children?" Sutton continued.

"On the Fourth of July. We had a family picnic at the lake."

Sutton leaned back in his chair and tapped his pencil against the edge of the table. "Mrs. Bayless, I ask you to search your memory very carefully and tell me the last time you had any contact at all with your nephew—whether in person, by telephone, by letter, or in any other way."

Mrs. Bayless wrinkled her forehead and pursed her lips in a characteristic gesture. "I haven't heard from him since the day of that family picnic," she said firmly.

"Would you say there are hard feelings between your family and the plaintiff here, Valerie Winston?"

Mrs. Bayless's face contorted with hate. "Of course there are hard feelings."

"Does that bitterness go all the way back to their divorce seven years ago?"

"It goes farther than that, all the way back to when they got married. John Ed had money and Valerie wanted it, so she trapped him the only way she could. She got pregnant and forced him to marry her."

"Your honor, I object," Mitch said vehemently.

"The witness is instructed not to continue this outburst. Her remarks will be stricken from the record." The judge was madder than a wet hen. This preliminary hearing was getting out of hand.

Valerie tried to rise from the counsel table but Mitch put out an arm to stop her. Her face dissolved into a red, weeping blob. "John Ed said he loved me and *wanted* to marry me," she whispered in anguish. "I didn't care about his family's money."

Jim Sutton shook his head in dismay. "Your honor, I apologize." Sutton hadn't expected Mrs. Bayless to go into ancient family history. It wasn't going to help his case if the judge thought the hard feelings went all the way back to the time of the marriage, instead of stemming from the divorce. "Pass the witness."

"How long is your cross-examination going to take, counsel?" the judge asked Mitch, glancing at the clock on the back wall. It was nearly twelve o'clock.

"Just a few minutes, your honor."

"Very well. I'll let you cross-examine now, and then we'll take a break for lunch."

Mitch fixed his gaze on the witness as though somehow he could make her tell the truth by sheer willpower. "Mrs. Bayless, you claim that you've had no contact at all with your nephew John Ed Winston since the Fourth of July?"

"That's the gospel truth," she said.

"And you claim you have no idea of his whereabouts since he left Gilbert to take the children to Disneyland?"

"Not a bit."

"You've never sent him money or telephoned him?"

She shook herself in outraged innocence. "How could I? I don't know where he is."

"Mrs. Bayless, you told your lawyer that there's a lot of bitterness between your family and Valerie Winston, the plaintiff, isn't that right?"

"Yes, that's true."

"And you say it stems from the time John Ed and Valerie got married?"

"Yes."

"And that Valerie was pregnant when they married?"

"Yes."

"How old was Valerie at that time?"

"Oh, about eighteen or so."

"And how old was John Ed?"

239

When she answered, it was grudgingly. "I suppose he was about twenty-four."

"Did they meet here in Gilbert?"

"No, they met over at San Marcos. They were in school there at Southwest University."

"If Valerie was eighteen, she was probably a freshman, away from home for the first time?"

"I wouldn't know."

"And John Ed was twenty-four. Isn't that a little older than most college students?"

"I don't believe so."

"Did he graduate from college that year?"

"No, he had to go to work and support his wife and family."

"I thought you said he had money and that's why Valerie wanted to marry him."

"He's going to inherit money. That's why Valerie wanted to marry him. She knew he'd get everything his father and I had."

"Oh, so she knew about the Winston family wealth at the time she was a freshman in college?"

Mitch didn't wait for a response. He simply looked at the notes he'd scribbled on his yellow tablet, then lifted his head. "I want to inquire about one other thing, Mrs. Bayless. You mentioned that Valerie forced John Ed to marry her, is that correct?"

"Oh, yes. I believe she threatened him with a paternity suit or something like that."

"How do you know that?"

"It was common knowledge in the family." She put a sarcastic emphasis on the word *common,* as though it were a substitute for Valerie herself.

"Mrs. Bayless, I'm wondering if your memory isn't a little faulty after all these years." Mitch asked the question in a kind, patient voice, trying to confuse the witness before he closed in for the kill. "Isn't it a fact that it was John Ed's *father* who forced him to marry Valerie?"

"Why, no," Mrs. Bayless sputtered.

"Isn't it true that John Ed had been running wild over at San Marcos and his father was sick and tired of it?"

"Not at all." Mrs. Bayless drew herself up like an angry pigeon.

"John Ed's an only child, isn't that correct?"

"Certainly."

"And you don't have any children either?"

"No, my husband and I were never blessed with a family."

"So John Ed was the end of the line as far as the Winstons were concerned? There wasn't anybody to carry on the family name except him?"

"I suppose that's true. I never gave it much thought."

"As a matter of fact, Mrs. Bayless, wasn't that a matter of grave concern to the Winston family? Wasn't John Ed in danger of being drafted and sent to Vietnam? And if that had happened and he'd gotten killed, the family line would've run out?"

"Why, no—we never—no." Mrs. Bayless was beginning to get rattled and looked to her brother for guidance.

"And when your brother, Harold Winston, found out that Valerie was pregnant, he bribed John Ed to marry her so that if something happened to his son, the family line would continue?"

"Objection, your honor," said Jim Sutton, angrily tossing down his pencil. "This is pure speculation on the part of plaintiff's counsel."

The judge wanted to hear the answer because it was a fascinating theory. But Sutton was right. It was pure speculation. "Sustained."

"No further questions." Mitch had made his point.

Sutton had to try to salvage something. "Mrs. Bayless, didn't your nephew remain married to Valerie Winston for nearly six years?"

"That's correct."

"So counsel's crazy suggestion couldn't be true, because if John Ed had been bribed to marry Valerie, he could've gotten a divorce as soon as the child was born."

"True." Mrs. Bayless drew a deep sigh of relief.

"Pass the witness." Sutton returned to his table.

"Just one more question, please, ma'am," Mitch said politely. "Was the first child a boy or a girl?"

"A girl, Shelley."

"So even if Shelley might carry on the family line, she wouldn't carry on the family name, isn't that correct?"

Mrs. Bayless shrugged her shoulders.

"Sorry, ma'am, but you'll have to answer out loud so the court reporter can get your answer in the record."

Mrs. Bayless's face twisted maliciously. "We have Michael and Jason to carry on the family name."

"No more questions."

"May this witness be excused?" Judge Nolan asked Sutton.

Sutton nodded. This testimony had backfired on him. He was going to have a busy lunch hour trying to patch things back together.

"Court will stand in recess until one-thirty."

"All rise," cried the bailiff, but the judge was already halfway out of the courtroom before people could scramble to their feet.

Kristina and Bud stayed in their seats until they were sure all the other spectators had left the courtroom and they would not be observed with Mitch and Valerie. The Winstons filed out with their attorney, leaving Mitch and Valerie alone at the counsel table.

"Mitch, this is horrible," Valerie wailed. "They aren't satisfied with taking my children away from me. They aren't going to stop until they destroy me."

Mitch tried to calm her fears, but she was too distraught to believe him. He was relieved when Bud and Kristina came to join them at the front of the courtroom, sure Bud would have more success with Valerie than he could.

While Bud went to Valerie and tried to comfort her, Kristina stood behind Mitch's chair and massaged his shoulders. "How are you doing?" she asked softly.

"You've seen it all." He pressed his face into his hands and let his spirits droop for a minute.

"I'm not talking about the case, Mitch. I'm talking about you. How are *you* doing?"

He stood and turned to face her. "Not too bad," he

243

said, rumpling the dark tresses of her wig. "Sorry about the photographs."

She blinked away tears. "That was a dirty trick."

"I should've been more careful. I knew they were vicious."

"Just tell the court we're engaged and that would solve the problem." Kristina put on a strong front, not letting Mitch see how devastated she'd been by the photos.

"I'm not going to let them drag you into this mess if I can help it," he said forcefully. "I care about you too much to do that. I'll handle it some other way. Besides, there's no reason for the whole damn world to know the intimate details of *our* relationship."

"Have you got any bright ideas?"

"I thought that was your department." He grinned at her. "God, I love you," he said. "No matter how badly things are going, it makes me feel better just to have you here."

"Is it really that bad?" There had been bumpy spots, but Kristina didn't think the morning had been a total loss. "How did you know Mr. Winston bribed John Ed to marry Valerie?"

"I didn't. That was a pure fishing expedition."

"I think you landed a big one, then. No matter how much they deny it, I think the judge is going to believe that's exactly what happened."

"Anyone who knows John Ed would make the same guess and probably be right. The way they're fighting to keep the kids even after custody was awarded to Valerie is proof enough."

"Will that make any difference to the case?"

"Probably not. They've established the old family bitterness between Valerie and the Winstons and the fact that the Winstons ran me out of town. Even if the judge disregards the photographs, they've given him a motive for the two of us to bring the suit as a vendetta. I thought I might be able to break the Winstons down on cross-examination, but I can see now that isn't going to happen. They've got their ducks lined up and they're all squawking the same tune." He slammed the fist of one hand into the palm of the other. "I need something to prove they know where John Ed is, and all we have is hunches."

"That's why you wanted their records."

"Exactly. It's a catch-22. I need their records to prove my hunch, but I have to have proof before I can get the records." He tugged at the brim of her lavender bonnet. "I hate this hat you're wearing. And I hate this stupid black wig. I want my own blond Scandinavian sweetheart." He was mad at the world and had to take it out on something. At least the disguise was inanimate.

"I wore it in case you needed me to do something."

"What did you have in mind? What we need is a miracle."

"What about the man at the Western Union office?"

"They've filed a motion to keep me from getting access to the Western Union records. I can't see the records until the judge rules on their motion and gives us permission." Mitch rested his chin on the top of Kristina's head and tried to think. "Wait a minute," he said, catching a glimmer of an idea. "I can't make him produce the records, but—" He snapped his fingers.

245

"You're onto something," Kristina said, feeling the charge of adrenaline that transformed Mitch.

"The district clerk's office will be closed during the lunch hour," Mitch said. "But when they open again at one o'clock, I want you to go in there and fill out an application for a subpoena, get the clerk to issue it, and then go over there and serve it on that guy. Do you remember his name?"

"Troy Blasingame."

"Right, Blasingame. Tell the clerk to give you a subpoena for two o'clock, and you sashay over to the Western Union office and hand it to him, then come back and fill out an affidavit of service."

"I thought the sheriff had to serve court papers."

"Not a subpoena. Anyone over eighteen can do it, as long as they're not a party to the lawsuit."

"You'd better write that down for me so I won't forget something important."

Mitch scribbled instructions on a yellow sheet, then ripped it out and handed it to her. "Here. Be sure to tell him two o'clock. I won't be able to put him on the stand until Sutton is through with his last witness."

"Who will that be?"

"I guess he'll put Chester Bayless on, but it shouldn't take long. He's just a brother-in-law."

"Do you think Mrs. Winston will come back this afternoon?"

"She'd better. The judge may hold her in contempt if she doesn't."

"Are you going to cross-examine her?"

"Probably not. Dealing with the Winstons is like dealing with a rattlesnake. The more you handle them, the better your chances of getting bit." Mitch glanced at his watch. "We'd better try to grab a bite to eat. Valerie, are you ready to go?"

"I'm not hungry," Valerie answered. "I think I'll just sit here with Bud and try to pull myself together."

"You've got to eat something, Valerie. You may have to take the stand this afternoon, and I don't want you getting dizzy on me. Besides, Bud looks like he could use something to eat."

"Come on, Valerie. You'll feel better if you get out of this place for a while, anyway." Kristina took her sister's hand and gave a firm tug. "Where are we going to eat?" she asked, following Mitch down the aisle and out of the courtroom.

"We can't go to the café across the street because that's where the Winstons and their lawyer will be. Why don't Valerie and I meet you and Bud at that barbecue stand out on the highway? There won't be any of the courthouse crowd out there."

"Barbecue? Yuk," Valerie said, her stomach already turning somersaults from nerves.

"We'll get you a bowl of vegetable stew and corn-bread. That'll give you strength for the afternoon." Mitch squeezed Kristina's hand. "She's going to need it," he added under his breath.

When they returned from lunch, Bud took a different route to the courthouse so the two vehicles wouldn't be seen together. He parked at the north end of the block, after he'd made sure that Mitch's car was parked diagonally across the street. By chance, the Winstons and their attorney were crossing the street from the café as he pulled into the parking space, so Bud and Kristina waited until the other group passed by before getting out of the pickup.

Mitch and Valerie came across the street just behind the Winstons and paused when Mr. Bayless stopped to put his wife's umbrella in his car, a 1968 Dodge four-door sedan, its blue paint faded by the Texas wind and sun. Even though the car was old, it was spit-clean and in good shape, as though the owner had taken good care of it. Mitch gave it a second glance. It wasn't exactly the kind of car he'd have expected one of the Winstons to drive, but then Mr. Bayless was only an in-law. No doubt Mr. W. Harold Winston drove something a lot fancier.

When the Winstons reached the courthouse steps, Mitch nudged Valerie forward but then remembered something he needed to tell Kristina about the subpoena. "Just a minute," he said, instructing Valerie to stay where she was while he walked back toward Bud's pickup.

Kristina met him halfway. "Something wrong?" she asked, edging in between the parked cars to give them a little privacy.

"I forgot to tell you to watch for that Blasingame fellow when he comes to the courthouse. I'm not sure how long it will take Sutton to finish up, and I don't want Blasingame in the courtroom until the Winstons are all through putting on their case. I don't want to tip our hand."

"What should I do, then?"

"Sit near the back by the door and watch for him. If the Winstons aren't through testifying when he gets

248

there, you get up and keep him outside in the hallway. I'll have the bailiff call his name when I'm ready for him."

Kristina nodded. "I can manage that."

Mitch smiled into her eyes. "No doubt of that." He gripped her hand. "Wish me luck."

"Oh, I do." Love flowed between them though not a word was spoken.

In another second he was going to kiss her. To break the spell, Mitch kicked the tire of the car next to them. "Would you have thought one of the Winstons would drive an old bomb like this?"

"I always thought people who drove these old Dodges were as solid and dependable as the cars are. This car is too good for the likes of a Winston." Kristina separated from Mitch, letting him go toward the courthouse while she walked behind the car, observing as Mitch had that the car was well maintained. "Mitch, come here," she called, noticing something unusual.

"What is it?" He glanced at his watch. He had plenty of time, but he wanted Kristina to get to the clerk's office and get that subpoena issued and served.

"Look at this," she said, pointing to the rear bumper of Mr. Bayless's car.

"Is there something special about that trailer hitch?"

"Look how shiny and new it is. See how the chrome has faded on the bumper?"

"Kris, this is a fine time to take an interest in the effects of weather on chrome."

"Mitch, use your head," she scolded. "If a person

249

had any use for a trailer hitch, wouldn't he put it on a car when it was new?"

"I suppose he would if he had any *regular* need for a trailer hitch. Maybe something just came up lately and he needed it for something special."

"That's exactly what I'm talking about."

Their eyes met. "So you think—"

"Remember the very first time I came snooping around to Gilbert and somebody was shushing up a rumor about a travel trailer?" They remembered their discussion in Mitch's office that day when they'd decided the rumor was a red herring to throw the police off the trail. "Maybe it wasn't a false clue. Maybe it was true and the Winstons really did have to squelch the rumors."

"You mean maybe somebody really did take John Ed a travel trailer?"

"I mean maybe *Chester Bayless* took John Ed a travel trailer."

"But why?"

"So it would be easier for John Ed to hide the kids. They could camp anywhere and lie low."

"But why didn't John Ed just take the trailer with him? Why involve Chester Bayless?"

"So Valerie wouldn't know how to hunt for him. After all, John Ed left here on a plane with the kids and they all had round-trip tickets. Valerie would never have let them go otherwise."

"How did he get a car after he got to California?"

"Who knows? He had an old friend in Los Angeles, someone we tried to contact after John Ed disappeared. Maybe that guy gave him a car. I know John

Ed didn't buy one in his own name because the police checked for that."

"Mitch?" Valerie called from farther down the sidewalk. "It's almost time to go in the courtroom."

Mitch muttered an expletive and looked at his watch. "I've got to get back in there. We're going to have to wing it and try to piece this thing together as we go." He quickly brushed Kristina's cheek with his lips and loped off down the sidewalk.

Kristina smoothed the skirt of her purple-flowered prairie dress and turned the other way. "I've got to get that subpoena," she called over her shoulder. "See you in court."

When court reconvened, Mrs. Winston had returned and was seated in her place at the counsel table next to her husband. After a hurried trip to the Western Union office, Kristina was now seated on the back bench where she could watch for the arrival of Troy Blasingame. News of the proceedings had spread through town during the lunch hour, so that the courtroom was now full of curious onlookers eager to pick up any juicy tidbits about the prominent Winston family.

"You may proceed, counsel," Judge Nolan said, nodding his head at Jim Sutton.

"We have one last witness, your honor, and his testimony will be brief. Defense calls Chester Bayless to the stand."

Chester Bayless made his way to the bench and took the witness oath. He was a small man with a wiry, compact body and hands calloused from ranch work.

251

His face had the leathery look of all Texas men who spend their waking hours in the wind and sun. He was out of his element in this imposing courtroom, and his fingers fidgeted with the brim of the cowboy hat on his lap.

"Mr. Bayless, what is your relationship to the Winston defendants?" asked Jim Sutton.

"Why, they're my in-laws. I'm married to Rose Ellen Winston, the sister of Harold, there," he said, pointing toward the counsel table. "John Ed is her only nephew."

"I'll ask you the same question I've asked everybody else," Sutton continued. "When was the last time you had any contact with John Ed Winston?"

"It was at a family picnic on the Fourth of July." His response was automatic.

"No further questions."

"Do you wish to cross-examine this witness?" inquired the judge, assuming that further questions would be a waste of everyone's time.

"Yes, your honor." Mitch leaned back in his chair and studied the witness. Chester Bayless seemed to be a perfect match for his old Dodge car, weathered but sturdy and reliable. "Mr. Bayless, you're not a Winston by blood, is that right?"

"Oh, no, sir, I'm just an in-law."

"Does your wife have close ties with her family?"

Chester reflected. "Yes, sir, you could say that."

"And she'd go to any lengths to help them if they needed her?"

"Objection, your honor. Counsel is leading the witness."

"This is cross-examination, your honor." Mitch gave Sutton a puzzled look. Jim Sutton knew as well as he did that opposing counsel could lead on cross-examination.

"Overruled. Proceed, counsel."

"Shall I repeat my question, Mr. Bayless?"

"Yes, sir. I've forgotten what it was with all these objections."

Someone in the audience laughed, and the judge glared over his spectacles.

"Would your wife go to any lengths to help her family?"

Chester cleared his throat. "I don't rightly know how to answer that." It was a true answer. When Mr. Sutton had called the family to his office to go over their testimony, he hadn't warned them that Mitch might ask this kind of question. Chester really didn't know how to answer it.

"I'd like to hurry this testimony along, counsel," the judge interrupted. "Will you proceed to another line of questioning?"

"Mr. Bayless, at noon I noticed you had a nice car, shiny trailer hitch, and all. You use that hitch much?"

Chester looked startled. He blinked his eyes and realized that Mitch actually expected him to answer. "Around the place I do, yes, sir." He stammered a little. "Haul my horse trailer and all."

"Mind telling us where you got that trailer hitch, and when?"

Chester shrugged. What could he do but answer the question? "Bought it from Wilbur Duffy over at the

253

Winston Hardware Store. He put it on for me, oh, several months back, I guess it was."

Kristina straightened in her seat. Wilbur Duffy, husband of Gladys Duffy, who worked in the county clerk's office. It was all beginning to tie together.

Mitch continued his cross-examination. "Car looks in pretty good shape. What kind of gas mileage do you get?"

Jim Sutton stood. "Your honor, I object to this line of questioning. It's totally irrelevant."

Mitch clenched his fists. "Please bear with me, your honor. I'll tie it all together if the court will just give me a few more minutes."

The judge frowned, turning his head from one lawyer to the other. "All right, counsel, you may proceed, but you'd better show me that this testimony is relevant or you'll never practice in my court again." The judge had just about had enough of these shenanigans.

"Thank you, your honor." Mitch sighed, but it was much too soon to relax.

"Answer the question," the judge instructed Chester.

"She gets about seventeen miles to a gallon." Chester was getting confused.

"What does she get when you're pulling the horse trailer?"

"Depends on whether the trailer is loaded or not." Chester loosened his collar a little.

"Let's say you're hauling a loaded trailer—not a horse trailer, but a small travel trailer. And let's say you're hauling it in the summertime so you're running the air conditioner." Mitch paused and let his words hang in the air, echoing like a guitar string that's been plucked too hard. Chester wiped his sweaty palms on his pant legs. Mitch's words jabbed like the clean blade of a knife. "And let's say you're hauling that trailer to Los Angeles, California. What kind of mileage would that nice little car of yours get under those circumstances, do you reckon?"

Chester popped his knuckles. All he could see was the deep blue irises of Mitch's eyes, blazing with a fire that looked as if it could consume the world. "Well, ah, that's a hypothetical question, Mr. McNaughton. I don't rightly know." Chester wiped his palms again.

"If I got my hands on your gasoline charge slips, would I find that it figured about eight or nine miles a gallon for you to take a travel trailer to John Ed Winston last August, at the very time Valerie Winston was begging her in-laws and the sheriff to help her find her children?" Mitch's voice rose to an uncharacteristic shout. "Mr. Bayless, is that what you used that fine old 1968 Dodge of yours for, to haul that trailer to John Ed so he could hide those children from their poor, distraught mother?"

The courtroom buzzed with excited whispers. The judge banged his gavel and demanded silence. The room stilled, and Chester Bayless cringed at the flames of conscience that licked at his feet.

"That's a hypothetical case, Mr. McNaughton," he answered, looking away from the dreadful fire in Mitch's eyes.

Mitch leaned forward in his seat until Chester could feel his warm breath. "Mr. Bayless, I remind you that you are under oath in a court of law. Perjury is a very serious offense. You're a decent man, Mr. Bayless. You're not a Winston. You're not the kind of man to commit perjury."

Across the counsel table Jim Sutton was objecting again, but neither Mitch nor Chester heard him. Inside Chester's mind the words *perjury, perjury, perjury* wailed like a guilty conscience. He put his head in his hands. The courtroom was as hushed as the grave, and neither man dared move or speak. Chester made a trip inward and found his soul.

When he lifted his head, he was no longer afraid of the fire in Mitch's eyes. His voice was so low that even the judge had to strain to catch his words. "That's just how it happened. John Ed told us at the Fourth of July picnic that Valerie was going to move to Austin and take the kids with her. Of course none of the Winstons could stand to let go of what was rightfully theirs, and those kids are Winstons. Rose Ellen was determined to help John Ed get the kids for himself, and I couldn't let her go off alone in the car pulling that travel trailer. The boy's parents had to stay here in Gilbert and make it look like everything was perfectly normal. They said it wouldn't do for Valerie to take the children away to Austin where they'd never see them again. They all got together and worked out a story, and nobody was ever supposed to find out the truth. We never dreamed you'd notice that trailer hitch on my car and start asking questions." Chester looked at his wife, sobbing while Mr. and Mrs. Winston stared into space, heads high as though nothing had changed at all. "I'm sorry, Rose Ellen," Chester whispered.

"Counsel will meet me in chambers immediately," the judge said. "Court will recess for ten minutes."

"Everyone rise," shouted the bailiff, but his words were unnecessary. People couldn't wait to get to their feet.

The hallway outside the courtroom was a scene of pandemonium. It had all happened so fast that Troy Blasingame hadn't yet arrived at the courthouse, so Kristina moved through the crowd hunting for him. She wanted to find Mitch and see whether he still wanted Troy to testify, but that was impossible, since Mitch was closeted in chambers with the judge.

She felt a glow of excitement. She'd never dreamed Mitch could take such a tiny piece of evidence and turn it into a battering ram against the stout Winston defenses.

"There you are," she said, spotting Troy Blasingame near the main entrance.

"What's going on, anyway?" he asked. He hadn't seen so much excitement in the courthouse since a big murder trial several years ago.

"I'll tell you all about it later," she promised. "Right now you're a witness and you aren't supposed to know about the testimony other witnesses have given."

"Me, a witness?" Troy was apprehensive. A timid soul, he had no interest in being forced into the spotlight.

"It won't take but just a minute," Kristina assured him. "Let's go sit down somewhere out of the way and wait till they call your name."

"Does this have something to do with that money order your friend sent you for your blowed-out tire?" he asked. He'd racked his brain ever since he'd been served with the subpoena, and all he could think of was that he'd done something wrong by not getting proper identification from Amanda Tucker that day.

"Oh, no, nothing like that. You don't have a thing to worry about," Kristina said, sitting down on a bench and patting the seat beside her. "You haven't done anything wrong."

The uproar in the hallway screeched to a halt when the bailiff called for order. Everyone rushed back into the courtroom, wondering what would happen next.

Judge Nolan was white around the mouth when he stormed back into the courtroom, the two attorneys loping through the side door a split second behind him.

"Your witness, counsel," the judge said, nodding curtly to Jim Sutton.

Sutton had lost his customary easygoing smile. His ego had just taken a severe blow to the solar plexus, and right now his biggest concern was to protect himself from the loss of his law license. "I have only one question on redirect," Sutton said. "Mr. Bayless, will you tell the court whether the Winston family told your attorney about these arrangements to help John Ed Winston during our consultations concerning this case."

"Oh, no, sir. Why, you wouldn't have taken the case if you'd known the truth."

"Thank you. No further questions."

"Counsel?" The judge turned to Mitch with a questioning look. Mitch could really make things hot for Sutton if he wanted to.

"No questions, your honor. This witness may be excused."

"You may step down."

Chester Bayless crushed his cowboy hat against his chest and walked slowly back to his empty seat at the counsel table. His wife scooted her chair away and refused to look at him.

Sutton stood. "The defendants have nothing further to present to the court at this time."

The judge turned to Mitch. "Mr. McNaughton?"

Mitch rose and glanced at the notes on his yellow pad. "Plaintiff would like to give the court a little more information before we rest, your honor. We call Troy Blasingame to the stand."

The bailiff called Troy's name, first inside the courtroom and then in the hall.

Kristina patted Troy's hand. "You'll do just fine," she said, following him inside and pointing him toward the witness stand at the front. She found an empty seat and sat down to watch.

"Mr. Blasingame, how are you employed?" Mitch asked after the witness had been sworn.

"I'm the manager of the local Western Union office."

"And is it part of your duties to send and receive money orders from across the entire United States?"

"Yes, it is." Troy swallowed hard. He'd known this subpoena had something to do with that money order for Amanda Tucker.

259

"Do you do that many times a day or only on occasion?"

"Not often at all."

"So when you send or receive a money order, it would be likely to stick in your mind?"

"Oh, certainly." Troy was now quite willing to confess his sins to the world. Surely the company wouldn't fire him for one little mistake.

"Do you remember sending a money order from here in Gilbert to someone in Granite Falls, Washington?"

"Huh?" Troy was confused. He'd thought he was going to be asked about Amanda Tucker and the Austin money order, not about the ones that went to Washington State. For the first time he looked around the courtroom and was surprised to see the Winstons sitting not ten feet away. His adam's apple bobbled as he tried to swallow past the lump in his throat. His wife Belva June had told him the lawyers were coming to argue their motions in the Winston case today, but nobody knew the Winstons themselves were going to be present. Usually nobody came to a boring old hearing on motions except the lawyers and the judge.

"Did you ever send a Western Union money order to someone in Granite Falls, Washington?" Mitch prodded.

"No, sir, I didn't."

Mitch looked at him in surprise. The man sounded like a person who was telling the truth, but it had to be a lie. Granite Falls was the name of the town he'd mentioned to Kristina. Mitch poured over his detailed

260

notes. "Oh, excuse me. What about Everett, Washington? Have you ever sent a money order there?"

"Yes, I have."

"Is there a connection between Granite Falls and Everett?" Mitch asked.

"Yes sir. You see I tried to send a money order to Granite Falls, but there was no Western Union office there. Everett was the closest town. So I sent it to Everett instead."

"To whom was that money order made out?" Mitch asked. He'd gotten to the hard part now, where he didn't know the answers and would have to follow his gut instinct.

"Someone named Robert Kensington."

That wasn't the answer Mitch wanted, but he didn't know how to back out of the hole he was in. "Did you send more than one money order to Robert Kensington?"

"In Everett, Washington?"

"Or anyplace else."

"I've been sending a money order to Robert Kensington about twice a month for the past several months, but only one of them went to Everett, Washington."

"When did you first start sending these money orders?"

"Oh, about the middle of August, I reckon."

"And when did you send the last one?"

"Why, only last week."

"Where did you send it?"

"I believe the town was called Port Townsend, Washington."

"Can you tell the court the name of the person here in Gilbert who's been sending these money orders to Robert Kensington?"

Timid Troy Blasingame squirmed in his seat and tried to fix his eyes on something besides the people sitting at the counsel table. "It wasn't always the same person."

"Was it always a person you recognized?"

"Oh, yes."

"Would you recognize them if you saw them again?"

"Yes, sir."

"Do you see them here in the courtroom today?"

Troy cast his eyes heavenward and said a silent prayer. "Yes, sir," he answered, pointing, "right there at the table beside you. Mr. Harold Winston, Mrs. Harold Winston, and Mrs. Rose Ellen Bayless."

"What about Mr. Chester Bayless?"

"Oh, no, sir. He's never been in the Western Union office the whole two years I've worked there."

"No more questions."

Jim Sutton thought his chances of salvaging anything from this fiasco were minute, but he had to give it a shot. "Mr. Blasingame, you don't know Robert Kensington, do you?"

"No, sir, I don't."

"Never met him?"

"No, sir."

"Don't know anything about him, where he's from or anything like that?"

"No, sir."

"Pass the witness."

"You may step down," said the judge. "Court stands in recess for fifteen minutes. When we come back, I'll announce my ruling on defendants' motions."

CHAPTER THIRTEEN

There was a hush in the courtroom when the hearing reconvened. Judge Nolan spoke with deliberation, as though choosing each word with care.

"There have been some unusual events during this proceeding today," he said, "and there have been many discrepancies and conflicts in the testimony that has been presented to the court." He peered over the top of his glasses at the group of people seated at the counsel table. "It is, of course, within the discretion of the court as to which witnesses are to be believed and how much weight to give the testimony of each witness. The court may believe all of you or none of you." The judge tapped his pencil against the edge of the bench, as though he still had some uncertainties.

"In view of the contradictory versions of the facts," he continued, "the court has decided to deny the defendants' motion for protective orders. I will permit the plaintiff, Valerie Winston, to proceed with discovery, and I direct the other members of the Winston family to make available to her all the bank, telephone, credit card, and other records in their possession. When Mr. McNaughton has had an opportunity to go through all the documentation, it should be evident whether there was in fact a conspiracy by the Winstons, and if so, he may present that evidence to a jury at the trial of this case."

Valerie turned to Mitch with a radiant smile and whispered, "Oh, Mitch, you did it!" Across the counsel table, Mr. W. Harold Winston audibly ground his teeth as his cheeks flushed bright pink.

"There is a matter which gravely concerns this court," the judge continued. "It will be some months before this case reaches the trial docket, and in the meantime, it seems possible that the plaintiff's children are being wrongfully detained in the State of Washington by their father. It also seems conceivable that they might be taken into Canada where it would be difficult to obtain extradition back to the United States. In view of this possibility, the court will entertain a request for an arrest warrant for John Ed Winston, and when the warrant is issued, the sheriff of this county will be ordered to go to Port Townsend, Washington, to locate the defendant and return him to Gilbert for criminal prosecution for kidnapping."

The judge turned to the Winstons and gave them an intimidating look. "The court expressly orders the members of the Winston family to have no contact whatsoever with John Ed Winston. Should any of you defy this order and make a long-distance telephone call or send a telegram, that fact will turn up on the subpoenaed documents. The entire family will be subject to jail and a heavy fine for contempt of court if that should happen, not to mention that they could be prosecuted for perjury. Do you understand me, Mr.

and Mrs. Winston, Mr. and Mrs. Bayless? I absolutely forbid you to contact John Ed Winston and tell him that a warrant has been issued for his arrest. If you do so, you will be subject to criminal prosecution."

The judge made a notation on his docket sheet and closed the file. "Is there anything further?"

Mitch and Jim Sutton stood and said simultaneously, "No, your honor."

"Very well. Court stands adjourned."

"All rise," cried the bailiff, as the stiff-backed judge stomped from the courtroom.

The Winston family huddled around their lawyer on the far side of the courtroom while Kristina and Bud made their way through the crowd to join Mitch and Valerie at the counsel table.

"Oh, Mitch!" Kristina cried, throwing herself into his arms. "You're wonderful!"

"Now, now," he said modestly, "it's not over yet. We've still got to get the children home."

"How long will it take?" Valerie asked, her face a strange blend of anxiety and joy.

"I'll go by the district attorney's office right now and get the arrest warrant taken care of. Then it will be up to the sheriff."

"Oh, no, what if John Ed gets away before then?"

Bud Thomas put a reassuring hand on Valerie's shoulder and massaged it in an absentminded way. "The Winstons might just go ahead and defy the judge's order," he speculated.

Kristina turned to Mitch. "Couldn't Valerie just fly

266

up there tonight and try to find the kids and bring them home herself?"

"Well, sure. That's a great idea. All she'll need is a certified copy of the divorce decree granting her custody, just in case there's any problem."

"You really mean it? If I can find them, I can bring them home?" Valerie clapped her hands together like a little girl on Christmas morning.

"You don't have a lot to go on, just that they were in Port Townsend recently."

"I'll find them, I know I will." Valerie slipped an arm around Bud's waist. "Will you go with me?" she asked shyly.

He hesitated. "I've got classes to teach tomorrow," he said.

"I'll cover for you," Kristina interrupted. "It's the last day of classes before Thanksgiving, so there probably won't be ten students there anyway."

"In that case," Bud said, grinning at Valerie, "I guess it's about time I met your kids. Especially since it looks like we're going to be spending most of our time together from now on."

The deputy sheriff who'd unwittingly helped Kristina on her previous trips to the courthouse came to the counsel table and cleared his throat. "Excuse me, Mr. McNaughton," he said. "Sheriff said for me to tell you that just as soon as you get that warrant issued, he wants me to beat it over to Austin and catch the first plane to Seattle."

"Oh," Valerie said. "Then does that mean you'll bring the children back yourself?"

"No, ma'am," the deputy answered. "I'm going on

267

official business to arrest John Ed Winston for kidnapping. Why, it may take me several days to work out all the extradition papers with the Washington State sheriff's office. I won't have time to do any babysitting."

"Then we're planning to fly out and find the children," Valerie said. "Do you think you'll be on the plane with us?"

"Yes, ma'am, if you're going to be on the next plane."

"Why, that's wonderful!" Valerie gave the deputy sheriff a dazzling smile.

"Do I know you from somewhere?" the deputy asked as he turned to leave. "You sure do look familiar."

Kristina turned her head to hide her laughter. The deputy hadn't recognized Kristina in her lavender-bonneted Amanda Tucker disguise, yet he'd noticed something familiar about Valerie, whom he'd never met. What an irony! And after all Kristina's worrying about being discovered!

Mitch opened up one of the files that was part of Valerie's case. "Here," he said to Valerie, "this is a certified copy of your divorce decree. Just in case you need it."

"Can we go now?" Valerie asked, "or do we have to stick around here?"

"You go home and pack and get your tickets," Mitch answered. "We'll finish up the details here."

Valerie's hand flew to her mouth. "Oh!"

"What is it?"

Valerie whispered in Kristina's ear, and Kristina reached in her purse. "Here, you go," she said, handing over a credit card. "I've been saving it for Christmas presents anyway."

"Thanks, Kris," Valerie cried over her shoulder as she rushed out the courtroom, Bud at her side. "I'll pay you back somehow."

Kristina snuggled into Mitch's enveloping arm. "We'll never be able to pay *you* back for all you've done for us," she said. "There's not enough money in the world for that."

He squeezed her against himself and whispered suggestively, "Maybe not enough *money,* but you might find some other way to pay my fee."

"Just what did you have in mind?" she asked, lifting her head to smile into his eyes.

"For starters, why don't you get rid of that damned bonnet?"

"Why, sir, do you want me to disrobe in this august court of law?"

"Not until all these other people leave," he murmured. "After that, we'll see." He took her hand and led her toward the exit. "Come on, I've got to go to the district attorney's office and get that arrest warrant taken care of so I can get on with the important business of the day. Namely you."

They walked past the Winstons, still deep in conversation with their attorney except for Chester Bayless, who stood apart from them, ignored. He noticed Mitch and Kristina walking his way and stepped into their path.

"Mr. McNaughton," he said, crushing the brim of his cowboy hat between nervous palms. "Do you have just a minute?"

269

Mitch stopped. The man looked bereft, and Mitch couldn't help feeling sorry for him. "Yes, sir. What can I do for you?"

"I did the right thing, didn't I, Mr. McNaughton?" Chester asked in a shaky whisper. "It was right for me to tell the truth, wasn't it?"

Mitch reached out to shake the other man's hand. "Yes, sir. It was the right thing. You don't ever have to apologize to anybody for what you did in this courtroom today."

Chester's back straightened visibly. "I knew I did, I just knew it. Rose Ellen says she'll never speak to me again, but I told her a man has to do what his conscience tells him is right." Chester pounded the brim of his hat and plopped it on his head. "I've been letting those Winstons tell me what to do for nearly thirty years. I reckon it's about time I stood up for myself. One thing for sure, I know I'm going to be able to sleep a lot better at night." There was a new spring in his step as he moved away. "Rose Ellen," he said, taking his wife firmly by the arm, "we'd best be going home. We've got a powerful lot of talking to do before suppertime."

As Chester and Rose Ellen turned to leave, Mitch and Kristina were only a few steps behind.

"Say, Mitch," called Jim Sutton, motioning for Mr. and Mrs. W. Harold Winston to wait while he spoke to his adversary. "I've been discussing things with my clients," Sutton said, "and they still maintain that you've brought this suit as a personal vendetta against them."

270

"I told you before, Jim. You know me better than that."

"I don't know, Mitch. They've got evidence that might sound persuasive to a jury."

"Like what?" Mitch felt icicles down his spine as the Winstons glared at him with malevolent expressions.

"Well, those photographs, for instance."

Mitch gave a mocking laugh. "I told you that isn't Valerie in those pictures."

"A jury isn't going to believe you. They'll see Valerie in person and they'll see the pictures. Even with a telephoto lens, you can tell it's the same woman."

Mitch's fist shot out and crumpled Sutton's lapel. "You just forget those photographs. If you try to drag them into court again, I'll—"

Sutton took a step backward. "Don't threaten me, son."

In another minute there was going to be a fistfight. Kristina took matters into her own hands. "Oh, for heaven's sake!" she exclaimed. "That isn't Valerie in the photographs, it's me!"

Mitch reached out to grab her shoulder. "Stay out of this," he commanded.

Sutton turned in her direction with a disbelieving glance. "A jury would never mistake you for the woman in the picture," he said. "She's a blonde."

Kristina yanked off her bonnet and the wig. "So am I," she said haughtily, shaking her silver-blond hair free with one hand. "I'm Valerie's sister, Kristina Neilsen."

While Jim Sutton tried to grasp the truth before his

eyes, Mr. Winston turned to Mrs. Winston. "So that's her sister," he murmured in agitation.

"Isn't she the one the investigator wrote about in his report?" inquired his wife. "The one who teaches at the University of Texas?"

Mr. Winston nodded. "Maybe we'll get to shoot the last arrow in our quiver before the hunt is over," he said. "One arrow may not be enough to be fatal, but we can certainly make it sting."

The brick building was almost deserted when Kristina finished up her last class the following day. True to form, most students had left early for the Thanksgiving weekend, and the faculty wasn't far behind. Kristina stopped by the office to pick up her mail, with the intention of going directly home and baking a pumpkin pie. She'd decided to cook a traditional Thanksgiving dinner, even though there wouldn't be anyone to eat it but herself and Mitch. They had a lot to be thankful for, and they were going to celebrate in the old-fashioned way.

To her surprise, there was a note in her box from Dr. Sherman Starling, the acting head of the department. "Urgent that you see me before leaving for the holidays," read the note. Puzzled, Kristina climbed the stairs to Dr. Starling's office and knocked at the door.

"Come in, Dr. Neilsen," he answered, his lips curved downward in a petulant frown.

"You wanted to see me?" she asked, taking the chair he indicated.

"Yes, indeed. I didn't feel that this matter could

wait until Dr. Perry returns." Dr. Vincent Perry was the chairman of Kristina's department but was attending a professional meeting in New Orleans, leaving Dr. Starling in charge.

"Is there a problem?" Kristina asked. Dr. Starling had sadistic tendencies and would let her squirm indefinitely unless she took the initiative.

"I don't know if there's a *problem,*" he said, with a persnickety precision in language. "But there's certainly been a *complaint.*"

"Concerning me?" She couldn't remember anything in particular, just the ordinary flak.

"One of the regents telephoned the Vice President for Academic Affairs, who telephoned the Dean of Arts and Sciences, who telephoned for Dr. Perry. In Dr. Perry's absence, I received the telephone call."

Would he never get to the point? He was trying to wear down her nerves with a battle of attrition, but Kristina was damned if she'd let him know he was getting her goat. "So?" she said, with just the right amount of defiant indifference.

"It's your instructional methodology." Dr. Starling lifted his head so he could look down his nose at her, a difficult feat considering that he was at least three inches shorter than Kristina. "Complaints about you have risen all the way to the top levels of the university."

"And what is it about my methodology that's created such a stir?" Kristina asked.

Dr. Starling's lips formed a vindictive smile that didn't reach his eyes. Glancing at his telephone notes,

273

he answered, "Your students have been working on their term projects, I understand."

"Yes, they have been."

"And several of them have been petitioning the City Council to adopt resolutions preventing further development in the southern part of the city where new industries are locating."

Kristina nodded.

"Others of them are circulating petitions throughout the city concerning pollution of Barton Springs and the spillway."

She nodded again.

"Two students have filed a protest with the utilities commission concerning price increases in utility service to consumers resulting from cost increases in the nuclear power project."

"That's right. Isn't it wonderful that these young people are becoming actively involved in local politics?"

Dr. Starling sucked in his breath. "Hardly. They're meddling in activities that involve huge sums of money. They're causing problems for the powers-that-be and are making a general nuisance of themselves. And you, Dr. Neilsen, are encouraging them."

"I have to agree, they're the best class I've ever taught. Quite frankly, Dr. Starling, I expect to win the faculty excellence award this year."

He tossed down his notes. "You can just forget that faculty excellence award. And if this furor doesn't cease, you may find yourself looking for another job." Dr. Starling had disliked Kristina from the start because of her popularity with students and the respect she received from professional colleagues.

Kristina was tired of these games. "Dr. Starling, let me be sure I understand what you're saying. Are you telling me that my job is in jeopardy because my political science students are learning about responsible citizenship firsthand instead of from a textbook? Or to put it differently, are you telling me that I might lose my job in retaliation for the exercise of my academic freedom?"

Dr. Starling was bright enough to know when he'd gone too far. Like many anemic administrators, he feared the thought of a civil rights lawsuit. "No, no, not at all," he said, quickly backing down. "I meant that you yourself might choose to seek a campus setting more compatible with your own views."

Kristina picked up her batik bag and stood. "I assure you, Dr. Starling, I have no plans to hunt for a job elsewhere. I like it here. I plan to go on doing exactly what I've been doing until I'm old and gray."

"Well, of course, if you get tenure, you'll be able to do exactly that, won't you?" He attempted a feeble smile. "Thank you for stopping by so I could make you aware of these telephone calls complaining about the activities of your students. What you do with the information is entirely up to you. You may wish to discuss it further with Dr. Perry when he returns after the holidays."

"No doubt I shall. Is there anything else on your list you'd like to mention to me?"

Dr. Starling really didn't know when to let go of something. "There is one last complaint," he said. "It seems that several of your students are accusing you of brainwashing them in favor of euthanasia."

Kristina couldn't help herself. She actually snickered. "If you want to wait a minute, I'll run down to my office and pick up a letter with a companion complaint. It seems that one of the students in that same class is accusing me of brainwashing students *against* euthanasia." She shook her head at the irony. "It's so good of you to give me that information, Dr. Starling. If I'm making people mad on both sides of a controversial issue, then I know for sure that I'm being absolutely neutral." Without a backward glance, she left the office. "See you Monday," she called cheerily over her shoulder.

Kristina's kitchen was full of the fragrance of pumpkin pie and sage dressing. She'd been busy all morning, slicing fruit for fruit salad, stuffing the turkey, chopping giblets for gravy, and doing with love all the other tasks that go into making a Thanksgiving feast. When Mitch arrived in the early afternoon, they watched the football game intermittently and kept sneaking into the kitchen to sample the food. In between times they sipped a white Riesling wine from stemmed glasses, happy to be alone together.

Kristina sprawled on the sofa in her raspberry-colored cashmere sweater with gray wool slacks, her head in Mitch's lap as she read the comic strips aloud and asked if he wanted to know his horoscope for the day.

"I already know what it says," he answered, tweak-

276

ing her nose. "It says I'm going to meet a tall, hand-some stranger and fall head over heels in love."

"Wrong, darling," she said, shifting in his arms. "That's *my* horoscope. Yours says you're going to eat a huge Thanksgiving feast and spend the rest of the night washing the dishes."

He pounded her with the pillow. "Why didn't we just pop a TV dinner in the microwave?"

"Because I've never cooked a meal for you before, that's why. I don't think you should marry a woman unless you know whether or not she can cook."

He rumpled her hair. "I'm not marrying you for your cooking, sweetheart."

She lifted herself until her head was level with his shoulder. "Oh, no? Then why are you marrying me?"

He muttered an obscenity. "Damn you, White, throw the ball!"

Kristina laughed and fell back into the cradle of his arms. "It feels like we've been married forever," she said. "You're already more interested in the football game than you are in me."

"Throw the ball, throw the ball!" Mitch shouted, dumping Kristina on the sofa as he abruptly stood to watch the play on the TV screen. "Wow, look at that pass! Come on, catch it—run, run, run, damn it! Touchdown, Kris, it's a touchdown!" He grabbed her in his arms and twirled her around the room. "It's a touchdown! Cowboys win!"

"The Cowboys always win in the last minute of the last quarter," she said, breathless from his hug. "I think they do it on purpose."

"It wouldn't be any fun if you could always predict

277

how the game's going to turn out. Part of the thrill is watching the Cowboys snatch victory from the jaws of defeat. And they do that on a regular basis." Mitch looked down at the beautiful woman in his arms. "You look like a raspberry ice cream cone in that sweater," he said. "Mind if I take a bite?"

"Help yourself," she said, stretching sensuously. As his head lowered, she slid out of his arms and onto the floor, pulling him down beside her. She closed her eyes to revel in the taste of his mouth against hers. "Mitch McNaughton," she scolded, opening one eye to catch him watching the TV screen, "don't you dare watch that instant replay! The real game is right here in this room, and if you don't take the offense, you're going to lose."

"Just one more minute," he pleaded, "then I'll turn it off."

"Never mind," she said, getting to her feet and pulling her sweater down over her waistband. "I'll go put dinner on the table. Your other appetites will have to wait."

"Krissie, come back here," Mitch said, beckoning her with his finger. "The game's over now. I promise you'll have my undivided attention."

"Too late." Her fanny switched as she marched into the kitchen. "I don't understand why things are so unbalanced all the time," she muttered. "I get in trouble at school because I get my students too excited, and yet I can't get myself in trouble at home because I can't excite my fiancé."

"What's this about getting in trouble at school?"

278

Mitch asked, reaching for a stalk of stuffed celery as he followed her into the kitchen.

"Oh, I got called on the carpet yesterday because someone made a complaint about me to one of the regents. It didn't take half an hour for the message to go straight through the chain of command." She explained what had happened, and Mitch became angry.

"It's the Winstons behind it, as sure as shooting. They've probably got connections with somebody who can put pressure on one of the regents. Do you think it's anything serious?"

"No, not really. I suppose it means I won't get the faculty excellence award this year, but the university isn't going to fire me. I'm a good teacher, so I don't have anything to worry about."

"Are you sure?" Mitch pulled her into his arms and rocked her body against his. He was surprised to feel so protective of her. He didn't want anybody to hurt her ever again. "Want a bite?" he asked, munching the celery while he thought of all the things he'd like to do to the Winstons to get even with them for trying to harm his darling Kristina.

"Quite sure." She pulled his face down and kissed his mouth. "But thanks for worrying about me."

"It's not fair for you to lose out on the faculty excellence award." Maybe there was something he could do, but what? he wondered.

"Oh, poo. There's so much politics involved in awards like that, Mitch, that it's not worth a second thought."

"I thought you wanted to win it."

279

"Well, of course I do. But it's not the end of the world if I don't get it."

"It's such a lousy, dirty trick, though. I'd love to get my hands on Mr. W. Harold Winston and wring his stupid neck."

Kristina held a platter and instructed Mitch to lift the turkey onto it from the roasting pan. "Can you slice a turkey?" she asked. "I've never been very good at doing this."

"Here, allow me. I've carved up many a mean old buzzard in my time. This turkey should be a cinch."

While she piled food into serving bowls, Mitch carved the turkey and arranged it in firm, juicy slices on the platter.

"Mitch?"

"Mmm?"

"You really mustn't mind about the faculty excellence award."

"Why not?"

"Because it's part of the price of fighting the Winstons, and it was worth it."

"Are you sure? The fight isn't over yet. Who knows what the next dirty trick is going to be?"

"Don't you remember what you told me 'way back when we first started talking about Valerie's case? You said that people have to pick their fights and calculate the risks because there are always going to be costs involved."

"We didn't figure on it affecting your professional career, though."

"We didn't figure that you might lose your law li-

280

cense over it either. We got into the fight and then the Winstons pushed the stakes way up high."

"Too high. We had to risk everything."

"But look what we won, Mitch. Look how much we have to be thankful for today. Valerie is well again and slowly getting back on her feet. If we're lucky, she'll soon find her kids and bring them back home. And she and Bud are falling in love—"

"And we have each other." He kissed her deeply.

"How much luckier can we be?"

The telephone shrilled. "Don't answer it," Mitch said.

"I have to. It might be Valerie." She reached for the wall telephone. "Hello. Why, yes, he's here." She handed the receiver to Mitch. "It's for you. Jim Sutton."

Mitch lifted an eyebrow in surprise. "Hello, Jim," he said. "No, we're just getting ready to have Thanksgiving dinner." Mitch cupped his hand over the mouth of the receiver. "Go listen in on the extension," he said to Kristina. "I think you're going to want to hear this."

She ran to the bedroom and picked up the receiver in time to hear Sutton say, "My clients are deeply distressed, Mitch. They had a telephone call early this morning that John Ed had been arrested in Washington and is being brought back to Texas on kidnapping charges. Frankly, they just never thought he'd be caught."

"And you never suspected the whole thing was a lie?" Mitch asked.

"Color me stupid," Sutton said. "I'll never be so

281

arrogant again as to think I can't be lied to. But I'm still their lawyer, and they want me to continue to represent them—and John Ed too, now that he's been arrested."

"That should keep you busy for a while," Mitch said, wondering why Sutton was calling him on Thanksgiving Day.

"Maybe we can find a shortcut, Mitch." Sutton paused, trying to find the right words. "As I mentioned, my clients are upset that John Ed has been arrested and faces a possible prison term. Of course the complaining witness against him would be Valerie Winston, and if she doesn't press charges, John Ed will never go to trial."

"You're probably right. I don't know what Valerie is going to want to do about that. I'll discuss it with her when she gets back. Do you know whether she's got the children with her?"

"I understand that she's on her way home with them right now. Listen, Mitch, I've talked to the Winstons about Valerie's lawsuit against them, and they're now willing to discuss the possibility of a settlement. They just don't think they want to continue with the case if a satisfactory arrangement can be worked out to dismiss it."

"Are you authorized to make a settlement offer?" Mitch asked.

"Yes, I am. They're willing to pay Valerie fifty thousand dollars cash, not as any admission of wrongdoing or liability, naturally, but simply to put an end to the litigation."

"It sounds to me like they're willing to pay Valerie

fifty thousand dollars not to press charges against John Ed."

"Now, Mitch." Sutton had warned the Winstons that Mitch was going to see through their offer. "There's no connection between these two separate matters. But now that you've brought it up, I don't see how it's going to do anybody any good for that boy to go to prison. Especially not Valerie's children. She's not going to want them to grow up knowing their father is a convict."

"Jim, do you remember that Valerie is suing the Winstons for half a million dollars?"

"Now, Mitch, you know no jury in Gilbert, Texas, is going to pay her half a million dollars, I don't care what you prove about the Winstons."

Sutton was right, of course. On the other hand, negotiation was a fine art. Mitch might be able to squeeze out a few more dollars. "I don't believe a jury will give her as little as fifty thousand either, Jim. So I guess we'll just hold off on any settlement and see if a jury won't do better by Valerie than the Winstons are willing to do. Do you have any idea which plane she'll be on?"

"I believe it's due into Austin any time now. Tell you what, Mitch, I'll see if I can't get the Winstons up to sixty thousand."

"Cash. Plus her hospital bills."

"How much is that?"

"Close to fifteen thousand."

"Ouch. Well, I'll see what they say."

"She wouldn't have had those hospital bills if it hadn't been for the Winstons. They owe her that."

"Have we got a deal?"

"Let's see," Mitch mused, "sixty thousand dollars cash plus her medical. Oh, lord, I almost forgot the most important item. Her attorney's fees."

"How much are you going to gouge us for that?" Sutton inquired glumly.

"I haven't totaled up my bill in quite a while. I'm guessing it's well past ten thousand dollars by this time."

"Itemize it."

"Jim, surely you know how I hate details."

"Never mind. Just round it off."

"I'm sure it will round off, say, to fifteen thousand."

"Sounds to me like you're expecting the Winstons to pay for your honeymoon."

"Poetic justice, don't you think?"

"Maybe so, Mitch, maybe so." He sighed. "Okay, it's a deal."

"One last thing."

"Not a dollar more, Mitch. I can't do it."

"Oh, this has nothing to do with the lawsuit, Jim. Just as having Valerie withdraw the criminal charges against John Ed has nothing to do with the lawsuit." Mitch cupped the telephone receiver and shouted to Kristina, "Kris, are you listening to this?"

"I haven't missed a word," she answered. "You're doing great."

"Mitch, are you there?" Sutton asked.

"Yep, I'm here. Get the Winstons to agree to this last item and we have ourselves a deal."

"What is it?"

"They seem to have a friend who knows one of the

regents at U.T. Ask the Winstons to send an urgent message all the way to the president of the university that Dr. Kristina Neilsen is a fantastic teacher, and she really ought to have top consideration for a faculty excellence award. I know the Winstons want to promote education, and they should be happy to use their influence to help a good teacher."

"I'm sure they'll be delighted. Anything else?"

But there was no answer to his question. Kristina had dropped the receiver when she heard Mitch's steps approach her bedroom. "Come on in, my darling," she whispered, lifting her lips to his.

Mitch found her mouth and gave her a deep, hungry kiss, then gently pushed her back against the pillows. "Dinner can wait," he said, holding her face between his hands while he kissed her eyes and nose, then buried his lips in the sensitive hollow of her slim neck. "The Thanksgiving games are just beginning."

JAYNE CASTLE

excites and delights you with
tales of adventure and romance

____TRADING SECRETS

Sabrina had wanted only a casual vacation fling with the
rugged Matt. But the extraordinary pull between them
made that impossible. So did her growing relationship
with his son—and her daring attempt to save the boy's life.
19053-3-15 $3.50

____DOUBLE DEALING

Jayne Castle sweeps you into the corporate world of
multimillion dollar real estate schemes and the very
private world of executive lovers. Mixing business with
pleasure, they made *passion* their bottom line.
12121-3-18 $3.95